MURDER AT ELMSTOW MINSTER

A Father Eadred Tale

MURDER AT ELMSTOW MINSTER

A Father Eadred Tale

LINDSAY JACOB

Matador
9 Priory Business Park,
Wistow Road, Kibworth Beauchamp,
Leicestershire. LE8 0RX
Tel: 0116 279 2299
Email: books@troubador.co.uk
Web: www.troubador.co.uk/matador
Twitter: @matadorbooks

ISBN 978 180046 244 1

British Library Cataloguing in Publication Data.
A catalogue record for this book is available from the British Library.

Printed and bound in Great Britain by 4edge Limited
Typeset in 11pt Adobe Garamond Pro by Troubador Publishing Ltd, Leicester, UK

Matador is an imprint of Troubador Publishing Ltd

To the people of East Anglia:
Past and Present

Prologue

Sister Verca was seldom open to temptation for she knew it led to sin. This virtue marked her from many of the other young, cloistered women but one morning she did succumb and thought she had gone to hell.

It was a precious time of silence, though painful for her body. The Sister-in-Christ slipped quietly from the sanctuary of her bed, shuddering when her feet touched the frozen ground. She paused awhile – no-one else stirred in the dormitory. Soon, she was dressed and with her candle guiding the way, she headed along the corridor towards the minster church. Through watery eyes she saw a single torch ahead, still issuing a faint glow.

The dawn service was yet some time away. Though the nun enjoyed communal prayer and praise, she was often dismayed by her companions. The whispers, the yawns, the chuckling and the other noises that were unseemly in the House of the Lord God! To be alone in God's presence was Verca's lifeblood. In the warmer months, she would steal away to the mere and stand, chest-deep, in the black water singing psalms but in winter the empty church was hers.

As Verca crept closer to the dying torch set high in the wall, a wisp of air scattered its last shreds. Her eyes followed them to the ground and to the furrows shadowed in the soil. The draught disturbed the door to her left; the wood creaked. It was a surprise to see it had not been closed, so was the prattle amongst the holy Sisters true? She stifled a giggle. Curiosity overcame her and she decided to find out. Verca eased the door open and peered inside – too dark – then a few steps more. She wished she had gone on her way.

Two bare feet swayed just before her eyes. Verca whimpered. She held her shaking wrist with her other hand and raised the candle, her eyes bulging. A man's body – completely unclothed – loomed. Verca looked higher. The shadows confused; the rope around his neck but something more. A ball of yarn had been pushed far into his mouth. Another gust blew through the window; the body turned, and more horror assailed the nun.

A woman; roped against him, back to back, also unclothed and hanging by the neck. Verca closed her eyes. Her heart pumped hard; her breathing laboured, she fell against the wall. The killers still lurked, veiled in the gloom, waiting to pounce. The nun struggled against a scream; she did not want to die.

Evil shadows danced in silence but they were of the dead. The perpetrators – man or fiend – had gone. Silently, the nun gasped a prayer.

"Oh, God have mercy." She stared up at the woman's face. A beast from hell could look no worse. A woollen ball had been similarly misused but this was enormous. The yarn had been forced so deeply and in such measure into the slender face that her cheeks bulged like those of a fattened pig and the wool spilled out from her gaping mouth. The poor woman's eyes stared upward, avoiding the monster she had become.

Another breath of wind and Verca's tiny flame was gone. She stumbled from the room and fell. Her hands felt for the wall; it guided her flight along the corridor and the minster woke to screams and cries of demonic murder.

ONE

Hereburg

The familiar chime drew a sharp gasp from Hereburg. Long awake, staring upward, she imagined herself as a wasted corpse, the blackness and chill of night her coffin lid. The Sisters-in-Christ – those she had once loved as daughters – filing past her worthless frame, gossiping and muttering their displeasure. Past redemption, waiting for judgement. How had it come to this?

Though the abbess was desperate for her plan to succeed, she could no longer pray to the Lord God for support, for she had deserted him. What she intended was a sin that would dismay the whole kingdom. She had been sorely troubled at its conception, but it would bring justice for one who was helpless, so she pressed on. Stone by stone, the fabric of her life had crumbled and stone by stone the plan developed. What she had condemned in others, she was now herself preparing to commit.

The joy she had felt when named the inaugural abbess of the community at Elmstow almost two years earlier was a memory that brought grief to her now. The sweetened words and the promise of leading a new house came from mouths that had since brought her to despair.

"I have been told that you will have authority over this community of chaste women and Elmstow will become a great fire to inspire faith and to guide our kingdom." Hereburg presumed that the thegn had sought to hide his embarrassment and inexperience in such matters behind the peculiar smile that accompanied his words. Later, she understood the truth. He had earnt no glory by his task.

She had been ready to give everything for her God and her king. To live as one with those of like mind, accepting the discipline and self-denial of a cloistered life. Her mind buzzed with ideas that she would bring into being to prove she was worthy of her selection over candidates that might have seemed to be more suitable.

"What a fool!" the abbess sobbed. "I lived for you, my God. But when I thought you were lifting me up, you were feeding me to my enemies. Why?" She rolled into a ball. "Was I too proud?" A memory of the past brought a fleeting smile.

"I was once, perhaps. If so, I am paying now."

It was all a lie, told by those born to privilege, schooled in deceit and with motives that Hereburg could scarcely believe. God's house was to be violated, his word insulted, and the abbess humiliated. It took a few months for her to realise the cruel deception and by then she had been implicated. She was to be a creature of base men and of women who were no better. There only to be a figurehead, while wickedness could be perpetrated.

2

Of the two dozen or so Sisters and priests at Elmstow, the abbess could count on less than half who had pious hearts – and these were mostly the old, the widowed and the poor. The daughters of the rich and powerful possessed different expectations. The empty rhythm of piety might still be observed at Elmstow but the soul was corrupt.

The effort of trying to fight against the worst of the world had worn her down and quickened the work of fallen nature. Once supple and unblemished, her skin, now flecked with wrinkles, hung loosely over diminished muscles. Her body arched forward and ached with movement. The words she searched for faded on the page and she read from memory.

Abbess Hereburg had lost the fleeting bloom of youth. It had seemed so immaterial for a while; her mind had been elsewhere, joyfully in pursuit of the spirit of the Lord God. But now, abandoned and surrounded by the excesses and arrogance of youthful flesh, she looked differently at the time remaining to her. Her opportunity would soon come to laugh at all those who had mocked her. They had no notion of the vengeance this insignificant hag was capable of – but soon they would pay an awful price.

Sometime in the coming day, Ceolfrith, ealdorman of the East Angles – the king's right-hand man – would arrive with his warriors. If he were impressed during his stay, King Athelstan himself would soon visit, rumoured to bring a great prize for the minster to add to its blossoming treasury. Bishop Aethelbert had long ago secured the king's promise but soon it would indeed happen.

Hereburg had fretted for months and not only about her soul; there were more immediate worries. She would be held responsible for the preparations for the ealdorman's stay and her plan depended on their success. She had lived on a knife's edge since the visit had been announced only a few weeks past and if ever her concealment were to see daylight, it was now. So much to do in so short a time.

In a momentary dream, she watched herself climb a stair with her secret cupped in her hands, as a parched seafarer would protect the last of his precious water. She cried out, seeing her enemies rushing down to meet her, eager to knock her to the ground, exposing her past. Hereburg woke, shuddering and moaning.

It had been the queen who had urged her husband to found a minster. King Athelstan had turned away when some in his army had executed the captured ten-year-old son of the Mercian king after a particularly vicious battle. His blood rarely had the better of his head – which is what made Athelstan a feared battle leader – so there were those who wondered why he had let so valuable a hostage be lost.

Whatever the reason, Athelstan was seized with a fear that the Lord God would demand a blood sacrifice from his own family in recompense. So, he undertook to endow the new minster with one hundred hides from his estates. The war had been costly and the full endowment was not immediately possible, so several great lords donated lands and gold from their own wealth to build the house for God's people and to deliver for themselves a heavenly reward with some temporal benefits. In fulfilment of the vow he had made on the battlefield, King Athelstan also dedicated his fifteen-year-old daughter, Cuthburg, to perpetual virginity. Her purity, pledged to God Almighty, would be his reparation.

She was an unruly girl, who had already caused her parents some anxiety. Her elder sister had been closely trained in the responsibilities of royal duties. Two winters earlier, she had contracted a fever and died.

When their grief had subsided, the king and queen saw in their remaining daughter their failure in not having prepared her similarly. She was a product of their indulgence – callow, selfish and conceited. Still, to despatch her to the cloister was a sacrifice Athelstan felt keenly. Cuthburg was a renowned beauty; there would be continental princes eager to tame her in the marriage bed and the ensuing accord would have enhanced Athelstan's influence over his enemies.

At least the king and queen could breathe more easily now that, at Elmstow, their daughter would be protected from temptation.

TWO

The King's Daughter

"At last, some deliverance from this boredom!"

The sound of the bell brought a smile to the young woman's face. It was a rare event to be so enthralled by the call to leave her bed in the freezing small hours – but Cuthburg was already awake.

She stifled her desire to shout aloud, whispering her happiness, then she pounded her fists joyfully into her bedding and danced around the room. As the king's daughter, she avoided the burden of physical labour and possessed her own chamber, as did a few of the other holy Sisters, although theirs were smaller. It was a sign of a rich foundation that not all the inmates shared a dormitory. But the tedium of endless services, droning voices and broken sleep drove her to distraction.

Cuthburg was owed loyalty as a duty by her father's subjects but she had tired of the fawning performances of many of the Sisters, keen to attach themselves to the rising royal star. The king's daughter had given up trying to hide her contempt. At least Mildred offered her excitement.

"Now, whom shall I bed after the feast?" Mildred asked playfully.

"A brave and lusty warrior!" Cuthburg affected a girlish voice, as she often did. "He must be worthy of you. Do not settle for anyone less."

Cuthburg's companion licked her impatient lips. Mildred was the daughter of a merchant who had died a few years earlier and the family's fortunes had waned, but he had been of good repute. Thus, the queen had taken Mildred into her household and chosen her to be her daughter's companion and watchful guard at Elmstow. If the princess' devout mother had known more about the girl, rather than the status of her father, she would have had Mildred exiled. Instead, she had engaged a temptress.

The two young women led each other into increasingly diverting games to relieve their boredom. There was one area of human interaction in which Mildred particularly excelled – exciting men's lust. A delectable distraction was planned for the feast on the following night and two men were to be their target.

"And your heart's desire arrives tomorrow."

"H'm," Cuthburg purred. "It has been four months since I saw him last. There are parts of my body that need his attention; they have lain dormant far too long." She squeezed her breasts then ran her hands down over her stomach to her thighs, giggling. "It will be a long night."

Cuthburg was grateful that her parents were miles away. Now, she could enjoy the feast. She could wear the bright, embroidered dress she had designed and do credit to the crystal pendant she ached to wear. It would soon bounce beguilingly and draw his eyes and warm hands to her chest once again. Perpetual virginity was an esteemed estate. She would nod when told this but say nothing. It might suit others but not a king's daughter – her needs were greater and responsibilities more complex. She would talk to her father when he came, and he would reverse his hasty decision. Besides, the dedication was inaccurate, but she had no intention of burdening her father with this knowledge – unless he continued with the travesty. Hers could be a symbolic virginity, she would tell her father – a pureness of mind – and that would surely be sufficient.

Cuthburg straightened her habit and performed a few final touches, enjoying what she saw reflected in her bowl of cleaning water. On whomever she bestowed her favours, he would feel as if he were in Heaven.

"I cannot abide this place any longer; to be separated from Aelfric night after night. It is unnatural – but all will change soon. I will talk to his father, the ealdorman. The king holds him in the highest regard and if he pleads for me, the king will listen."

"But your father will not let you marry Aelfric. Once you leave here, the king will choose you a husband from another kingdom and he will be richer and more powerful than Aelfric can ever be."

"That will not happen! I have done my father's bidding and now he must free me. He must!" The princess fell back onto her bed. Despite her plea, she knew Mildred was right. The king would choose her future husband. Cuthburg began to weep. Mildred turned to her and smiled.

"There is a way through this. It carries great dangers but if it succeeds, all will be well. Listen."

Cuthburg adopted her usual position, scurrying through the icy darkness to catch the tail of the other handmaidens of Christ, who were gathering in the minster church for the three o'clock service. The melodic chanting of psalms gently broke the silence, linking the community to their God, but for many of the congregation their minds were elsewhere.

God would bide his time, for they would soon call on him and weep for his protection.

THREE

The Ealdorman's Warning

"Lord Ceolfrith." Father Eadred bowed to the man who had summoned him. The ealdorman – the second most powerful man in the kingdom – continued to steer his horse along the path.

In the early light, cautious hooves picked their way forward. The liminal track struggled to stay above sheets of glistening ice that reflected the vast blue expanse stretching above. Many years earlier, the trees had been cleared from the route to remove the risk of thieves, murderers and outlaws from hiding in wait. Their place had been taken by marshy fenland that had made the track impassable in the colder, wetter months. An earlier king had resolved to strengthen the pathway by having piles of wicker hurdles spread over the lower reaches then topped with bundles of reed and sedge. Repairs were needed constantly, but undertaken infrequently, unless war was in the air. For this was the sole route linking the heart of the Kingdom of the East Angles through the fens to its south-western corner and the border with Mercia.

Once in a while, the line of horses and men thread past a lopsided figure made of the same material as the track, some almost the size of a man; others, small and visible only to careful eyes. The decaying sentinels had been placed there by the builders to enlist the help of the spirits of this corner of the fen country in protecting the track from sinking and its users from danger. Now the minster has been built, followers of Christ journey along this way and have raised wooden crosses where prayers are said for the same purpose. Use of numinous wicker spirit figures is discouraged – but who can forbid what happens silently in a man's heart?

The ealdorman's flint heart remembers a time, several years earlier, when he drove his mount through this same ground to victory, snatched from the kingdom's greatest enemy. King Athelstan had led the army with Ceolfrith at his side to finally break Mercian control of East Anglia. Raiding by both sides still continues to cause uncertainty, distrust and bloodshed. Though the Mercians are not the power they once were, fear of large-scale invasion continues to weigh on the East Anglian leadership and a military presence in the contested region continues. Much depends on Ceolfrith, the ealdorman.

"I am not enjoying this." He coughed, spat to the ground and swore. "I never liked this minster. So, a boy is killed. War is war; there is no point in feeling remorse afterwards. This should be a fortress, built to celebrate our great victory. I almost died fighting here. The closest death has ever come to me but in the cauldron of battle, I defeated

11

it. This minster is built on weakness, churchman, and will never bring anything other than weakness. How much further?"

"Little more than an hour, my lord. Over that hill and we should see it." Aelfric – the ealdorman's eldest son – pointed into the distance. He looked for some acknowledgement but, as usual, none came. Despite being his eldest, the ealdorman exhibited little obvious warmth for Aelfric, while the hunt and the feast often entertained the ealdorman and his two younger sons. Some thought it was the ealdorman's way of toughening Aelfric for his future responsibilities, but others thought his coldness was strange and unnecessary.

"And you, priest; you are here to spy?"

Eadred winced and spoke the words the bishop had told him.

"No, my lord. I am here as Bishop Aethelbert's representative to ensure that the holy relic we hope to obtain is installed properly by masses, prayers and fasting. The bishop is, as you know, too ill to travel."

"Priest, do not insult me. I know when I hear lies. You are here to see whether the abbess and her girls are behaving properly. Is that not so?" He spoke without looking at Eadred.

How a man could instil words with such menace. The priest shivered.

"The bishop has a responsibility to God and to the king to ensure that the minster is a beacon of faith and that the cloistered Sisters live their lives as true descendants of—"

"You are his spy," the ealdorman interrupted. "I understand that men like you choose words carefully to mask unpleasant truths in fog and to sound learned but I

12

am plain, uneducated and speak simply. I also see clearly – very clearly. My life depends upon it." He stared suddenly with such venom into Eadred's eyes that the priest recoiled.

"Let me use simple words now. I loathe everything about Elmstow but one thing. I am told it can put on a good feast. I have not seen my home in three months of fighting off raiding parties and negotiating with the Mercians deep into their land. I risk my life daily. I sleep with one eye open. I would be home now if the king had not ordered me a few weeks ago to come to Elmstow. We have not come to fast or pray but to rest, eat, drink, recover and be entertained, as is our right. Do not interfere. This is the king's property, not the bishop's. It should have been land bestowed to a warrior thegn to bolster our defences, not for women. It was built as a fort, not a church!" And with that he rode off, shouting back at Eadred.

"And the bishop has now persuaded the king to free Elmstow from all renders. You are bleeding us, churchman. Elmstow's wealth should be repairing this shit of a road! In peace, you think we are the devil; in war, you want us as your saviour! We are not both. Think carefully which table you eat from."

The ealdorman wheeled his horse around. Unfortunately for Eadred, Ceolfrith had not finished.

"When the kingdom is threatened. When enemies slice your throats and hack your bodies. When your holy Sisters, stripped naked, scream as men take their turn. Who do you expect to protect you? Do not think that I will hurry. You may dream of Heaven but remember you are part of this kingdom while you live and when it suffers, you suffer. I will make sure of that.

13

"Have you seen what a settlement looks like after a raid? Have you?"

"I have not." Eadred's voice quaked.

"You should. Step carefully, churchman, my patience is wearing thin."

Eadred had hoped he would have shouted back that the kingdom is the stronger if the Lord God is honoured; that a people cannot stand together or beat their enemies by their own strength but need to call upon God to help defeat darkness – but his courage failed him.

The bishop had warned Eadred that his visit to Elmstow would not be easy, that the ealdorman would bristle at any curbing of his rights, but to remember that the queen was a God-fearing woman and she would protect the privileges of the minster.

The priest should have accompanied Bishop Aethelbert to Elmstow but the old man had fallen into bouts where he struggled to catch his breath and would not risk a long winter's journey.

"I have not abandoned you, dear boy." Aethelbert had shaken a subdued Eadred by the arm. "I would be a burden to you. But I have prayed that you will be protected from any evil on this journey and will continue to pray thus. Our God is stronger than anything that might come against you. I cannot let anyone else accompany you. You will understand why later." The bishop smiled but had refused to elaborate. "Come, you are ready for this task. A good priest must face such challenges. Now, if you leave soon, you will be able to join the ealdorman's troop for part of your journey – for he also travels to Elmstow."

It was an uneasy priest who sat on an old tree stump beside the road and watched the ealdorman and his men ride past. Hard faces stared down at him. Men with daunting frames and muscles that could snap Eadred's bones without effort. A rider steered his mount to push hard into Eadred, who resisted being toppled. The priest looked up and wished he had not. Sneering, the warrior spat into the priest's tunic and drifted on. Eadred swallowed hard.

He waited until the last of the troop had disappeared over the brow of the hill then he fell to his knees and began to pray. The desperate hunger to be free of his torments twisted the priest's face. He tried to calm himself and a gentle, pensive, finely featured face appeared briefly before the anguish returned and Eadred's doleful brown eyes stared skyward. His slight frame shook beneath his tunic. He fought to control the tremors but each time he started to pray, the thoughts and words splintered, struck and cut by a stream of violent images – from his past and from the last few minutes – all aimed at him. No matter how hard he tried, the path to the Lord God was blocked by taunting memories. It was a familiar circumstance for the young priest – overwhelmed by the aggression and evil of others and bedevilled by his own weakness.

He had joined the cloister to escape the brutality that oppressed him, only for the bishop to say that he had more need of priests than monks. Not those who desired to withdraw from the world but those to go into the dark corners of men's souls, to face evil and to beat it – to show God's love to the wicked and to bring them to confession and penitence. The bishop had tolerated no complaint. Eadred wandered slowly towards the minster.

In a while, he was a few steps from the summit of a low hill – the only rise to be seen for miles – that drifted away to the left as two ripples in the skin of the earth. As with the rest of the track, the surrounding tree cover had been removed but the forked ridge and the deep depression between the spurs remained covered by a dense wood.

Ahead lay Elmstow Minster, a substantial collection of stone and wooden buildings. It had, in ages past, been a fort constructed by the Roman legions and still possessed the bearing of a military establishment. The cloistered women lived protected behind a curtain wall curling upon a bank and faced with a formidable ditch.

Beyond the ramparts, in all directions, fields and meadows spread out; some in pasture dotted with livestock, a few part-covered with the green hues of vegetables, and some with the black earth of the fens exposed by the plough. From his vantage point, Eadred could discern that the enclosed minster and its ring of bounty rested on land rising, in places almost imperceptibly, above the fen pools that stretched into the distance with their banks of reed and occasional stands of trees. The ealdorman may have railed against the use of Elmstow but certainly it had been fortified against Mercian aggression.

The young priest looked out in awe at the holy vision ahead of him. His eyes had never rested on such a reflection of God's majesty. The community of buildings focused around an immense church with a tower rising high above the surrounding flat countryside. The sunlight, though pale and cold, transformed the cream-coloured stone of the tower into rich, golden butter. Eadred surveyed a scene of God's glory and man's faith and pious works that took his breath away.

"Is it not a joy to see such a wonder?"

FOUR

Tatwine

Eadred turned so quickly that he tripped and fell. The figure who had spoken chuckled gently and extended his hand.

"Forgive me, I did not intend to startle you, but you were preoccupied."

Although Eadred's heart pounded, the stranger's compassion and soothing smile were disarming, and the priest's anxiety melted. He looked at a monk – at least, he thought him to be one. His head was tonsured, albeit irregularly, but rather than a cowl, the man wore a crude, sullied tunic made from animal skins under a rough pelt cloak. Whatever beasts clothed this monk had also bestowed their smell.

Piercing blue eyes grinned out over a thick black beard, stippled with grey. Eadred took the hand and was pulled effortlessly to his feet.

"I am Tatwine, the sole Brother attached to the minster you see before you, but I live a solitary life not far from here. I watched unseen while the troop rode past and would have left then but I saw you kneel at prayer and I saw the sorrow you brought to our Lord."

Eadred's face reddened.

"No. Please, feel no shame. There is no need; on the contrary."

Tatwine took Eadred's hands in his and squeezed them firmly until the priest looked into his eyes. The hermit asked Eadred for his name and why he journeyed to Elmstow. The priest repeated the words he had given to the ealdorman about his mission.

"Indeed, our bishop trusts you with a great responsibility. He has much faith in you, and I do not doubt that it is well-placed.

"Father Eadred, come, sit on this rock, for I must tell you something that has come to me."

It was baffling to Eadred that he felt at comfort with this strange figure who had burst into his life not five minutes since. Though the hermit had facial features suggesting he was quite older than Eadred, his voice and supple movement indicated their ages were perhaps closer. It would not be long before this peculiar-looking figure would astonish the priest.

"You should know first that this is the second winter I have lived a solitary life. I pray and contemplate our Saviour by day and battle the forces of evil by night. I have avoided too many earthly disturbances thus far but as I edged closer to the heart of God, the attacks from demons increased – even more so than I expected. They assail and abuse me each night, but with the Lord God's help, I am still prevailing. I

18

will tell you more about the wiles and temptations of the fiends of hell later for it is an instruction you will need to call upon in the coming days.

"As I grew in relationship with our God, to my amazement and joy he granted me the gift of prophesy." The hermit stared into the distance with an expression of wonder. "I give thanks many times each day that I was blessed in this way for I am no special soul. He has given me eyes to see into the future, not at all times and often as if a fog envelops the figures and their actions. And I have been given an understanding as to why much can remain unclear and confused. For it is the free will that we have all been granted. A man can choose between good and evil. I am able to see some fragments of what is in a man's heart and what might transpire but none of this may come to pass. It is his choice.

"I cannot prophesy through my own strength, as hard as I might try. It comes as a gift from the Lord God when he sees fit. Though I am awake, it seems like a dream and when I leave the presence of the Lord's Spirit and realise what has happened, my mind tries quickly to remember it all. But there really is no need, my friend, because when I pray for understanding about the vision, what I need to know comes to me, when the Lord God deems it so."

Eadred found himself drawn along by Tatwine's wonder, and felt himself blessed to be taken into the monk's gift, but soon he would feel overwhelmed.

"I have had four such visions over the past several years. On each occasion, I have been able to interpret the prophecy through prayer, although not always immediately. Father Eadred, when I saw you in deep misery and supplication, the Lord God took me into his spirit and began to speak to me – and it was about you. He has a message for you!"

Tatwine glanced at Eadred, as if to satisfy himself that the priest was listening carefully. He need not have been concerned. The priest's forge-flamed eyes blazed, fanned ever brighter and larger by the monk's words. He stared, motionless and silently, into the distance.

"This is what the Lord God showed me.

"I saw a great prize to be had and it rested on a plinth. Around it, there were many men brandishing sharp blades. Some swagger, drumming their weapons on their shields, eager to earn glory for themselves by winning the prize. You are there, in your priestly clothing. You plead with them on your knees and in gentle speech not to fight because the prize is not theirs to have; they have no right to it, and it will bring them unimaginable sadness. They laugh at you; call you weak. You see the hostility and arrogance in their faces that they direct at you. You withdraw quietly and with doleful eyes.

"As they look upon the trophy, which seems to gain in brilliance, evil also grows. For some, it is greed. For others, it is pride and aggression that take hold and they begin to slash at each other. Before long, many terrible wounds have been inflicted. Limbs are cut from their bodies; heads are rent open. The warriors become as slaughtered beasts littering the ground. Most are dead and the few who remain alive are horribly injured and disfigured.

"From out of the shadows a figure slinks; slowly and furtively, it steps through the butchery, looking left and right. One of the wounded warriors cries out for help – the newcomer takes his knife and cuts the warrior's throat.

Another of the wounded tries to grab his leg and the silent stalker pierces him in the back with a spear point. He creeps around, stabbing and extinguishing the remnants of life. When all are dead, the culprit removes his hood and smiles. He raises the prize in his hands, his eyes glowing with happiness.

"It is then that I see you, covered by a shining cloak, walking in prayer through the entrails and the severed heads and limbs. The murderer, thinking everyone dead, is startled by your appearance. In a calm voice, you tell him that his crime is far greater than that of the dead warriors, for he has murdered and stolen secretly to avoid justice and that he must answer with his life.

"He laughs, saying you are a fool – for he is blameless and only picked up the prize because it was lying in the dirt after others had killed for it – and that it is his by right. You demand he stops his lies for they are an affront to God, who knows all things. He goes to attack you with his dagger, but it breaks on your cloak. Although he has not uttered his name, you know it and you shout it aloud three times. At the first two cries of his name, the man writhes in pain and at the third, his body and his spirit die in agony. You take the prize from his dead hands and offer it to the Lord God, for you know it is his."

The monk sat back and made the sign of the cross. Eadred stared at him, his chest heaving.

"Brother Tatwine, what does this vision mean?"

Tatwine smiled at Eadred's open-eyed eagerness.

"Part of the meaning seems clear, but I will need to pray for insight."

"Will you pray now?"

The monk nodded.

The unkempt hermit shut his eyes and rested his hand on Eadred's shoulder. He prayed that he would be capable of discerning the true significance of his vision and with his eyes still closed he began to speak, slowly and with his expression animated by the sights that moved before his mind's eye.

"Rightly, you do not seek to glorify yourself by the gifts you have been granted but instead you honour he who blessed you with these abilities. You live the virtues of humility, restraint and faith. Yet, Father Eadred, you are weighed down by feelings of inadequacy and often misery. You give the voices of others too much power – the unrighteous mouths that spit the lie that restraint is weakness."

Eadred attempted to pull away but Tatwine held him fast.

"Listen! Listen to the word of God. These are words he wants you to hear." The hermit spoke with increased force.

"These thoughts that curse you come from the evil one, who wishes to fill your head and heart with darkness and failure. Blessed are the meek, for they shall inherit the earth. Our Lord Jesus Christ was meek, but he was strong. He accepted freely that he would be killed upon a cross, yet he was the Son of God and had power beyond measure. Do not feel intimidated by the outer appearance of aggression for you have been given the measure of it – if you have the faith to believe.

"You have a great gift that has been granted by the Lord God. Others may seek confrontation and ignite generations of feuding and bloodshed, but you are a peacemaker and reconciler. The devil wishes to blunt this gift because it gives life. You have the power to break the legacy of violence that is so often destructive to our families. It may seem hard to seek peace, when those around you want war, but it is worth the struggle.

"And our Saviour has granted you another great gift. It is shown in the vision, but I cannot yet discern it – but it is great indeed. Are you able to understand it?"

Eadred's mind was still dwelling on Tatwine's earlier comments.

"No, I have no idea. I struggle in my own skin. If I have another gift or any gifts, they elude me."

Tatwine put his arm around Eadred's sunken shoulders. The priest's initial keenness to comprehend his gift, as the hermit had seen it, soured with the awareness that it involved reaching out in danger to dissuade those who would do harm to each other.

"The devil has held sway over you for too long, my friend. You have given too much of the storehouse of your heart and mind for that black creature to fill and there is scarcely room left for your God-given nature. He has worked to squash your talents, but that time is over. Many men serve out their days with little understanding of their gifts, let alone to see them flourish – but this is not your fate. Each time I have had a vision from the Lord, it has been for a great purpose – and it will be no different for you."

"I do not understand any of this; any of what has happened. Yet, I do trust you." Eadred stared at the monk.

"I am pleased that you do. When the Lord God makes paths to cross, he has bigger intentions. I am sure that you will discover them in the days ahead and I will also. I am glad that our lives were meant to meet, Father Eadred."

Eadred nodded in agreement.

"You must tell me though, how can you live alone? I crave my times of solitude, but I think I would despair if I were separated from my Brothers-in-Christ for too long."

"I am one of those men who best lives without others for most of my days. I will tell you the reason sometime but for now, come. I will take you to my home down there between the two ridges and we will eat and talk for a while for I must prepare you for your time at Elmstow. It is not what it seems. There are those there who pray to God but serve the devil."

FIVE

The Moneyer

If this were God's house, it was like none other that Eadred had witnessed. The entire community seemed caught up with frantic preparations and anticipation for the feast. Sisters laughed and pointed as they watched the minster's slaves unload the last of the wagons. For two days now, the wheels had creaked with their burdens from the storerooms at the minster and from nearby farms, and from the river and fishponds. Great joints from sheep, pigs and cattle, flitches of bacon, hams, chickens, wildfowl, hares and baskets of fish, eels, oysters, crabs, eggs, cheeses, bread, vegetables and fruit. Vats of ale and jugs of wine – greeted with claps and giggles. All manner of foods and drink had been unloaded and checked by the senior Sisters. The smells of cooking filled the air.

"What saint's day are you preparing for, Sister?"

"I am uncertain, Father, but it must be one. I think it is

the ealdorman's favoured saint. It is to his honour that we will hold this celebration."

"The saint or the ealdorman?"

The cloistered woman chuckled.

"Great feasts might be allowed on holy days, if the abbess agrees, but not just to sate the flesh. Surely, there is enough here to feed the community and the ealdorman's men for a month?"

The woman had lost interest in the conversation and hurried off to watch the preparations.

Eadred was beginning to believe that the lurid picture of life in the minster painted by Tatwine might not be a fabrication of a mind that had avoided as much human contact as possible. The priest recalled what the monk had said.

"Though I have only once set foot in the minster since I embarked on this solitary life, I am visited sometimes by one of the priests, who comes to join me here to share the struggle against the demons who live in this place. He tells me of the brazenness of the inmates, of the laxity in standards and how there is all but war between those who cherish the Word of God and those who see the minster as a place for their personal pleasure of the basest kind. He tells me that the abbess once struggled to maintain proper control of the foundation in the face of hostility from those who have endowed the house for their own purposes, but is now exhausted and frail from her efforts. He fears she has lost the battle and will fight for truth no more."

Eadred seemed to be the only person unhappy to be there. Even the ealdorman, who despised the thought of the place, was laughing now he was out of the saddle and with a drink in his hand. It made Eadred hate the man even more. Alcohol was no stranger to the priest – they were warm friends, who had had many conversations. Eadred understood and believed that lack of self-restraint was a sin, so for him inebriation was seldom accompanied by mirth but to ease the anguish that came upon him when the demon elves had their way.

"This is a fine establishment, is it not? The bishop, whom I know well, is rightly proud of its harvest."

Eadred turned to see a crimsoned smile gulp another mouthful of wine. The speaker was even better dressed than the ealdorman and three times the girth. Critical as he was already of the frivolity underway around him, the priest felt vexed at the seemingly genuine praise from this most immoderate of beings.

"This is the most defensible place in the kingdom after the king's capital. See, the walls were devised by Roman men, who built their fort here. It is said by some that the gods who protected the soldiers of Rome who once lived here, can still be raised through special words said over the weapons of the legions. King Athelstan shaped his minster within this great curtain and strengthened it with a ditch. It has always been a temple to God and a fortress for men.

"The flour milled here is the best in the land of the East Angles. Take my word for it. I have tried to persuade the bishop to produce more and to let me market it in the north, where I have connections, but he does not seem interested. It is such a waste of the possibilities of the minster. A man in his position needs to be more concerned about the Church's wealth. Do you not agree?"

Eadred bowed slightly but had no interest in discussing the question.

"You should hide your disinterest better, my young friend. Listen, you know the ealdorman's view. I travelled here from the border with his men and overheard what he said to you. The king's support for this house is not assured. One more nasty Mercian attack on our borders and Ceolfrith's arguments could well sway the king against this place. This foundation will only flourish if it secures its own wealth. Believe me, I know these things."

The man possessed a confidence that Eadred lacked, which made him feel instantly uneasy. Yet, this was not the arrogant and brute attack that the ealdorman had inflicted on him. The priest spluttered a response.

"But the queen! The bishop is certain of her support."

"There are no certainties these days. I can see you are troubled by what I say. The queen, God bless her, for all her piety has visited Elmstow but once, and that was at its foundation. Its reputation has declined since then," the speaker rolled his eyes, "but that has been masked by the good character of the abbess. There is no-one who has the courage to tell the queen. What would she make of all this?"

The man shifted to survey the commotion behind him.

"H'm, the promise of this place is shamelessly debauched. Even the court on victory days rarely sees this excess. I do not criticise luxury, of course, for men spend their lives to gain comfort, as have I, but should those who have apparently given their life to God be so enslaved by the world?

"I was to be a cloistered man many years ago. It is hard to believe now, I know. That is when I first met the bishop, who was then a young priest. But my two elder brothers were killed in the wars and my father removed me before my vows so I could support my parents as they grew old.

"When I saw you – and I have seen many like you – ready to serve God with open-hearted zeal, I remembered, as you do as the years pass, the joy and eagerness I felt at your age. But my life took a different turn, and I forgot my former self. The path of life is strewn with rocks and wild animals and other dangers, and we are often forced to take another route to our destination. It is only later that we realise that our purpose has also changed, and it is beyond our power to find our way back." He smiled wistfully.

"It was not long after leaving the monastery that I realised I liked the world too much to have lasted anyway. I lack the discipline that constant faith requires." The moneyer slapped his ample stomach. "Fasting would kill me and I still enjoy the warmth of younger women, now my wife is dead." He licked his lips. "These are the benefits of wealth as age lays waste to the body." His face changed, to be shaped by melancholic recollections, then returned so quickly to that of a practical man of business that Eadred wondered if he had imagined the transitory slip of the mask.

"Let me give you this advice. Take it if you wish. I have shared it often enough with old Aethelbert but he does not understand. The cloister is not free of the vices and wickedness of the world; far from it. You will see it at its worst over the next few days, I wager. It is more vulnerable than my world. While ever you rely on the wealth of others, they will control you, even when you least suspect it.

"There is always a contest for valuable estates and the powerful will bicker and fight over them. The land on which this minster was built was to be granted to the ealdorman's eldest son, but the queen intervened, and her husband granted it to the bishop. While the ealdorman lives, Elmstow will never be safe. And there are many who have bought a place here for their delinquent daughters. They pollute the cloister, but it is easier to take their money, rather than earn your own. Do not imagine that the parents of these rich and beautiful ladies give gold to Elmstow without conditions.

"You clearly have the bishop's ear for him to send you in his stead. Persuade the bishop, where I have failed – secure your own revenues and property. Aethelbert is old and sick. Powerful men want him gone so they can get their hands on this source of wealth. He should never have let this place fall into ruin.

"I am Regenhere, moneyer from Gippeswyc. Watch carefully over the next few days and you will see the truth of my words. Now, I must find my son. In the first hour he was here, he found the best wine this place has to offer; the best meat in the second; and by now he will be offering one of the young, attractive Sisters a dazzling – but inexpensive – jewel. But at heart, he is a good Christian soul.

"I journey to the court to have my son accepted as my replacement as moneyer. Death has whispered in my ear. He comes to us all. Tell old Aethelbert that I would mend the wrongs I have committed in my life – he knows what I have done – and I stand ready to help him free this house from the web of sin and the black spiders who weave it. There are markets eager for the produce grown here. Better to grow and sell the abundance to buy your freedom, than have it consumed by gluttons. I can make it happen." Regenhere swilled back the remainder of his wine and disappeared between the wagons lined up and disgorging their contents.

Eadred had little experience of such men and as he wandered off to find the cell that he had been allocated, the weight of his ignorance of the ways of the world dragged at him. He thought himself useless to fulfil the tasks expected of him.

He recalled one of the warnings from Tatwine that he should expect that many of those he met at Elmstow would lie more readily than the men Eadred was used to, for they had dark secrets and ambitions and much to lose. They would threaten or charm him – whatever seemed most effective – to keep him from causing trouble. The moneyer had proven strangely disarming for one so rich and powerful, so Eadred doubted that he had said the complete truth, but what he had remarked was distressing and there was one inescapable fact.

The bishop he loved more than any man alive was responsible for the state of Elmstow. Aethelbert's sacred duty was to ensure that the Church of the East Angles followed the example set by the Apostles. But, through decrepitude or laziness, he had failed, and now sent a boy to give the appearance that the bishop was concerned with the filth that polluted the House of God.

The feast in the ealdorman's honour was only a few hours away. Eadred dreaded that he would have to attend. He would rather eat paupers' bread alone in his cell than witness a celebration of excess but that would not be possible.

Female eyes absorbed the sturdy contours of the warriors. Smiles that invited and tempted. Provocative movements and playful giggles. Muscles were flexed and lewd banter exchanged. Blood was rising all around the young priest. He felt sick and alone.

SIX

Midnight

Eadred rose from his knees. The greatest joy he knew in this world was to leave it – temporarily – and to let God speak to him of the wonders of Heaven. At one special time, during the Night Office, half-asleep, chanting and singing psalms, he had felt his life force muscle suddenly against his tainted flesh. At first, he thought death was upon him when his soul burst free. He sensed the wings of angels lifting him and he came before the very spirit of God. No words he had ever learnt were able to explain the explosion of joy and love within him – but he was not dead.

He opened his eyes to see a gaggle of faces staring towards him and heard cries of happiness erupt. The Brothers tripped over each other in their questions and their descriptions of his death-like swoon. Words failed him again when the bishop probed him to understand what had happened in the length of time when Eadred had lain still with the slightest smile, repelling all attempts to revive him, including a forceful kick to his thigh from Brother Cuthbert.

The priest apologised when Aethelbert's voice rose angrily as he accused Eadred of keeping the truth from him. Later, the bishop also asked for forgiveness, saying with moistened eyes that only twice in his many years, and that many seasons earlier, had he been given the privilege of seeing some of the glories of the Lord God's heavenly home but it had sustained his faith.

Occasions of deep communion with his God were exceedingly rare for Eadred and he yearned for others. Yet even alone in his cell, after thanksgiving, prayer and petition, he found it impossible, now piled with cares, to peel from his mind the routines and concerns of the world. His soul was trapped, unable to be free to rest and to listen to his God.

One night, in a dream, he was granted a vision of his prison. He saw a net but not one cast out lovingly to fish for souls but one that confined a soul to the world of flesh. He saw himself struggling, held fast within a meshwork. Each square was a detail of his responsibilities and cares, in themselves trivial, but together they held him down – a thousand seemingly harmless tasks that kept him from his eternal Saviour. Ale, and sometimes wine, when the ruby liquid was available in sufficient quantities, never brought Eadred to that inner peace but did afford some flicker of calmness that led him to his rest on difficult nights.

This was not a night when Eadred might gently approach his Saviour. What the moneyer had said vexed him. Man was born sinful. Eadred had witnessed many times how the devil had corrupted men by greed, lust, pride, jealousy, revenge –

leading them to the most vile of unrepented sins, and to the loss of their eternal souls. The priest held that those who had chosen a religious life – most of them – did so because they rejected worldly self-love and the dictates of the flesh. Their desire was to dedicate their lives to worshipping God and to fighting against their sinful natures. The key was to keep the Church and its community pure.

But the moneyer exposed a dilemma. Holy Church could never escape the temptations of the world – it was rooted in them. Eadred knew of no holy house that did not rely on endowments from rich benefactors; they were all beholden to the wishes and whims of the rich, and a pawn in their squabbles. Yet, if it sought to create its own revenues, by producing and selling what was surplus to the needs of its community, and to building its wealth, then the ways of the world would inevitably creep into the heart of the Church. The desire to harvest gold would replace the harvesting of souls. A man might seek to leave the world by joining the cloister, but the cloister could never part from the world.

He envied the hermit, Tatwine. Here was a man who relished the gift that God had bestowed upon him, who had escaped the demands of the world to combat evil in the unseen realm. It was a purpose that the priest wanted for himself, but God in his wisdom had another road for him. It was not one that Eadred welcomed.

He had waited for the bell to call the community to their midnight service. When it became clear that such a sign would not be forthcoming, he hurried past the rising sounds of the feast towards the church. A door to Eadred's left opened and two young women, as agitated as he at their tardiness, burst from the dormitory a step or so ahead of him. They mumbled for his forgiveness and after a moment's hesitation, hastened along the dimly lit corridor towards the church.

The priest did not expect a full assembly of Elmstow's community, but when he arrived, he just shook his head. The three lonely figures waited in awkward silence for a minute or so but none other appeared.

"Father, how should we proceed? There are so few of us. We are only postulants with little understanding of how to worship in the correct way. I am Leoba and this is my sister, Edith."

"But you surely attend the services? Tell me that this woeful sight is a rare departure from the minster's usual practice? The duty of the whole community with its postulants and novices is to observe the cycle of daily prayer and praise."

"We are seldom allowed to, Father. We were slaves in Mercia and would be treated as slaves here if not for the abbess. We were captured during a raid by the warriors of your kingdom. Our brother works in the minster's fields. The lords of the East Angles and Mercia squabble over land and wealth and enslave each other's people but the abbess showed us the love of Christ and paid for our freedom and brought us here last summer."

This was a side of the abbess that Eadred found surprising, from what the bishop and Tatwine had told him. He could not hide a hint of scepticism.

"The abbess has done you a great service, to be sure, but it is her responsibility that you be allowed – be required – to share in the community's worship of our Almighty Saviour. Her duty is to save souls, not just bodies."

Leoba replied with a weary smile, "You would know that many of the Sisters here come from powerful families, Father. They are used to lives of privilege and take food and comfort for granted but we have always known poverty and hunger."

Leoba stopped speaking and thought carefully about her next words.

"The abbess has a good heart – that is certain – but from what we have seen she has little control over this house and leaves it to some of the senior Sisters to do what is necessary to run the minster."

"She has many tasks, and it is right that the more experienced Sisters share in the load. It is sensible."

Again, the postulant held her silence for a few moments before replying to Eadred.

"My words were poor, Father. These are Sisters who run the minster, as they see fit. It is not right. They ignore our Holy Mother and show her no respect. There are some good people here and they speak of the abbess having lost the will to lead. We have been told by the elder Sisters that we must be patient and humble and learn to serve others as Christ did, before our instruction begins. Christ served even the poorest and most wretched and we must imitate him. So, we perform duties that the Sisters tell us to do – cleaning and helping in the kitchen, serving at the benches, and we have skill at weaving and sewing, so we do this for the wealthy Sisters, who are keen to look enticing tonight at the feast. Thus, we wait and serve as part of our instruction."

Then, with a nervous glance that suggested Leoba feared she had said too much, the postulant continued.

"Yet, Father, it is better – far better – than our former lives and we give thanks to the Lord God for that."

Eadred nodded, although he knew that, at least for the moment, the sisters were treated barely better than slaves by the rich and indulgent community.

"It seems that you alone of the community are absent from the feast. Are you also forbidden to attend?"

The figure of Edith drifted from the shadows into the candlelight with a brief smile at the priest. Eadred failed to contain a gasp.

Before him stood the most beautiful woman he had ever seen. The flickering light danced across a face that was beyond his experience, framed by a white headpiece, with the effect that Edith's perfect features seemed to float out from the cover of darkness like those of an angel. Eadred's intruding eyes moved briefly over the shape of the postulant's body. The subdued candlelight hid his crimson face, but he stuttered over his next words. Leoba responded.

"Father, most of the community was given leave to miss the midnight service, in order to attend the feast and to flatter the ealdorman – but we were not. I was told I might be called upon to serve later, if the slaves cannot bring food, ale and wine quickly enough to meet the appetites of the ealdorman and his warriors. They use all manner of words but in truth, they do not want my sister there." Edith reached out to hold her sister's forearm and the two women smiled warmly at each other.

"I have been cursed by the kind of beauty, many tell me, that men crave." Edith spoke cheerlessly. "All I ever wished for was to worship the Almighty and to draw closer to him. But the evil one placed a curse on me as I grew from a child into a young woman. I was plain and unnoticed then the

37

bane worked within me." Edith moved her reproachful eyes to meet Eadred's.

"Even those who have chosen to give their lives to the Lord God and to renounce the ways of the flesh are tempted by the most outward allurements. I give no encouragement." Eadred nodded in response.

"When the abbess bought our freedom and we entered Elmstow, we truly believed that we had been delivered from the traps of the flesh – but Father, sin walks these cloisters without fear and with many friends. Who is to clean out this foul nest?"

"The bishop does know of the decay of this house and has sent me to gather information that he might use to root out the offending maggots." As soon as Eadred had spoken, he wished he had kept quiet about the purpose of his visit, as Bishop Aethelbert had demanded.

"It is important that this is not known. I explain it to you to give you hope. Now, swear on the Holy Bible that you will keep this knowledge secret." Both sisters did as they were asked without hesitation, although they said it was unnecessary.

Edith continued, "One of the nuns told me in blunt words that she and her friends had decided that I alone of all the community would be forbidden from attending the feast. They have waited for tonight. They have had us working late into the night to make fine, embroidered clothes that flatter their bodies. Few of the younger nuns expect to go to bed alone. I was told of their worry that men are shallow about their choice of women at a feast and, if I were at the benches, the most manly of warriors would want me over any of them. I would have no power to refuse."

"What!" Eadred could not believe what he was hearing. It was even worse than the image painted by Tatwine, although that was bad enough. "I will speak to the abbess."

Edith shook her head.

"For what purpose, Father? She will not forbid the activities of the nuns. It is known that the ealdorman hates this place and wants us gone. Her one desire is to please him and his men and to change his mind. As for me, if I am spared a night of having to please men, I am grateful. I am a gift to merchants and thegns who visit, and some of the priests in this Holy House," she spoke the words bitterly, "use my body in turn. It is the price I must pay for being here."

Eadred groaned, holding his head in his hands. He felt impotent, unable to protect or support these women in their desire for the cloistered life. It led him once more into dangerous territory.

"My duties to the bishop call me to the evening meal, although it disgusts me to participate in such a swill. However, I will return for the three o'clock service and I will have the community also called. They have been excused once and that is enough.

"I have no confidence that the designated Sister will ring the bell tonight, so would you undertake this duty to rouse our fellow warriors of Christ?"

Leoba raised her eyebrows, imagining the effect the three o'clock bell might have on the Sisters and their activities.

"I will, Reverend Father. I will do as you ask."

"The evening may have been stolen by the ealdorman, but the night service belongs to God in his own home and I want all the community to attend. Now, ring the bell on time and loudly, so we proclaim that this is God's house."

"I will, Father. I will not let you down. I swear it. And Father, do not judge our dear Holy Mother too harshly. I see the sadness in her eyes. She has been abandoned by those whose support she had every right to expect. It is they who deserve your condemnation."

Eadred sighed. He had already said too much.

"Now, God be with you both." With that, Eadred led them in the Lord's Prayer then the sisters hurried away.

What manner of place is this? the priest thought, on his return to his cell. The church almost empty, while holy women arrayed in tight dresses barged past him, swooning at muscled warriors. The words that issued from their mouths were as far from Christ as east from west. The sounds of excess and debauchery waxed and assailed Eadred's ears. He knew he should pray for their return to God's ways but, in his dismay, he urged God's wrath to strike down all those who had turned from him.

SEVEN

Demons

Black-faced and so close that its spear-sharp bristles cut into the hermit's skin, the demon stared into Tatwine's eyes. Each breath blew the stench of rotting flesh. With a grunt, the creature from hell extended its tongue. The blotched, disfigured muscle pushed hard against Tatwine's lips. The grin was malicious. Mouth firmly closed, the hermit stood his ground, his back against a great oak.

Armed through hours of prayer by the might of the Lord God, every fibre of his body and every thought that possessed him exalted in the battle. Night after night, the hideous creatures rose from the depths of the pit to reclaim their domain that the monk had invaded. Each night they fail. So now, they try a new path. Their words – not spoken but yet in his mind – recall the hermit's youth.

When he stole food many times from an ageing neighbour who died, feeble and hungry, in winter's bite. When he followed a slave girl on her journey to collect water, ripped the tunic from her budding body, and would have forced himself inside her, until he saw the scared child in her face. When, ale-addled, he had fought his friend over a forgotten slight and killed him with an axe blow. Compensation was paid for his crimes, as required by the king's law, which took his kin years to pay, for Tatwine had few resources of his own. The weight of these sins had grown and refused to leave him. Then one day, God's spirit entered his heart in a flash of light and Tatwine gave his soul to his Saviour and entered the cloister.

With joy, not guilt, he faces the demon now and when its defeated tongue withdraws, the monk shouts the sacred name of the Creator in its face. The fiend shrieks then slinks away with its slimy entourage, having again failed to remove the monk from their realm.

"Praise to the Lord God. You foul creatures of the devil; I have no fear. Do your worst for you know the Creator of all that is good will never be defeated." Tatwine raised his numb arms and laughed. "Praise to the King of the Mighty Armies of Heaven."

The sickly, sweet odour of corrupt flesh begins to fade.

"I am ready," the hermit shouts, his face wild with expectation, his muscles tense. A source of light radiates from behind him. Tatwine turns quickly and steps around the trunk that protects his back to greet it. He peers as the light moves closer and begins to take shape. The darkness dissolves, his nostrils are bewildered by the scent of spring flowers. Still unfinished, the shape moves ever nearer, until it stands fully formed an arm's length before him.

Tatwine gazes upon a woman's form. He blinks and his resolve to command that it return to the underworld falters.

"See what you have sacrificed, my brave warrior. My master is weak and close to death. I am the slave you wanted so badly. I can be yours now. He will sell me to you for next to nothing. He will have no need of money or me soon. Leave the hole that you live in and this stinking fen. We will live together, and I will fill your days and nights with joy. What do you say?"

The words to hurl the apparition back to hell do not form. Tatwine stares. He recognises the face. It had appeared to him in dreams many times in earlier years but never as perfectly as this. His desire had been desperate that afternoon when he had followed the girl but her face – the face of an angel – had conquered his lust. Her scented fingers loosen her tunic. It falls.

"See how I have grown. Come, lie with me now." She reaches out a hand.

The words struggle to emerge from the hermit's mouth.

"You appear as her, but you are a demon." He closes his eyes. "Be gone from here. In the name of the Lord God, be gone." He strikes out with his fist. His further commands are lost in the sudden tumult of voices. "Go!"

The beasts from hell shout and scream but in the voices of men and women.

"The Lord God will help me fight. You have no power over me."

Again, a plea. A demon would never call on the Living God. The hermit pushed himself away from the protecting tree, dragging his feet through the oozing mud in the direction of the noise. The shouting grew louder; more distressed and fearful then muffled. The hermit bellowed out an alarm.

"I am coming." His foot hit a fallen branch and Tatwine was launched forward onto the ground. Winded, cold and with his ankle throbbing with pain, the cries and moans urged him on. Then silence. He stood still, wincing, breathless – nothing but the sound of feet pounding into the distance.

Tatwine reached the main track to Elmstow, just after the summit of the hill before it descended towards the minster. He slumped to his knees. The clouds opened and moonlight poured from the heavens, bathing the frost-covered country. On any other occasion at this season and time of night, he would sit and wonder at God's creation. The bare, silver-green branches; the vast expanse above, glowing with pulsing candlelight; the rich lands of the East Angles, glinting as a million jewels, stretching to the horizon; the damp, potent scent of winter; and the bell chiming from the minster church. But not tonight. He saw two figures disappearing down the slope towards Elmstow. Had he been torn from his vision or still at its edges? One of the figures limped along behind the other but there was urgency in their movement.

The hermit raised himself and turned to walk back to his shelter. Between the forks of the ridge, not ten minutes' walk from where he stood, there was a pit that had been dug into the chalk by giants many generations beyond memory, and marked at its mouth by huge rocks that had been fashioned into a roof. The rocks bore the deep grooves and scratches from the effort of dragging them from their birthplace. The place was shunned by men, who feared entrapment by the dark creatures that had made their home there. Yet Tatwine, to atone for his sins, chose here as the place where he would live and daily battle the infuriated monsters.

Not long after leaving the track and making his way towards the tree cover, Tatwine saw a mound on the earth some way ahead. He knew the area well, so the sight was unexpected. The time when he confronted demons had passed for the night – he detected none of the familiar signs and smells that told of the infernal realm. Perhaps a sheep or pig that a slothful servant had let wander off the track on the way to the minster's lands and that had been killed by wolves? Still, he was curious. The monk drew closer and his breathing quickened. The form was human.

The figure lay partially curled, looking away from Tatwine and covered in a hooded cloak. There was no movement, but the hermit advanced cautiously. He had no weapon, as was his usual practice, and felt uneasy. Silently, he bent and searched the frozen soil for a fallen branch and soon he found a solid stake. Though fearless in confronting demonic beings, Tatwine began shaking when thinking of his next move.

"What afflicts you?" His voice trembled. With no answer forthcoming, he repeated his question and poked the figure gently with the stake. Still no response. Tatwine pushed harder, then harder still, while repeating his question. With apprehension growing, the hermit did the inevitable and decided to touch the figure on the shoulder. First gently, then he shook it harder. With his heart in his mouth, Tatwine took the body by the shoulders and turned it.

"God in Heaven, what is this?" He stared down at the silvered face of a woman – the slave he had once desired and who had appeared to him earlier that night as a demonic being. Fear contorted her lifeless expression. Tatwine sat paralysed and confused. Why would a woman from his youth, whom he had not seen for several years or more, suddenly appear to him – in spirit and now in the flesh? Blood gushed from a wound between her breasts. He knelt beside her and prayed.

"I will not leave you to be torn apart by wolves. Though I prayed for the strength to forget you, you were often in my dreams for many years, until the Lord God helped me overcome my coarse and lewd desires. I had wanted to touch you but not like this." Tatwine pushed his hands beneath the woman's body then braced himself and lifted. He began the slow walk back to his home. Several times the effort almost proved too much, even for his strong frame, but he fulfilled his word and lowered her into his pit and covered her in shallow soil and stones at the back of the shaft.

The hermit sat near the mouth of his strange home, in fitful contemplation and prayer, weeping. Such pain in his heart that a memory he had prayed would be healed had now been poisoned. What purpose did the Lord God have in this agonising night or had the demons gained a victory? Sleep released him sporadically.

He awoke, bewildered, saddened and seized with fear. The men who had killed a defenceless girl could already be in Elmstow and what harm was it possible for them to wreak? Though it would be several hours yet before light smeared the eastern sky, he would need to alert the community. The hermit felt the knife he had tucked beneath his belt and set off.

EIGHT

The Feast

"Priest, sit here; sit here!" Ealdorman Ceolfrith's tone and gesticulations were polite enough, eased by considerable volumes of alcohol, but with no intention of accepting refusal. "Next to the abbess and me, as befits the bishop's representative. And this is the Lady Cuthburg."

The ealdorman reclined in a chair more imposing than that of the abbess. His was the smile of the blissfully relaxed and secure. The excess of food and drink accounted for part of his demeanour, but he was also presiding over a feast with his beloved hearth-group of warriors and he rejoiced in their company.

Eadred bowed politely to the king's daughter, to Hereburg and to the ealdorman and sat beside the abbess, whom he had not met before. The ealdorman banged his cup down, twice. The woman who was dispensing ale and wine to the vessels thrust in front of her moved quickly to

47

the main bench, ignoring the slurred complaints of those who had missed out. She stopped where the ealdorman sat and poured. Eadred watched her carefully. She raised her head for a moment then drifted away, head bent forward, avoiding scrutiny. It was Leoba – but she did not go unnoticed.

The ealdorman's son, Aelfric, stood and grabbed at the forearm, stopping her from disappearing through the door. He spun her around and, though Eadred could not discern his words, his action was clearly fuelled by anger. She tried to free herself while he continued to fire questions, his fury and her fear mounting.

From the disordered mass of the feast, the moneyer, Regenhere, appeared. He spoke to Aelfric with urgency, pulling his other arm, trying to persuade him to withdraw. The jug fell to the floor and smashed. Aelfric pushed Leoba away and fell back into his seat. Regenhere spoke closely into his ear; it was to reassure, that much was clear, but Aelfric's stony countenance signified a lack of success. The noise of the feast continued unabated, but the ealdorman had not missed the incident.

The young priest understood that this was not going to be a restrained and reflective meal, but his senses were assaulted by the sights, sounds and smells of near-pagan indulgence. Warriors sprawled in their chairs and, having sated their stomachs, were moving their attentions to the adoring cloistered women, only the elder of whom wore the prescribed dress. The others had arrayed themselves in embroidered garb and flashy baubles and they laughed and giggled at the lewd implications of the kingdom's heroes. The air was thick with the stench of meat, fat and intestinal vapours.

Eadred knew well enough where the surfeit of alcohol and the allure of warm, compliant bodies would lead. The priest was no saint. He had fallen often enough onto his bed senseless from drink and had accepted the favours of several young women he had attended. Was the gluttony and debauchery of each soul he looked upon now a worse sin than his own?

It was – of this he had no doubt. They enjoyed their debauchery with no regret. He did not. The shameless men and women falling over each other in front of him thought it harmless amusement; he knew it was a sin. After each of his failings, he wept, confessed and prayed for forgiveness and for the strength to resist temptation when it met him once more.

"Reverend Mother, in the name of our Lord, thank you for your hospitality. The bishop has been ill and has charged me with his usual visit. I have a letter from him in my cell and will give it you when you wish." He bowed again, watching the abbess' response carefully, as the bishop had asked of him. She smiled vaguely, with eyes staring in front of her, then began mumbling the Lord's Prayer.

"Please thank the bishop on your return and I pray that your opinion of our poor house is favourable. Come, take some refreshment."

Her next words were lost as a shriek of laughter caused Father Eadred to flinch. It was like a nightmare. A slave played the cithara and sang a song to glorify pagan warrior heroes. The curling sea of flesh heaved. Hands stalked and squeezed responsive breasts. In the shadows, one of the odious men and an immodest Sister-in-Christ had begun their rhythm of obscenity.

"Abbess Hereburg, I must insist…" Her eyes remained closed; she waved away his complaint. It was too much. The bishop had told him to watch and note all that transpired but not to attempt to alter any of the behaviour he witnessed and that it would all be used when the time was right. It was well enough for the bishop to speak thus but he was not looking at this flagrant abuse of God's house. Eadred would say nothing yet but he could stomach no more. The priest rose, knocking over his chair. The tide of laughter, grunts and groans surged from wall to wall.

"Priest, sit down!" Eadred heard the ealdorman's words and the disgusting string of abuse that followed but with little thought of anything other than escape, he ignored them. It was the least of the abhorrent profanities assailing his senses. Eadred hurried to the door. He did not get there.

A massive hand fell onto his shoulder; Eadred crumpled under its weight. He groaned, as it squeezed tighter, and even more when he heard the ealdorman yell out, with slow determination, "Bring him here!"

"Let me go! Leave me alone, please!" Eadred struggled and pleaded but with a warrior to either side of him, it was futile. Effortlessly, they took him by the tunic at his shoulders and lifted him from the ground. The sounds of bawdy feasting turned to laughter and ridicule. Eadred still demanded his release but as he saw the faces – not only warriors but also nuns – laughing until they wept, pointing at a sight they found so comical, tears began to well up in his eyes. He was dropped to the ground the other side of the bench from Ealdorman Ceolfrith.

"This is God's house, and I am the bishop's representative. I—"

The ealdorman shouted over his shaking voice, "What did I tell you, priest? This is the king's property, and I am the king's chief minister. The bishop is far away, and you would do well to recognise that you show your displeasure at your peril. I will have my position honoured."

A few of the warriors shouted out their views on what should now happen – from tying Eadred to a chair and filling him with ale to cutting off his ears. The drunken hall filled with the pulse of feet and hands, drumming out a sickening beat, while voices roared for some sport at Eadred's expense. The ealdorman leant back in his chair and smiled.

"Honourable sir, your men are tired after their feats in battle and deserve the best this poor house may serve. Please, give this priest leave to depart so that you and your warriors may enjoy this feast without further hindrance." Hereburg bowed again, as she had done when she moved to stand directly in front of the ealdorman. The noise around them continued unabated. Ceolfrith had winced and moved forward in his chair, trying to understand the abbess' words. She may have had to compete against the clamour, but the ealdorman had no intention of doing so. He stood, drew his sword and smashed it down on the bench. The laughter and shouting died away and there was silence. The ealdorman began to speak.

One of the warriors, well and truly inebriated, collapsed to the floor, bringing half of a bench's contents with him.

"Take him out and throw him in the fishpond!" Once Ceolfrith's order had been carried out and silence restored, he started once again.

"The priest should be allowed to depart, I agree, but not before an apology and the correct behaviour. It was surely impertinent to leave our bench without requesting leave from me, the princess and you. There is a proper way of doing things." Hereburg nodded and turned to Eadred with expectation. He was more than happy to comply and did so in a quiet, tremulous voice.

"Reverend Mother, Lady Cuthburg, Lord Ceolfrith, please excuse my poor manners. I am but a simple priest. I ask for your permission to leave the hall and to retire to my cell to pray." The two women nodded and the ealdorman, once he had overcome his annoyance at being listed last in Eadred's apology, did likewise.

Eadred moved quickly through the benches towards his escape. The noise rose again. He ran across the courtyard towards his cell, turning fearfully to see if he were being followed. The screams and moans beside a fire near the dormitory wall brought terror. The white arse rose and fell and the nun, with her tunic pulled up to her chest, and the warrior drove their enjoyment to its finality. The priest swerved past them and on to his sanctuary.

Eadred leant against the door of his cell, shaking and weeping into his hands. Disgust, sadness and loneliness overwhelmed his fragile heart. In the house of God, in the community of handmaidens of Christ, in a Christian kingdom, Christ was a stranger. He gave scant thought then to how the abbess had taken him from the lion's den but later he prayed for her. He had no understanding of why the ealdorman, who seemed ready for his blood, had acquiesced to the abbess' request. None of it made sense.

"My Father, protect and save me from my misery." Eadred's words fell into weeping. He slumped into his bed, exhausted, but the knot in his stomach and the images of his ridicule kept him from sleep. He had never felt hate that burned inside him until he met the ealdorman.

"Send your angels to cleanse this place of evil, so it becomes a fitting home for those who hold you highest. Give me the strength to act as a warrior for you."

NINE

Murder

Less than an hour later and barely twenty yards from Father Eadred's lonely suffering, in her chamber, Cuthburg and Aelfric had disposed of their clothing and were blissfully celebrating their reunion. After their accumulated passions had been gratified for the moment and before Aelfric returned to help guard his father, the princess spoke of a plan that could lead to her freedom from her father's vow and secure for Aelfric the king and queen's unending gratitude and acceptance that the two would marry. Encouraged by their joyous bonding and plans, they laughed at the vile trick Cuthburg and Mildred had played on their two lovers – sending them to the wrong rooms, where their salacious whispers had brought aged nuns to open their doors.

The clanging bell thundered in Eadred's head. Had he slept? Misery must have exhausted him and granted a few minutes of peace. The peal filled the minster, louder and longer than the usual alarm. Leoba had fulfilled her task admirably and not a soul could avoid its urgency. But there were those who would never wake.

"Murder! In the name of God, bloody, demonic murder!" Then screams and wails. Eadred heard running along the corridor outside his cell and more voices. He dressed quickly and sped towards the mayhem. The passage was blocked by holy Sisters and warriors; some half-dressed, emerging from the same doors. The priest managed to find a way past them until the hulking form of the moneyer, Regenhere, facing away from the priest, obstructed further progress. Eadred shook his shoulder. He turned, his face devoid of colour for once, and his frog eyes bulged in terror.

"I am ruined." He squeezed his temples and groaned. "I am ruined." Eadred pushed past him.

"God in Heaven!" Eadred shuddered. It was a scene from blood month but not of beasts' carcasses. The priest's eyes rose to see two lifeless faces.

"Dear God, I did not pray for his death, only for the minster to be purged of evil."

Ceolfrith had been tied to a young woman, back to back, hanging by their necks from a rafter; both naked. But it was the woman that caused Eadred to cry out. Both of the dead had balls of woollen yarn pushed into their mouths, but her face had been distorted almost beyond recognition.

"It is the Princess Cuthburg." Voices wailed. One rose above the others.

"Let me pass! Out of the way!" Aelfric pushed through the door of the princess' chamber.

No words formed; just the howl of a dying beast. The

ealdorman's son fell back against a wall, then he wailed, "No," four or five times, and slumped to his knees.

"Out! All of you, out!" Aelfric's and the ealdorman's men stood still, confused. "Leave me. All of you leave!" Then he screamed, louder than before, "Do not stare at them! Proclaim it to all that if anyone attempts to flee this minster, they will be found out, hunted down, disfigured and executed." Aelfric bellowed to his most trusted hearth companions, "Secure the gates. Whoever committed this atrocity will die in agony. Go, quickly. Scour the whole minster."

The warriors left, pledging to Aelfric that they would let no-one leave and that his father and Cuthburg would be avenged.

"You, priest. You must stay."

The ealdorman's son closed the door and, falling against the wall, let out a low groan of wretched pain. Eadred knew too well the moans and cries of anguish from men and women who had lost those close to them. Sometimes, their misery affected his own demeanour and he sobbed together with them and performed his priestly tasks with love and tenderness, as though he were saying farewell to his own sister. With others, he felt distant and looked upon the tears and forlorn state without emotion. But this was a new experience. Eadred stared at the earthen floor, unable to share Aelfric's sadness. A weight had been lifted from him with the ealdorman's death. Time passed slowly.

"Priest, Elmstow is full of vermin. You know this already. There will be foul talk of this terrible crime; that my father and the princess were naked in her room. I tell you that some fiend has made it appear that there was some disgusting behaviour – some vile connection – between them. That is a lie and if I hear of anyone spreading this poison, I will have them flogged.

"You are not from here, which is good, for you will help me cover the bodies and to pray for the release of the princess' soul and for her to be accepted into the Lord God's house." Aelfric breathed deeply, refusing to look at the bodies. "I will be truthful." Though the door was closed, there were still the sounds of crying nuns and angry warriors not far from where Aelfric and Eadred knelt. Aelfric lowered his voice to a whisper.

"I will talk about my father. I have accepted the Lord Jesus Christ as my saviour and rejected all other gods and spirits, as the Church demanded, but my father was a stranger to the Lord God. He said the words that were needed for the king and queen to believe he had turned from our family's ancestral protectors – but he had not altered his heart. He did still commune with spirits that the Church has condemned."

"With demons?"

"Hush!" Aelfric put his hand to Eadred's mouth. "The ealdorman had many difficult responsibilities. His warriors saw him as the bridge to the spirits of their ancestors, but the king demanded he be baptised. He did so through loyalty to King Athelstan, but it was shallow. Father, is this the work of some dark force from the underworld? I fear for his soul. Is it lost?"

Eadred did not want to answer. It was a question he had been asked before – more times than he wished – but he could not lie. The Church was clear with its belief and that the truth had to be spoken, as often as needed. The bishop had told him of the pressure he was under from noble families to mellow his position, but he could not in conscience go against the Holy Bible.

"Lord, we cannot serve God and the devil. If your father did consort with demons then yes, he turned from Christ and there is no place for him in God's hall. It was your father's decision, and we are powerless to remedy it.

"It is possible that a demon has done this but not alone. The devil does his work through men by twisting their minds. If your father knew demons, then all manner of obscenity is possible."

Aelfric nodded. The priest had expected an argument, but none came. Before Eadred had time to speak further, the ealdorman's son continued but in a softer, more sensitive voice.

"Princess Cuthburg was devout in her love of the Lord Jesus. There is no taint upon her. I cannot imagine who of this world would have committed this outrage. Someone in the minster – my father or others but not her – has communed with creatures from hell. You must pray that her soul is safe, and help me cover her body – their bodies – and her poor face. They must not be left to hang like animals."

"My lord, I will pray for the princess, most assuredly – but if your father turned from Christ, my prayers shall have no purpose for him."

"He has chosen his own fate. We can do no more."

"My lord, we will cover the body of your father, but I will go now and ask the abbess to come quickly with some of the cloistered Sisters to care for the body of the princess."

"No, you alone will help me with both bodies." Aelfric's pointed finger shook a few inches in front of Eadred's eyes.

"But my lord, it is wrong for men to touch her naked body. I cannot. You cannot command me to do this, which is against the rules of my house."

"I will not have any of the women here touch her. Do you hear? They are unworthy. They are corrupt. I know something of them. I cannot do this alone. You have no improper thoughts, priest, so you will help me."

Eadred closed his eyes, tormented by what had been asked of him.

"Remember, priest, you have few friends here. You would do well not to make me your enemy. Come, they cannot be left as they are."

The ealdorman's son was right. Eadred started to pray aloud.

"I am sorry how you were treated at the feast. I spoke to my men afterwards. It will not happen again.

"I will send for clean clothing for both of them."

Aelfric shouted to one of his men to bring blankets and cloaks. Eadred continued to pray for the souls of both victims, despite what he had said to Aelfric, until the guard and one of the Sisters returned laden with blankets and cloaks for the corpses.

The woman was soon running back along the corridor, crying loudly, after receiving blistering abuse from Aelfric for having assumed she was to care for Cuthburg's body.

"We will cut them first from each other then we will more easily be able to lower them in a proper fashion." Eadred agreed. It was a dreadful task but at least he would be able to give the dead the dignity that was their right.

With the door bolted, the two men commenced their task. They stood on a bench, so they could unknot the rope that bound tightly around the chests and trunks of the two bodies.

Each man avoiding standing in front of the ghastly corpses but placed themselves at the sides. Eadred kept his eyes focused on the task, at pains not to look upon Cuthburg's nakedness or to touch any part of her but her hands. Had he looked at the ealdorman's son, when he reached up and struggled unsuccessfully to wrest the huge ball of wool from her mouth, he would have seen such a sight of dejection and sadness that could not hold its silence.

"I am alone," Aelfric moaned. "What creature could have done this?"

Eadred did not answer but continued his work. He knew that the devil worked through men to create fear and discord. Murder by secretive hands sowed dissension in the community, setting neighbour against neighbour with enmity spilling down the generations. This monstrous crime had been committed by one or more of those who had been in the minster that night. Someone so soaked in sin and depravity that they had lost the fear of God.

Accidentally, the priest's hand touched Cuthburg's thigh. Eadred recoiled with such panic that he almost lost balance. When he had recovered, the priest appeared thoughtful, and surreptitiously moved the back of his fingers so they brushed against her thigh once more. It was cold. It entered the priest's head to touch the ealdorman's corpse similarly. Without alarming Aelfric, Eadred managed to lightly brush Ceolfrith's thigh. There was still a hint of warmth, though the night had been bitterly cold. He reached up to take the ball of wool in his hand and began to prise it from the ealdorman's mouth. When the offending object passed by Eadred's nose, he flinched from its unpleasant odour.

When the last of the bonds around the bodies fell away, the corpses separated and the tension in the ropes around their necks caused the bodies to turn gently, like some grim dance of death, until they faced each other. Eadred gasped at the sight of a savage wound to the back of Cuthburg's head and the ghastly veil of blood and juices that had dribbled down her back. The ealdorman's son stared in horror.

"In God's name, no! Leave her be." Aelfric held his father's arm and moved him back, so he again faced away from Cuthburg. As he did so, the princess turned, and Aelfric looked up into one of her sightless eyes.

"How can I live?" He buried his head in his hands and wept, muttering some words of affection. His right hand moved and rested on her thigh, where it gently caressed her cold skin, and tears welled in his eyes.

Eadred blinked several times, trying to understand what he was witnessing. He had overheard some of Aelfric's whispers; he wished he had not. Surely, the intimacy of Aelfric's contact and his words – their gross indecency – could not suggest that he had been in some improper relationship with the princess? She had been promised to the Church as a perpetual virgin by the king and it was the sacred obligation of any man, let alone one of Aelfric's status, to observe this holy state. It was beyond anything Eadred's imagination could conjure. Aelfric's soul was in danger and the priest needed to act quickly.

The ropes that had hanged the two unfortunates had been thrown over the central rafter and were fixed to an iron ring embedded in the wall of the cell.

"Lord Aelfric, it is time to release each of them." He would have said more but the priest's troubled mind told him to speak only a few words. Aelfric looked distracted but eventually nodded. They climbed from the bench and while the ealdorman's son took the strain of the rope holding Cuthburg, the priest used Aelfric's sword to saw through it. Once her body had been lowered to the ground, the two men knelt on either side of the princess.

Eadred started to move her right arm so it was tucked closer to her body, but Aelfric raised his hand. The priest moved away. He watched while Aelfric attempted to dislodge the enormous ball of wool from Cuthburg's mouth. It had been forced deeply into the confined space.

"What animal could have treated her like this?" The ealdorman's son wept, trying to pull the object from her throat and from where it had caught around her teeth. It finally gave way and both men moaned.

An image of a monster's face could not be more grotesque. The cave of her mouth gaped open with distended cheeks. Unless a person already knew of her beauty, it would be impossible to perceive it now. Aelfric cupped her chin and pushed but the mouth would not close. He placed a finger on her eyelid, but it would not shut.

"I swear, priest, when I find who did this, their death will be heard from one border of the kingdom to the other." Aelfric turned his attentions to the rest of the princess' body. It was increasingly awkward for the priest to watch. Each touch from the ealdorman's son was like a caress, not only on the extremities of her limbs, but, as he covered her nakedness with blankets, his hands appeared to linger on her thighs and stomach and elsewhere. Rather than turn away, Eadred seemed frozen by what he was seeing. Without thinking much but knowing he had to end this behaviour, Eadred spoke.

"The soul has left this peerless lady. Her time in the world of the flesh is over, my lord, and her spirit waits on the judgement of the Lord God."

"Pray for her then, priest. Aloud, so I can hear your words."

When Cuthburg's nakedness had been covered, the two men freed the ealdorman's body in silence. Both were keen to break the unease of the last few minutes and proceeded quickly. Nonetheless, again Eadred sensed a discordance between the behaviour Aelfric had shown towards the princess and the treatment of his father's body. He expected the eldest son to exhibit more than the almost hostile indifference and lack of sentiment that was occurring. It was left to the priest to straighten the ealdorman's body and to spread the cloaks over the extremities of the limbs. Aelfric stood silently facing the wall, playing no part, as Eadred went about his uncomfortable task.

"Thank you, Father. You have done me a great service. Now, if you would leave me."

It would have been a completely reasonable and unobjectionable demand if Eadred had not witnessed Aelfric's behaviour over the past half-hour, but he did not dare disobey. Eadred bowed but had one request.

"Lord, it may be useful in finding the killers if I could look at the garments that the princess and ealdorman wore? They may hold some reminder of what happened."

The ealdorman's son appeared displeased.

"If you must but be quick and they stay in this room."

Eadred bowed once more and knelt beside the pile of clothing. He could feel Aelfric's annoyance playing out behind him. The priest hurried, looking over the gore-soaked back of Cuthburg's linen night tunic. He opened the ealdorman's tunic and cloak; they were clean.

The priest had overstayed his welcome and left, saying he wished he could have done more for the ealdorman. He took with him the two balls of yarn, noticing that the one from Cuthburg's mouth had no hint of the foul odour that imbued the ball from the ealdorman.

It was a troubled man who wandered slowly along the corridor towards his own cell, especially when he heard Aelfric bolt the door. Elmstow was sinking into the pit of its own sin.

TEN

Eadred's Task

Bishop Aethelbert struggled to dismount. He winced in pain, almost falling sideways, but waved Eadred away tersely. Then he relented, extending his hand. The priest knelt and kissed the episcopal ring. The bishop's hand was shaking, his condition clearly far worse than when last they met. If the old man were in his bed, Eadred would have thought his last day would soon be upon him.

"I am sorry." Aethelbert rested his hand on the priest's head. "Up you get. It is good to see you again, my boy, despite these awful circumstances, but I am tired and I ache. The journey from Snailwell has not been easy; my old body does not take kindly to riding distances these days and I have more worries than I can bear."

"The Lord God will help carry them." Eadred blushed at his own words. How glib they sounded.

"He will. I hope it." The bishop smiled at his favourite

son-in-Christ, but his face soon changed. "Though I cannot hand them over yet but pray that our Saviour will give me the strength and the wisdom to do my duty – and show me mercy. Now, where is my chamber, for I must talk alone with you?"

They walked slowly to the room that had been allotted to the bishop and once they were seated and he was certain that they could not be overheard, Aethelbert continued. "The king and queen are grief-stricken and the king's need for vengeance almost without bounds. Only the queen saved me from exile. It would have killed me. The king railed against me. He blamed me for the pitiful state of this house. He thought he was sending his daughter to a place of safety. The king takes seriously his sacred duty to protect the peace of the kingdom and the health of God's Church, but both now face ruin.

"And the words he used against me. I have not heard such vile language since I was young – and the king said them against me!

"But the queen, God bless her, she reminded him that some of his own nobles had treated this place as their whoring nest and had stood against its cleansing. He had to own that, and it saved me. She is blessed amongst women, for I do not care to think what would have happened to me. As it is, he has had me on horseback for three long days. I have little concern about my own life, but I cannot die before we find the animals that did this. It weighs heavily on my soul.

"The king and queen cannot believe that their daughter and the ealdorman were in her chamber, naked, of their own choice. It is too wicked to think upon. Somehow, they must have been forced there." The bishop threw his arms into the air.

"One moment, he screams for blood and throws whatever is before him against the wall. The next, the king weeps and broods in his loss and his fear. The minster was under his protection, yet two of the greatest in the land have been murdered here in the most evil and shameful of ways. Our king and queen are suffering from the most terrible loss and the king's honour has been stained. He lives in fear for his soul that he has failed the Lord God, who has taken his only daughter. The kingdom has felt God's wrath and more will fall upon us in the days and weeks ahead."

It was not rare for the bishop to shed tears these days but Eadred was moved to pity by the old man's sobbing. For a few seconds, it overcame his mounting anger that the bishop had let Elmstow slide almost into hell itself and the kingdom might well follow.

"The queen knew of the condition of this house? I thought she was ignorant of its state. She is God-fearing. How could this happen? Did she not tell the king of her fears?"

The bishop raised his hand to stop Eadred's string of questions.

"Answer me this, first. Is it not possible that the men who killed the poor girl on the hill nearby also committed these atrocities? Tell me that it could have been, for if not them, it was someone who was already here in the minster."

Eadred sighed.

"The hermit, Tatwine, has told me that they were running towards here and could have arrived that night before the murders happened, but the gate was guarded well, and no-one entered the minster."

"How much can I bear?" the bishop sobbed.

"You may think that the queen and I failed to do what

we could to cleanse Elmstow when we first knew but there are reasons. I will tell you soon. The queen has no more tears to shed. I heard her wailing in her chamber. Her ladies carry concerns for her life and for her mind.

"The Lord God himself is coming in fury and none of us will be safe from his wrath. The two souls who have died are just the beginning. The wound has festered, and the limb must be removed from the body."

"Could our God be that vengeful?"

"Who knows the mind of God? I know that I cannot absolve myself and the time to act is now – and you have a task to do."

Aethelbert moved himself slowly, groaning as pain convulsed through his back and legs.

"I tire of this body, but it must carry me awhile yet. The evil one tempts us all, Eadred, and I have not been free from his attacks. As age has wearied me, I have sought more comfort than I ought. I understood soon enough what these lords were planning but I did not question them when they offered their gold and I turned away from disputation. All for my own ease."

"But they are powerful men," Eadred replied. "It would be hard to stand against them."

I serve a God who is all-powerful and yet I slithered from the fight like a snake. What, I wonder, do they think of my faith – of my God – if I stand by to let the excesses of the flesh drown this minster? What do I think of my faith? Is it waning as my strength departs? The bishop shook his head, as he contemplated his question and his answer. He did not speak it, but his answer did not favour him.

"Listen hard, my dear boy, I will tell you the truth and

68

what must be done for there is little time left to right these wrongs. Your chaste ears may wish they were deaf but do not miss a word that I speak now.

"It was at the time when the king established this minster that various lords began to endow it with gold and lands. At first, I thought it was their faith and desire to thank our Lord God for all he had done for them and their houses. They came and spoke to me in pious terms and each praised the worth of a nun, whom they said would serve the minster well as abbess – her name was Hereburg. As they were giving their gold to the minster, it was only right that I speak to her. I sent for this nun and despite her lack of experience, compared to others whom I thought had merit, finding her full of the love of our Lord and anxious to serve him, I proposed her name to the king and queen and she was duly made the first abbess.

"In the first months that followed, all seemed well. The new abbess, in her own right, drew together a family of righteous Sisters, whose hearts she searched diligently. The lords who had endowed the foundation also sent young women who were known to these great families to be considered for entry to the cloister. There was nothing exceptional in this, but the abbess told me of a concern that was growing within her that the patrons were seeking for her to accept postulants she did not consider to be worthy candidates. They seemed to have no desire in their hearts to deepen their knowledge of the Lord God, or to praise him, or to tame the desires of their bodies. Yet, these were powerful men, used to being obeyed, and who had endowed the minster richly. The abbess did not wish to cross such men without my support.

"Eadred," the bishop sighed, with his eyes closed. "To my great shame, I asked the abbess to accept the postulants without question and not to cross the great lords. My health was poor, and it sapped my energies and dulled my mind. I had not the will to fight, for the powerful fight hard and long and these are weapons I do not have." Eadred watched carefully as the bishop sat with his bowed head resting on his clasped hands, deep in reflection. Without looking up, Bishop Aethelbert began speaking once more.

"I met and did speak to one of the lords – I shall not mention his name. I spoke courteously about the intentions of the young women he had proposed to enter Elmstow to become Sisters-in-Christ and that he might question them on whether the cloister was suited to them. He said he would but that he found it surprising that anyone would question their piety. I heard nothing more.

"Nor did I hear more from the abbess and I suppose I took her silence as… well." The bishop began to mumble. "I hoped it meant that her concerns were considered carefully and the worst excesses dealt with, but to be honest, I knew then, as I know now, that they were not. Poor Hereburg was left without protection to manage as best she could." The bishop stared at the walls around him then took Eadred's hands in his.

"Do not judge me too harshly, dear boy. These are difficult times for our Church, and I have grown old trying to serve our Lord in the path he set for me. At your age, you would not understand but not all who give wealth to God's Church do so for good reasons and the powerful in our land do not always think of securing God's favour for the kingdom. But I have done what I can in repentance.

Listen carefully now. I have told you much but what I am about to say concerns you directly.

"When I went to court last Easter to deliver Holy Communion for the king and queen, I took the opportunity to talk to Her Majesty. She is a great woman, Eadred; noble, pious and wise. She has a wonderful skill in putting men at their ease, so they talk, perhaps more than they should. So, I found myself telling her my concerns about Elmstow. I think she may have already had some idea. But what affected me most was her concern for Abbess Hereburg. I think perhaps she understood what trials the abbess faced better than would a man.

"From what she said, I also think she did not like the ealdorman. She warned me that he was not a man to be crossed and that the king was blind to his faults. I can tell you this now the ealdorman is dead. The queen advised me not to take the state of Elmstow any further, for she thought that those powerful men who abused the minster would seek the protection of the ealdorman and it would not go well for me or the Church. 'Let it fester,' the great lady said. And so I did."

Eadred waited for the bishop to continue. Aethelbert just stared past the young priest, gently shaking his head. Then he moaned so loudly that Eadred flinched.

"The king is sending his armed men here with the tools to administer the ordeal of hot iron. I am to officiate."

"But we do not know who is accused! Do they mean to put everyone on trial?"

"Ah, that is the case. Everyone who was here on the night of the murders, other than Aelfric and the abbess. All will be tested and those who fail will die a traitor's death.

"This is where this wretched matter involves you, dear boy. Now, listen carefully. What I say to you now is of the utmost importance to the Church in this kingdom, to the kingdom itself, and to me. You must tell no-one what I tell you now. Do you understand? No-one!" Aethelbert waited for a visibly agitated priest to whisper his consent.

"The kingdom is at risk. Not only with the murder of the princess but the king has lost the man who held his forces in readiness, who did his daily bidding to preserve peace and order. There is no man who came close to him. The ealdorman was no friend to the Church, but the king relied on him – too much – and the warriors loved him and love him still and would have gone to the gates of hell for him. Without the ealdorman to gauge the movements of Mercian forces and to direct and lead our army, our borders are unsafe. The world beyond these walls must not discover that Ceolfrith is dead, until the king has re-ordered our defences. He must quickly choose the new ealdorman."

"Lord Aelfric?" Eadred looked and sounded alarmed.

"And what of it? He is the main contender. His father has schooled him well. Tell me what concerns you?" Eadred maintained his silence, wishing he had said nothing. "I have no time for secrets. Too much is at risk. What do you know, boy?" The bishop still spoke in a whisper but there was anger in his face and his whole body shook.

"Aelfric asked me to pray for the princess. He also ordered me to help him take down the bodies – just us two. All others were told to leave the chamber. When we were alone undertaking our task…" Eadred's voice quavered then he drifted into silence. The bishop grabbed his shoulder and shook him roughly. The priest continued, "He had tears in his eyes, and he touched the body of the princess in an unseemly fashion. He spoke immodest words to her." Eadred's face flushed red. The old bishop remained still, waiting for Eadred to continue. "And though his own father rested beside the Lady Cuthburg's body, he gave him no sign of respect."

Eadred sat back against the wall. The silence continued. Finally, the bishop spoke but not until he had cupped his face into his hands and sobbed.

"Oh, how will this end? Now, you must say nothing of what you saw to anyone. I am the only one here who you will confide in. Trust no-one else. Is that clear?" The priest whispered that he understood.

"I have more to say. There is no doubt that the king will close this minster and the Sisters will join other houses if they are fortunate. I would have fought for it once but not now. It is a den of iniquity and has sealed its own fate. We are close to the border here – the king will reclaim the land and grant it to whoever will strengthen his arm.

"The queen believed that the king would not do what was needed to heal the sickness in this place until it raged as a fever and could not be ignored. The poor woman could never have imagined that the fever would take her daughter. The killers will be found, one way or another, and face justice. It will be terrible. Many innocent souls will die as well. The net will take many to catch the few. The dreadful truth is that the murderers came from the armed men or from the community here. It is awful to think on this."

"There are others here though, my lord."

"I know of them," the bishop replied. "Regenhere, the moneyer, is rich and well-respected at court. He has a worldly skill but his son, Raedwulf, lacks the father's ability. He is rather dim-witted, if truth be told, and enjoys an easy life and boasts of his success with women – gained with his father's money. The father must, I think, be disappointed at the son but is too lenient. He indulges his vanity. That must happen when you are rich and have only one child. The moneyer also has other weaknesses, now his wife is dead. There are stories of his liking for younger women.

"I know that Regenhere has set his heart on his son being chosen to replace him as moneyer, but it is the king's decision. Whoever mints the kingdom's coins must be trusted. It must be galling for Regenhere to desire greater esteem for his family but for it to depend on an aimless child."

"Regenhere tells me that he has spoken often to you about how the minster could free itself from those who seek to control it."

"He may have spoken once," the bishop replied, scratching his head, "but if so, it was many years ago. My memory is not that good these days. But, if he says that, I think he might exaggerate."

"Or lie?" Eadred mused.

The bishop said nothing but Eadred saw that the trembling in his hands had worsened. Eadred was also troubled.

"Reverend Father, surely the Sisters-in-Christ will not have to face the ordeal by hot iron?"

"They as well. It was the queen who questioned me closely as to whether any of the religious men and women in this place should have the privilege of undertaking the ordeal by sacrament, if their behaviour had already made them guilty of the worst debauchery. I answered her truthfully that they had sullied their vows. How could I condone the use of the Blessed Sacrament to discover who had committed these murders, when so many of the inmates were already saturated by sin?

"In her anger and sorrow, she demanded trial by hot iron and King Athelstan agreed. No-one will be spared – not even you. I do harbour a fear that the boundless offences that this house has committed will be exposed in the ordeals and many will be found guilty of crimes against God but in the general swill the murderers may escape being identified for their particular grievous sin. God will be wrathful. But there is one way to avoid this dreadful outcome.

"I told the king that I know a man of great faith whom God has blessed with a special gift of prophecy. A man who can look upon the scene of a murder and see an image in his mind of how it was committed and who perpetrated the deed." Eadred began to feel singularly uneasy. The bishop looked him straight in the eyes.

"It was not a prophecy, my lord bishop. I discerned Brother Cuthbert's murderer by studying where his death had occurred and by finding mistakes that Brother Wilfred had made in attempting to hide his crime; and asking questions of him and others. Then the truth that Brother Wilfred wished to keep secret became clear to me."

"But you prayed to the Lord God to shine his light on the crime?"

"I did, of course. I pray for guidance in all I do. But I also used the mind that I was given. I have only detected the culprit this once. Lord Bishop, please tell me that you have not told the king that I can find the murderer? I am not able…"

"Enough, enough! By all that is sacred. If we fail, blood will run like a river. You will do as you are commanded!" The bishop shook with rage. "We are not sitting in the peace of God's house; we are at war with the devil's hordes and you are a soldier with a duty. Have you not heard me? You are the only man who stands between all the men and women here now and the ordeal – and there is enough sin in this abominable house for half of them to be executed! Is that understood?"

Eadred could not face the fury in the bishop's face and looked to the ground. He nodded.

"I pleaded with the king on my knees. He has given you two days to discover the murderer then, if the truth eludes you, the ordeals will start. Now, use the time well – every second. Pray for guidance and I will pray for you. You have until this time the day following tomorrow. Search the hearts of all those you meet.

"Remember, the gift you have is God-given. It is your sacred duty to use it to glorify him. Use it to bring the guilty to justice and to save the innocent. If there is more than one, we must discover them all and root them out. While the murderers are free, further atrocities are possible. Uncover the reasons for this infamy.

"Lord Aelfric knows of your mission – I was told to tell him – and he has said he will support it. Yet, given what you saw, do not put your trust in him or anyone, man or woman, of any station, other than me. And I should tell you that Aelfric has been given charge of all the warriors who are here."

The stern face of Bishop Aethelbert softened and he squeezed the back of Eadred's hand.

"Forgive me but you must understand the enormity of what has happened here and what will follow if you fail. Be cautious, my boy. There is more danger here than in the darkest fen. You are special to me. Beware. Now, is there anything else you need to know?"

Eadred felt heavy with his unwanted responsibility but he knew there was no way he could avoid it.

"One question, Reverend Father. I have heard that the land on which this minster was built was expected to be granted to Lord Aelfric, but the king was persuaded by the queen to grant it instead to the Church. I know from Ealdorman Ceolfrith's own mouth how angry he was that it was endowed to God's work. The moneyer even said that while Ceolfrith lived, Elmstow would never be secure. I would know what more you might know of this?"

The bishop sighed and rubbed his forehead.

"Regenhere knows far more than I but I have heard a different story. Ceolfrith never seemed close in his heart to his eldest son. No-one knows the reason. I remember being told by Ceolfrith's wife, God bless her, in the time before she died that the ealdorman had urged the king to grant this land to one of his other two sons. The charter was even drawn up but when war with Mercia flared again, it was forgotten and then following victory in battle, the land was granted by the king to the Church." The bishop managed a wry smile. "If the ealdorman were alive, he would be a happy man now to see the minster about to be taken from the Church."

Eadred fell against the door of his cell. He poured a cupful of wine. It barely knew the vessel before it was tumbling down his throat. Could Aelfric have killed his own father? It was too dark a thought. Could the abbess have organised the ealdorman's death? Both had reason. But who would want Cuthburg dead? Certainly not Aelfric. Eadred took another cupful then another to dull the whirlpool in his head and fell asleep.

ELEVEN

The Bodies

Eadred woke with a cry. He lay breathing heavily and with each breath he struggled to master the panic swelling within him. He had no time to sleep. Flustered, the priest looked at the candle he had lit; still burning brightly and barely reduced in size. Eadred tried to gather his thoughts. He forced himself from his bed and onto his knees.

Despite every effort, he found it impossible to calm himself. His head spun with fragmentary thoughts and glimpses of the two carcasses and the room that felt their last heartbeats. The priest's mind relived snatches of the conversations he had heard and his mind's eye risked drowning in the sights and faces he had seen around him in Elmstow. Fear drove him into action.

He knew what he had to do before the afternoon closed in. After brief conversations with the two nuns and the priest who had cleaned and dressed the dead, he hurried to the minster church where the two bodies had been laid out.

"Forgive me, Reverend Mother, for disturbing you." Her pale, distressed face when she turned shocked the priest. Only some small signs of life disproved her being dead. She rubbed away the tears with her sleeve. "I did not expect to see you here. Are you ill? Should I send for some of the Sisters to care for you?"

Hereburg muttered some annoyance, rejecting the offer. She knelt before Ceolfrith's body, which lay in an open coffin before the altar with his face exposed. The princess lay in a coffin some six feet away. The air was scented by sprigs of herbs that had been positioned within the coffins and strewn over the floor.

"I have been praying for them." Her voice faltered and drifted almost to silence. "They were of the highest stature in our kingdom and met their deaths in my house. This is weighing on me. It is my duty to pray for their souls, as I have each day, now that the masses we would normally hold for the dead have been forbidden by Lord Aelfric."

"Most assuredly, it is right for you to do so."

"I know of your task, Father Eadred. You must keep me informed of any discoveries you make. Is that clear?" The priest agreed. Hereburg struggled to get to her feet but waved away Eadred's offer of help.

"Reverend Mother, I must thank you for your kindness on the night of the feast."

The gaunt face looked confused.

"For freeing me from the attentions of the ealdorman and his men."

"He would have done you no harm – just entertainment," she gasped, then shuffled from the room.

Eadred had not met Abbess Hereburg before the night of the feast but this surely was not her usual self. She had acted strangely at the feast and now added to his impression by her furtive and distracted behaviour. Her eyes had darted around the room and she emitted little cries of concern for no apparent reason and then shook. She was shaking now, once almost falling against the wall, as Eadred watched her walking slowly along the corridor. She was as if drunk. Her left hand sought the comfort of the stones and when she turned, she looked straight into his eyes. He moved away, feeling awkward, and listened for her steps to disappear. It was his time now to see what the dead could tell him.

On Aelfric's orders, the bodies had been brought from the small stone building where they were being stored and would be returned there at day's end. It was the coldest enclosure in the minster and thankfully the destruction of the flesh that comes once the soul has left its earthly home was not as pronounced as the priest had feared. Still, the odour, though eased by the herbs, was obvious once he drew closer to the bodies.

The ealdorman lay regaled in his fine clothes and Cuthburg in a simple habit and veil that covered her face. They were guarded by two of Aelfric's men and two of the elder holy Sisters. The women continued their sewing, and the men resumed their low-volume chatting. Eadred avoided meeting their gaze but sensed well enough the warriors' annoyance as he began to survey their master in his coffin. The priest prayed silently that Aelfric had been true to his word and had proclaimed the task that had been imposed on Eadred and given his protection.

Ceolfrith's face still possessed the assurance and arrogance of one used to wielding power. Despite his violent death, the ealdorman exhibited no hint in his expression of fear or concern. The man who had threatened Eadred and would have had his men bait him for entertainment still made Eadred uneasy. He bore the ugly mark left by the rope around his neck. When Eadred had helped lower the two bodies, he noticed surprisingly that the hands of neither victim had been bound and bore no mark that they had been tied at any time. It was just as odd that a man of the ealdorman's strength and belligerence did not exhibit more obvious signs of a struggle on his body. The priest who had washed and dressed Ceolfrith had told Eadred that he too had noticed no fresh wounds or other signs of conflict, other than the numerous scars from a lifetime of fighting.

Eadred recoiled in horror when he lifted the veil from the princess' face. The features which had been renowned for their beauty and refinement had disappeared, to be replaced by swollen, discoloured meat. The large woollen ball that had been pushed hard into her mouth had gone, leaving a face misshapen in a ghastly, open-mouthed distortion, as if the princess sought to scream out her killer's name. The bluish bulge of a heavy bruise and the red lines of grazed skin discoloured Cuthburg's left temple, and her neck bore the burn marks of the hanging rope.

Eadred had been contemplating the vicious wound to the back of Cuthburg's head and hoped he could have looked more closely but was under Aelfric's strict command not to touch either body. The holy Sisters who had been charged with washing and clothing her body had said little to Eadred, for Aelfric had angrily dismissed them before they were far into their task and replaced them with his own nurse.

"Did the abbess come alone to pray?" Eadred asked of the two guards. Indifferently, they nodded their agreement. "I thought I saw her looking for something on the ealdorman's body before she knelt?" The guards had no intention of saying anything if they could avoid it. It was clear that they had little regard for the priest and stared at him with barely concealed malice. Eadred responded to their silent aggression. "Then I shall go to Lord Aelfric, whose orders I am following, and tell him that you should be the first to be tested when the king's men arrive to administer the ordeals." Eadred turned away from the two massive warriors to hide his anxiety then returned to face them.

One of the guards then spoke but with a continuing reluctance.

"The abbess did touch our lord's clothing and seemed to look for something."

"Did she take anything?"

"No, I think not. She mumbled some words and cried a little. Then you arrived and she moved away."

Eadred moved to the two nuns and questioned them about any interest the abbess may have exhibited in Cuthburg's body; whether she had touched it or spoken anything? They also seemed annoyed to be asked such things and looked to each other for guidance.

"Did the abbess look first at the ealdorman's body or that of the princess?" Eventually, one of the cloistered women spoke a few words.

83

"Our Reverend Mother went first to the ealdorman's body then you arrived."

"So, I disturbed her from praying for the princess?"

"She had not been here long, so I think you must have done so. It would have been her intention to pray next for the Lady Cuthburg."

The abbess had been there for more than prayer. Eadred had seen it in her eyes. He had disturbed her. It was curious, he thought, that the abbess went firstly to pray for the ealdorman and not Cuthburg. She was both a princess and an inmate of the minster.

"Do you know who found the bodies?"

"Yes, it was Sister Verca."

"Both the princess and the ealdorman are clothed in new garments. Where are the clothes they had on the night of the feast?"

"They were burned, by order of Lord Aelfric," one of the warriors replied.

With nothing else to be gained from talking to those guarding the bodies, Eadred left the dead and went to where they had lost their lives. He had gained the key from Aelfric, who seemed to exhibit no unease about the prospect of having the princess' chamber examined now she was no longer there.

Eadred hoped that without the distraction that the bodies and Aelfric's tormented behaviour had caused on the morning after the murder, he might be able to see something that would aid him in his pursuit. The priest looked carefully over the earthen floor and walls, the rafter over which the ropes had been thrown and the iron hinge to which they had been secured. He came upon a smeared patch of blood against the far wall around the height of his chest. Blood had also flowed freely into the earth away from the wall, where the priest imagined that Cuthburg's head had spilt its contents.

Eadred sat with his back against one of the walls and looked once more around the chamber. In one of the corners, there were half a dozen blue-grey woollen balls, similar to those that had been used to stop the victims from shouting out. None were nearly as large as that pulled from Cuthburg's mouth. Surely, the two souls had died in this room? Someone would have noticed if they had been dragged or carried there. Unfortunately for Eadred, he could see no signs in the earthen floor of the chamber or around the outside of the door to help him; any marks had been obscured by endless feet, coming and going.

Why were the princess and the ealdorman together in her room after the feast – and naked? It horrified Eadred that Cuthburg and Aelfric had been in some immoral relationship; it would be beyond debauchery to imagine that his father had been similarly connected to her! Eadred wished that he had been given the opportunity to look more closely at the clothing they had worn that night but what he had seen showed him that Cuthburg was dressed in her night tunic when she was hit from behind and that later she was stripped.

Someone would have heard, seen or known something. But whom could Eadred question and would they answer truthfully? The ealdorman's son had behaved strangely but his stature protected him from suspicion – at least for now. Reluctantly, Eadred acknowledged that he had to talk again to the abbess and try to uncover the reason for her peculiar actions; then he would talk to Sister Verca.

With darkness and its chill taking possession of the minster, Eadred pulled his cloak closely around his shoulders and hurried towards Hereburg's chamber. It was familiar voices that caused him to slow his pace then to press against the wall in the shadows.

"The king will listen to me now my father is dead but there are other voices – yet I will do my utmost."

The moneyer nodded.

"And my other wish?"

"I have told you; I will see what I can do."

"Good; there is gold and silver if you succeed."

TWELVE

The Sacred Mere

"Almighty Father, forgive me. I am burdened by a great sin."

The bitter gusts bit into her wet body like a blade. Sister Verca bent forward, groaning. The mere lapped at her waist. Her tunic gripped her shivering body. She could endure no more.

Darkness was falling and soon the sky would be as black as the fen soil that nurtured the crops that prospered in the minster's fields. The nun knew the track well. She could feel her way home to the protection of the minster and the warmth of the dormitory, without light to guide her.

One last prayer. A few more seconds of pain then she would end her vigil. All her short life, she had wanted to join the cloister and her wish had been granted. Her life was full of joy but one mistake – one that she had barely understood as wrong – had placed her soul in jeopardy. Now she understood that she had knowledge of the crime.

"I am stupid, so stupid but I am not evil. Heavenly Father, believe me. I was too innocent to understand that I was listening to evil counsel," Verca wept. "I never knew that my silence was wrong. Have mercy on me. I am too young to understand how simple it is to fall away from your spirit.

"You are a merciful God. Free me now from this filthy skin. Lead me back to your ways. There is still time. I swear before you that I will confess to the abbess what I saw." The Sister-in-Christ raised her hands to the skies imploring a miracle – and it happened.

The frenzied wind that had thrashed the naked branches and reeds subsided, until it was still. The heavens opened. Verca felt her soul rise. In rapture, she looked below and saw her own body collapse into the charnel mere. She closed her eyes and prayed, so many words, over and over, giving thanks for God's grace – his forgiveness.

Verca opened her eyes and she saw herself standing once again in the sacred waters. She no longer felt the cold but a wonderful warmth that seemed to cover not only her body but her thoughts, memories and deeds. A parade of faces greeted her. Some she had loved and admired; some she had disliked. But she saw all of them now as her God saw them, and they were wonderful creations. She smiled then burst into tears.

It was a while before she waded ashore and covered herself with her cloak and set her feet on the path back to Elmstow. She knew she had been given a glimpse of God's house and been stripped of her sins. She would never be the same again and was prepared for whatever she had to face in the world of men. Verca began to pray for the one who had led her into wickedness and who had used her innocence.

When she opened her eyes after being clubbed to the ground and felt herself being dragged up and onto her knees with her hands bound behind her, Verca knew that the devil was trying one last time to tempt her back into evil. The young nun heard the strident demands about whom she had told about the morning she had discovered the princess and the ealdorman. Yet the words were like a dream. The voices tried to convict her of her own involvement – she smiled in return. Not one more word would she speak to them; not one more risk of being implicated in the wicked endeavour.

The fists that slammed into the holy Sister's stomach and face were like a child's caress. She sang out the words of praise even louder. Ugly faces, twisted by frustration and fury, spewed profane words a few inches from her eyes.

When the knife sliced off her ears, Verca was unmoved. When her tongue was ripped away, her heart gave thanks that she could never speak untruths again. The rope tightened around her throat and she felt herself being pulled from the ground. Verca's heart rejoiced that she could sin no more.

*

"Lord Aelfric, let me speak to him. Send for his return."

"Enough! I never want to see that face again." The ealdorman's son hammered his fist onto the bench. "He will never be named or seen again in our kingdom." Aelfric's stare kept Eadred's next words from leaving his lips.

When the priest had heard that morning of the discovery of Sister Verca's body and the exile of the warrior who had let her and her murderers somehow leave Elmstow, he hurried to the hall to confront Aelfric to halt the sentence. It was vital to question the man further, he had said.

"What if he were part of the group that had killed the young nun in such a terrible way? What if he were implicated in the murders of the princess and ealdorman? He should be questioned!"

"It is done!" Aelfric shouted. "I knew him well and his father. He would never be deceitful or treacherous. He was a fool and that is all. I trusted him and gave him charge of my guard only last month. My father told me then it was a stupid decision." Aelfric threw his cup against the wall.

To be exiled was a fate worse than execution for the soldier. He was already well on his way to the kingdom's border, where he would be released without weapon, money or horse. For every day that remained to him he would be friendless, remembering his shame. His lands were forfeit and his wife and children left dependent on her family.

He had protested that the walls of the minster were impossible to guard. Some of the length of the perimeter was formed from the original fort built by the Roman legions. It was still strong. In other places, stones and bricks from a ruined villa had been employed by the East Angles in earlier generations to develop the encircling defences. In a few spots, the construction had been thrown together poorly and could be dislodged. The warrior had confessed that he had lately discovered a hole at the base of the wall at the back of an unused pigpen, concealed behind piles of firewood. It was here that those who wished had left or entered the minster, hidden from prying eyes.

"The ealdorman told me that the oaf had no brain and was lazy and he was right. The idiot came from a noble family and I thought that enough. Priest, he had no part in the murders but let the murderers escape. Now, leave me."

Eadred left the hall. Aelfric would have to answer to the king for the escape of his daughter's murderers and the weight of that failure was crushing the ealdorman's son – or so it appeared.

The priest went to the minster church where Verca's body lay. He took one look at her disfigured, mangled face and fell to his knees. He wept and prayed. Eadred was shivering with misery when he stood and gazed once more at the young nun.

"Blessed Sister, I will find whoever did this to you. The Lord God will show me the way and they will face justice. They will not escape and most surely, they will not avoid the wrath of God. But you are now at peace and with our Lord."

Verca had been discovered earlier that day by some of the slaves on their way to the fields. She was hanging naked, her face and body mutilated. Eadred forced himself to look once more at the nun's face and the tears started again to roll down his cheeks. In disbelief, beneath her discoloured flesh and hardened blood, Eadred glimpsed not pain and anguish but a slight smile; an expression of peace.

"Father, you cared for your daughter until the last. Her body faced barbaric treatment, but you strengthened her at the end of her earthly life." The priest felt an upsurge of faith and to his dying day, this would be one of the few moments he remembered when he had come face to face with the immeasurable power and mercy of his creator.

As he looked again at the victory in the young nun's expression, a thought came to him and it led him to rush back to the hall. Two guards barred his way at the door. At odds with his usual caution, Eadred bellowed at the top of his voice, "Lord Aelfric, there is still a way of finding the killers. Let me talk to you, I beg you. Listen!" There was no response. One of the guards took hold of Eadred's cloak and began to drag him from the door.

"Lord Aelfric, listen. Sister Verca has spoken to me. She has spoken to me." The guard's disquiet rose with every word Eadred shouted and he knocked the priest to the ground with a string of oaths.

"Let the priest be." Aelfric stood at the open door. "If this wastes time, I'll have you thrown out of Elmstow." Eadred nodded in response.

"Sister Verca died with a smile despite the violence inflicted on her. I have just seen her; it is marvellous to see such peace. God was with her to the end. Her murderers silenced her, but they did not get from the holy Sister what they wanted. Her smile showed me that the victory was hers."

Aelfric did not seem persuaded by the priest's words.

"What importance is this? She was killed to silence her tongue, or in revenge; or simply killed by ruffians who came upon her in the fens. What does it matter? She cannot speak now, and the killers are long gone."

Eadred appeared thoughtful but not disconcerted.

"My lord, Sister Verca's body was found near the fen mere where she went often alone to commune with God's Spirit. Other Sisters have told me it was her favoured place – and also that she was not one of the delinquents in this minster but a true daughter of Christ. I do not think she was involved in the murders but could have seen or found something when she discovered the bodies that the killers wanted to be kept secret. She would not break your command that all inmates remain within the minster walls unless she needed to take something important to our Lord. Whatever it was, the Lord forgave her.

"Evil men followed her and sought not just to kill her but to inflict terrible pain on her poor body to make her talk – to give up some knowledge, whatever it was, but she did not give in.

"Lord, I do not think the murderers have left the minster. There is some piece of their crime or some task that escapes them still. Do not repair the hole where they entered and left but guard it well. Have your most loyal men swear to secrecy for this may be our only chance. Tell your men to look closely at the faces they see and to shout the alarm if they see one that is unfamiliar – and to search all the minster buildings. With stealth, we may still catch the culprits."

Aelfric sighed.

"I cannot understand this. I pray that this is not false hope."

Eadred stared in expectation; willing the words he wanted to hear.

"Very well, it will be done. Now go and continue your work."

As Eadred left Aelfric's company, he asked for permission to question the warriors and this was agreed. He felt encouraged by the insight the Lord God had given him and that the ealdorman's son had been swayed by his reasoning. Though, as he hastened to the bishop's chamber to tell him what had transpired, it came upon him that he had ignored the bishop's advice to trust no-one.

"What else could I have done?" he said in a whisper,

rehearsing what he would say to Bishop Aethelbert. "I will tell Lord Aelfric no more than I need to, but I have to share some things. The hole in the minster wall may still catch the murderers and it had to be left open." *No*, Eadred thought, *I will say nothing to the bishop and trust in God that I have made a wise choice.*

So, with time slipping by and seeing Abbess Hereburg returning to her cell, Eadred scurried to intercept her, his mind working through the questions he hoped she would answer. She seemed intent on avoiding him and, hearing his request, let out a whimper, her eyes flashing around, like a hare desperately searching for an escape. But with none appearing or forming itself in her frantic mind, she nodded her agreement and disappeared.

The discovery of the secluded breach in the perimeter wall gave Eadred further hope. The two figures that Tatwine had seen heading for the minster could have entered and killed the princess and the ealdorman, which would mean that the community and the warriors would be innocent. But why were they murdered?

THIRTEEN

Questions

Close to half an hour later Eadred knocked on the door of the room the abbess used for small receptions.

"Reverend Mother, thank you for this audience. You asked me to let you know what I had found. Sadly, not as much as I had hoped, and the evil is spreading and with it more darkness. There are now four murders."

"Three! There are three," Hereburg replied in a shrill and angry voice, staring with unnatural eyes. Eadred gulped and after an awkward silence, resumed.

"Reverend Mother, I have heard that a young woman was killed on the night of the feast, on the nearby hill to the south. Her body has been taken to rest in one of the minster's outbuildings. Her death might be connected to the others; it might not. Whoever killed her could have entered the minster somehow and also killed the ealdorman and the princess. It is possible. So, there are four souls who have died unnaturally."

Hereburg sat slumped in her chair, whimpering. The bench before her was cluttered with cups, a jug and several candle holders – some upright, some lying on their side. The abbess had not given Eadred permission to sit but the priest noticed that if she were to give that consent, he would have to remove a pile of dishevelled clothing. Other cups and stubs of candle had fallen to the ground.

Her response to Eadred's explanation was to wave her hand dismissively and she burst into tears.

"I am ruined," she wailed, taking another gulp of wine. "My throat, it burns with fear. I am thrown to the wolves."

"I have found nothing yet that helps in discovering the murderers. But Reverend Mother, did you perhaps find something on the ealdorman's body that might help me?"

Hereburg wailed and shook her head.

To each question he asked, she cried out that she was lost and took more of the wine to her lips.

Eadred pushed on.

"We will all face the possibility of death over the coming few days unless we discover the perpetrators first. Reverend Mother, what is so concerning? I plead with you; what knowledge do you have that causes such distress? The Lord God will not abandon you." But the abbess had dissolved into uncontrollable weeping, babbling incoherently to invisible figures, staring at the ceiling, pulling at her hair.

It was beyond Eadred's experience to know how best to console the abbess. Her behaviour was perverse; even demonic. He would need to talk to the bishop, for if there was a way of freeing her from the dark spirits that assailed her, he would know. There was no point in continuing with the audience.

"With your permission, Reverend Mother, I will talk to the Sisters-in-Christ."

She continued her demented weeping, so with a bow of his head, the priest removed himself from the room and shuddered. Had the abbess' treatment at the hands of others caused her mind to become so troubled that it had warped or had others taken advantage of – or even called upon – an attack by evil spirits?

Eadred spoke to each of the twenty or so holy Sisters and postulants. Most of the stories were the same – they had attended the feast and then retired to bed – alone. No sound of struggle was heard. It was a lie, of course, and had been agreed between many of the nuns. The three priests also had heard and seen nothing.

Eadred's time with the warriors was similarly fruitless. None admitted to liaisons with the Sisters. All said that they had attended the ealdorman at the feast then slept on the floor of the hall but when they were awoken by cries, he was not there.

Each story was the same and monotonously conveyed. Of the female inmates, only Leoba, her sister Edith, and a nun called Tetta had versions that differed from the concocted approach. But he had yet to talk to Lady Cuthburg's companion, Mildred, and would seek her out later. With the gloom of evening approaching, Eadred managed only a brief and anxious time of prayer before the remarks from the women who had expressed anything different from the others entrapped his thoughts once again.

Tetta was one of the older cloistered women at Elmstow – one who had worn her prescribed habit at the feast and who had looked uneasy at the direction in which the celebration was heading. Unlike her slender Sisters-in-Christ at Elmstow, she was solidly built, with muscled arms that spoke of years of hard physical labour. Her face was a similar contrast. Not milky and fine-featured but ruddy, weatherbeaten and puffy. There was a strength about her, physically and also with an air of practical determination. She came towards Eadred with her arms and fists tensed by her sides and with her jaw set, almost as if she were preparing to hit him. She sat on the front of the stool, arching towards the priest.

"I do not remember the time when I saw her. I confess that my head was perhaps awry from ale. I am too old for that sort of celebration and do not take drink well – so I left the feast earlier than the young ones and went to my cell." The nun managed a slight smile. "Even Lord Ceolfrith was fuddled with wine. I did not sleep well; there was too much noise from people moving past my door, laughing and speaking the most unseemly things. Someone knocked – then again. I heard more laughter, as if already in my cell, then fast-moving feet. When I looked, there was no-one. I was about to return to my bed when I saw the abbess. She was leaving from the princess' chamber."

"You are certain it was her and from the Lady Cuthburg's room? It is important, Sister, that you remember carefully what you saw."

Tetta retreated on her stool and remained quiet for a few moments of recollection.

"My eyes are not what they were when I was young, but it was her. She has a way of shuffling these days that marks her out from others. I could not see clearly that she was leaving from the princess' chamber; the wall bends a little between my room and hers and obscures some of the corridor, yet it seemed that she was closing the door. It was not expected, so I looked carefully. It was her but she was stumbling about even more than usual, as through excess of wine, and I heard weeping. It was the abbess' voice."

"Did she see you?"

"I do not know. She said nothing and dragged herself off into the darkness."

"Did anyone else leave the room?"

"Not while I was watching, and none entered, but I did not stand gawking. I heard more people coming towards me, so I closed my door."

"Sister Tetta, one last question. Have you seen any unexpected faces since the night of the feast?"

"I cannot say. There are so many new faces – all of the warriors – they confuse me."

"Sorry, before you go – the few times I have spoken to the abbess while here, I have found her manner odd. So odd, she seems at times affected by dark forces. She cannot always have been as this?"

Tetta shook her head and sighed.

"Poor woman. I remember when she first arrived to become our abbess. The love of our Lord burned in her spirit and shone through her eyes. She inspired me then, but the devil's brood has worn her down. I helped her where I could, but her faith was not tough. The fight proved too much for her and the pious were pushed aside. Father, it is obvious that Elmstow is not the place it should be – and the abbess must take some of the blame; though not all.

"She is afflicted; perhaps by demons but more likely by her treatment from those who should have supported her. The abbess has been destroyed. She is a sad, lost creature.

Even if somehow the minster survives, our abbess will not. I do not care if you tell the bishop this."

Eadred had found Leoba and Edith alone at one of the minster's gardens, gathering vegetables and herbs for the evening meal. He planned to speak to each individually but was met with reluctance, so with time escaping, he accepted the inevitable.

"After leaving the church with you we went back to the dormitory. A nun came looking for us and said we had to serve at the feast – to go straight away or we would be in trouble. I did go," Leoba said. Edith replied differently.

"I disobeyed, Father. Better to face extra work and less food for ignoring the nun than have a drunken idiot take me for the night. I could see clearly enough where the night was heading. Many of the warriors were beyond control."

"I served at the feast, then once the princess, abbess and ealdorman left, I went quickly to the dormitory before anyone who had not found a woman picked on me," Leoba added.

"Lord Aelfric argued with you. What was that about?"

"You noticed," Leoba smiled. "I suppose everyone did. He asked where Edith was. I said I did not know, and he grew angry and demanded that I fetch her."

Eadred creased his brow.

"Surely, he had no ill intentions? I have heard lately that it is commonly known that Lord Aelfric and the princess were close and wished to get even closer. I myself had witnessed his tenderness for her."

"I know the way men look at my sister when they want her in their bed." Leoba's voice was weary with experience. "The ealdorman's son had that look from the first time he saw her several days ago. And I think, Father, you have very little knowledge of the world of the rich and powerful.

"It was the ealdorman who wanted his son to marry that vain princess, if her father freed her from the pledge of virginity. Lord Aelfric has simpler tastes. And he has had other women. There are stories – and I do not doubt them. He pays for their silence – or rather his father did."

"But this makes little sense. I saw the way the ealdorman's son looked at Cuthburg's body…" Again, Eadred wished he had kept quiet and said no more. He left the two sisters, feeling more confused than before. Even Edith could be guilty. She might have been jealous of the princess. He had no time to think further and hurried to the room set aside for needlework and such tasks, as this was close to Cuthburg's and the ealdorman's chambers.

The accoutrements for spinning, weaving and sewing lay scattered around the room. Four chairs sat upright. There was a bed with half a dozen cushions spread haphazardly. It seemed to Eadred to be ill-placed in the room. There was also a distinct smell to the bed – like mice. It was the same smell the priest had detected on the ball of wool that had been pushed into the ealdorman's mouth.

Eadred lit several candles and peered closely into every corner of the space. He could find nothing else that seemed unexpected. He sat on the bed, disconsolate at his lack of progress, and scanned the room again, holding a candle at arm's length. A small pile of woollen and linen offcuts and a spindle that had snapped caught his attention. Eadred moved closer; caught on the jagged end of the splintered wood were a few strands of blue-grey wool. The offcuts were dark brown. He brought the threads close to his nose

– though faint, they possessed the same odour as was found on the bed. The priest lifted a handful of the offcuts and smelt them – they were free of the smell.

Eadred knelt and looked under the bed. He reached into the shadows and felt an object. With a murmur of satisfaction, he retrieved the other part of the broken spindle and pulled more threads from its jagged end; they were of a rusty brown colour. He knew where he had seen cloth of this hue – the ealdorman's rich cloak from the night of the feast. They possessed no displeasing smell. Taking his discoveries, the priest left the room and went to continue his questioning.

Only two men had different stories for the night of the feast – the moneyer and his son. He was already suspicious of the moneyer's veracity, so Eadred warned that any falsity would have the direst of consequences.

"I know the king well. He will support our oaths – we are completely blameless, I assure you. Question those who are questionable; not us."

"The king is beyond fury and sadness. He requires more than our oaths. He expects us all to be truthful about everything we saw and what we did on the night of the murders. Let no-one attempt to conceal what they know, or their lives may be endangered – whoever they are."

This was not a message the moneyer took to and he exhaled loudly. He stared into Eadred's eyes and the priest stared back.

"Ask your questions if you must. I have already told you that I went to bed drunk and slept until I heard the screams when the poor souls were discovered."

"Your son was with you?"

"His bed is in my chamber. I assume he was there. I have no recollection."

Raedwulf turned crimson. The awkward silence made his condition worse. With the father leaving the son to explain himself, Eadred asked about his actions and sleeping arrangements that night. Raedwulf spoke slowly and quietly.

"I fell asleep in a lady's company, in her chamber, and awoke only with the uproar from the discovery of the murders."

"And her name?" Raedwulf glanced at his father. His bulging eyes stared back.

"Mildred, Lady Cuthburg's companion. We were together at all times that night after the feast." Seeing the priest's obvious dislike at this behaviour, Raedwulf continued, "I am unmarried and seeking a good wife. My desires got the better of me with drink. I am not perfect."

Eadred understood how this might happen but Raedwulf's smile and bearing annoyed him.

"Did you know of any hostility between Mildred and her mistress?"

"No, of course not. They were happy in each other's company. Very happy," Regenhere answered for his son. He banged his fist on the bench.

"I have known Mildred since she was a child. Her father was a successful merchant. His fortune ebbed during years of poor health, but his lineage is well known. And we – we have no reason to harm either the princess or the ealdorman. I have grown rich in this kingdom – why would I jeopardise it all?"

Mildred was the last person Eadred needed to question. Her annoyance was even greater than that of the moneyer.

"When did you leave the princess on the night of the feast?"

Mildred was blunt and shameless.

"I spoke to her only when we played a trick on two men then I left her to take one of them to her bed."

"Lord Aelfric?"

"You seem to know already."

"And when did you see her again?"

"You have no right to ask me these questions. I was Princess Cuthburg's companion, chosen by her mother, the queen. You are a common priest. You know your humble duties – do them. Do not think of acting above your station."

"This is my humble duty. The king himself has given me power to find the murderers." Eadred raised his voice, staring into Mildred's icy face. "You would do well not to stand in my way. The king will not rest until the killers are found and executed."

"We all know that you must find the murderers before Vespers tomorrow or Lord Aelfric will take over. He is a man – you are a boy." Mildred chuckled when she saw the effect of her words.

"Such small muscles."

Eadred's voice trembled when he repeated his question.

"When I awoke with the commotion and I saw her poor body on the rope."

"And where did you go after you left her when she was still alive?"

"I saw you talking to Raedwulf, so I think you know already. I took him to my bed. It was Cuthburg's idea that I have him beside me that night."

Eadred was so perplexed by Mildred's last comment that

he asked her to repeat it. Why would Cuthburg want her companion to bed Raedwulf?

"She was mischievous."

"Did you already know him well?"

"No. I encouraged him before the feast and, as with all men, he took the bait. I had not spoken to him before then."

"But your father knew Raedwulf's father well? You would have met him before?"

"Maybe. My father knew many powerful people and I met many through him – but I cannot be expected to remember them all."

"So I am clear, did the Lady Cuthburg ask that it be Raedwulf or were you free to choose the man?"

"She told me that it had to be Raedwulf. I do not know why. I did not care. She played with people's lives. I was not foolish enough to refuse her. You may think little of me, but she was not a good person. She was not here of her own choice and made of it what she could. But now, I have lost my patron; my only protector."

Eadred swallowed his disgust at Cuthburg's companion and thanked her for answering his questions.

"You would do well, priest, not to try so hard to find the murderers. No-one expects much to come of your task but if you do chance to come closer to those who did the crime, expect them to deter you. They have killed the greatest in the kingdom without remorse. You cannot imagine the depravity within these walls. You are not a strong man and they would use a blade to separate you from your life with no pity."

Eadred slumped against the wall after Mildred left. His back dripped with sweat and he felt himself a child. He had not contemplated that his own life might be at risk, but that woman had spoken what was obvious. The contempt towards him that was stamped across her face kept returning. How many shades of evil possessed Elmstow?

There had been little hint of sadness from Mildred about the murder of the princess, other than its impact on her. Some of the recollections of what had happened the night of the murders troubled the priest. Someone was lying but how could he move forward?

Where was the light? Some small candle that lit the path forward. There was nothing, now he could not talk to Sister Verca, just gloom. A gaggle of voices and a few odd memories.

Eadred would talk again to the abbess about what he had been told about her strange movements on the night of the murders. With the midnight service now only a few hours away, he could think of no other path.

"I will fail the bishop. This is more than I can do."

FOURTEEN

Revelation

The gentle tapping on his door caused Eadred to cry out before stifling the sound. The silence was again broken by a persistent low drumming.

"Father Eadred, my friend. It is Tatwine. Come, let me in."

"Are you alone?"

"Yes, of course. Now, let me in. I have no wish to be seen."

Tatwine closed and bolted the door behind him. Eadred could not help but issue a fleeting smile. The hermit's face was creased with such joy, then he grasped the priest's shoulders and shook them with indecent familiarity.

"I am happy to see you, Brother Tatwine, but this is unexpected. I confess that I do not think I have smiled since I saw you last. That is a sad thing to admit."

"My dear friend – I will call you my friend because you

are my Brother-in-Christ – do not let your smile fade. I have something to tell you. In prayer, our Saviour spoke to me. He admonished me that it is not enough that I shared the prophecy I was granted about you. I must share your burden – and more. You feel abandoned, alone, with a task that seems impossible. I am here to say that you have not been abandoned.

"I have now seen the truth of the vision I had. Put aside any fears that you are not adequate for this task for you have not been chosen by any man but by your Heavenly Lord."

Eadred began to shake; not only from the words the hermit spoke but from the force with which they were delivered. He had barely talked with Tatwine, yet Eadred already understood that he was so blindingly different from the others he had met at Elmstow. This was a man who was closer to God's heart than the priest had ever been. The priest's spirit had been crushed. He felt helpless and divided from the bishop but here were words that took the weight of failure from him. Could it be that simple? Eadred's tears fell freely.

Tatwine extended his arms and Eadred fell into them, weeping. Then, at the hermit's invitation, they both knelt and prayed. As his voice joined with Tatwine's, he felt a joy that the Lord God had put a friend in his life to walk this painful, demanding and dangerous path. Eadred knew that he would break the bishop's injunction not to share his discoveries or progress with anyone for he needed to talk about these things and to trust someone. If he were wrong about the hermit then so be it. God would guide him and make the path clear – and as clear as a bell, he did.

"Eadred, I felt unease at returning to Elmstow because

the journey started with the murder of a defenceless woman but I know that I have been sent by the Lord God to help you, and we will both rest on his strength and wisdom.

"My Brother, after prayer and fasting, I now know the full meaning of the prophecy. Listen!"

Eadred not only listened; he watched. The hermit's eyes seemed to inhabit half his face and light shone from them. His expression glowed with the knowledge that he was speaking something sacred.

"What is happening at Elmstow is creating suspicion and enmity and will fuel far more before the end of this dark time. Some of the greatest in the kingdom have been murdered and any one of those who were here that night could have done this. The evil one will use this to turn good Christian souls against one another and the effects will ripple through the kingdom and destroy the faith of the people. You have been chosen to stop this happening."

The young priest sat silently, as if paralysed by Tatwine's words, his child-like hands resting on his lap. The hermit raised his own hand to ensure that Eadred would not attempt to speak.

"There is more, my friend; far more. You will remember that there was another meaning that I could not discern at the time but now it is clear. You challenged the murderer – do you remember?"

It seemed an eternity had passed since Tatwine had explained his prophecy but the young priest remembered it clearly.

"My dear Eadred, you were the Lord God's tool to find the murderer and to bring him to earthly and heavenly justice." Tatwine smiled gently, extending his hand to rest on the priest's shoulder. He struggled to speak against an outpouring of emotion and weeping. "And you are now. In the spirit and in the flesh, you are our Lord's warrior in this fight and he has granted you his protection and gifted you the skill to win and through you darkness will not prevail!

"You are as David and you will be victorious over Goliath. You have better than earthly armour for the Lord God clothes you in his own."

The two men continued to pray silently, side by side. Gradually, the elation in both calmed but though the rains had stopped, the rivers now ran stronger and deeper.

"I have not divulged this revelation to anyone but you as is my practice with others whom I have seen in my visions. It is your decision whether you wish to keep this to yourself or to let others know. But share your thoughts and troubles with me, my good friend, as I will with you. We are now bound together by the Lord God and he expects much of us."

Eadred nodded.

"I fear I will still struggle. There is the truth of it. My light seems small and fragile. Once in a while it has fallen upon some small scrap of their evil acts, but the candle has been too weak to follow their path."

Tatwine put his hand to Eadred's lips.

"Enough! Have you not heard me? Perhaps it is because you have not journeyed near to the heart of our Lord, as I have. There is a power there that no man and no demon can vanquish. There will be more hard times to come and shadowy paths to travel but make no mistake, you have been armed to win. Remember what he has promised. For the Lord loves the righteous and keeps them for eternity but the seed of the wicked he destroys.

"This place has grown even fouler since I was last here. I should not be surprised that lives have been taken; this minster is a temple to the flesh and to sin. But believe, as I do, that the battle is not lost.

"The Lord and his army of angels is coming, Eadred. He is coming with fire and sword and he will smite the wicked. They will cry for mercy but there are those here whose cries he will not hear. And we, my dear friend, we will prepare his path."

The hermit reached for his waist and produced a key.

"Now, to work. I secured this from one of Lord Aelfric's guards. He was once a postulant and is a good man. Lord Aelfric heard my story about the murdered woman I found on the southern road and asked that I bring you to see her body, but I do not think he expected us to go tonight. Yet, there is no time to lose."

Despite the lateness of the hour, Eadred accepted the monk's appeal and followed him to the outbuilding where the slave's body lay. On the way, Tatwine told Eadred the bewildering connection between the slave and himself.

"It is one of the strangest stories I have heard and at the very least, the men you saw running from the body could well be here, in Elmstow. Are you certain that this is the slave from your past and who appeared as a demon in your vision?"

Tatwine moved the candle closer so the light danced over the woman's marble face. His voice turned doleful.

"Sadly, my friend, it is. I can see no reason or purpose to her death. There she lies, the woman I coveted in my youth. Cold as ice. The smell of death fills this room. Her name was Eanswith. I cannot guess what she was doing on the

111

Elmstow road late into a winter's night. And there she met her lonely death at the hands of two thugs."

"What if they were travelling with her?" Tatwine returned Eadred's gaze, looking thoughtful at the question.

"Or what if she were journeying to find you? She knew you from your youth and discovered where you were and needed help?"

The monk sighed – that Eanswith might have sought to meet him. Had she kept a memory of him, as he had of her?

"I would have helped her, Eadred. But I wish you had not said that, as I would have done almost anything for her." Tatwine sniffed and looked away. "It is wrong, I know, that a memory of a brief encounter from my former life still affects me so." Eadred put his hand on his friend's shoulder.

"I am sorry. It was stupid of me to voice thoughts that have no basis. It is not wrong to be moved by this. I spoke to the holy Sister who washed Eanswith's body. She died of a single dagger wound. It would have been quick, and we will discover who did this. They might still be within this minster and they will face justice."

Tatwine nodded in response.

"Lord Aelfric thought that you might want to look more closely at Eanswith's body, within, of course, the bounds of decency, to see if there are any signs that might help you find the murderers. He thought that all the murders could be connected in some way."

Eadred passed his candle closer to the body, moving the folds in Eanswith's crude tunic, banishing the shadows, peering closely. The stench of death twisted his stomach. Tatwine had moved away and was staring at the wall. It was a blessing, Eadred thought, that he had done so for ugly bruises had formed on the woman's thighs. The Sister who had washed the body had whispered to Eadred that she had seen signs of rough treatment there and higher. No more needed to be said about this and Eadred prayed he would be forgiven for uttering a lie to his friend about Eanswith's final minutes.

"Eanswith is in the gentle hands of our Lord now, my dear friend. I can see nothing more to help me, but we will find her killers. Go to your rest now for tomorrow will be busy and fraught. When we awake, I would welcome your company. There are many dangers here." Tatwine agreed without hesitation. He locked the door, saying that he had to take the key back to the guard. As he was leaving, Eadred tugged at his sleeve and whispered sheepishly, "Your gift of revelation, is it able to see who committed these murders – or to guide us through the tangle of deception?"

"My dear Eadred, I have thought often about this, as have others. I am feared by some in this place who wish to keep their secrets hidden. There are many who also seek me out for they wish to know God's path for them when they have difficult decisions to make. I tell all who come that while it is my duty to pray for them, I have no influence on when my prophetic visions happen or what they show. They are always a gift from God. The visions he has given me have never shown the evil perpetrated by anyone I know. They show the goodness and the gifts particular men and women have, that the Lord God wishes them to use for his glory. As with you."

The priest appeared somewhat downcast by Tatwine's words. The hermit took the priest's shoulders and shook them firmly.

"Have you understood nothing? The Lord God wants you to grow and to become the man he knows you are capable of. How can this happen if he does your work for you? You will remain as a child.

"Come, be cheered by what he has shown you. The gifts of Father Eadred, the warrior for Christ, are beyond measure. It is time to use them for his glory. And now that your eyes have been opened do not close them again or pretend you are blind and helpless. That would be an affront to he who made you."

FIFTEEN

A Step Closer and a Step Further Away

The midnight service was not far off but if he hurried, Eadred might persuade the abbess to talk to him briefly. She was fragile and it was possible she could accidentally divulge something if he asked the right question.

"Reverend Mother, may I speak to you, please? If you are at prayer, I am deeply sorry, but this cannot wait." His insistent hammering soon caused a knot of observers to gather around the abbess' door.

"Calm yourself, Father Eadred. The abbess is often at personal prayer now. When she is with God, the things of this world cannot reach or trouble her. She is being shown the wonders of Heaven. Feel envy, if you wish, but not annoyance."

Eadred nodded. He asked God to forgive him for his

impatience. He would talk to Hereburg at the end of the service.

He was the first to arrive and sat biting his fingernails in agitation.

"Lord God, help me. I have so much to do and so little time. Please, Father, shine a light in this darkness and I will surely follow it."

Within five or so minutes every nun, priest and postulant and many of the warriors and visitors were crammed into the minster church. Most were silently pleading for God's protection and mercy but for a few of those souls within the minster enclave, their thoughts were darker. Then the mumbling started.

Eadred spoke quickly to Lord Aelfric and left the church with two of his guards. He pounded on the abbess' door with increasingly urgent pleas that she open it. With no response, he left it to the warriors to kick the door in.

The room was empty.

"Let no-one in." Eadred's appeal was ignored, as holy Sisters pushed their way into the abbess' chamber. "Let me search. I must find the truth. Get out!" From the corner of his eye, the priest saw a woman's hand reach for the goblet on the bench. He grabbed her wrist but not tightly enough and the hand was gone.

"Stop her. Who reached out?" No-one answered. "I must know. Tell me!" The room was soon full of nuns and of noise. "Touch nothing. Do you hear?" Eadred turned to the guards. "Your lord will know from me if you let anything be stolen and the abbess' whereabouts go undetected." The soldiers disregarded the Sisters' dignity and dragged several unruly and raucous women from the room. The others backed away. "Now, keep them out!" the priest yelled above the commotion, and pushed the door closed.

Eadred slumped against a wall, his chest heaving. He beat his fist against the floor and groaned – a chance had been missed. He scanned the room. A bed with a blanket, a small bench, chair and chest were the sole furnishings. There was a single candleholder on the bench and one on a shelf against the wall. That on the bench contained a stub of candle and the other was barely a quarter used. A goblet and the abbess' personal psalter rested on the bench. Eadred leafed through the pages.

The room possessed the same mousy smell as Eadred had detected in the room set aside for spinning and weaving and that pervaded the ball of wool that had been stuffed into the ealdorman's mouth. He brought the goblet to his nose. It too had that unpleasant trace. The chest was unlocked and contained several items of conventual clothing, neatly folded. Eadred removed them but found nothing untoward, other than again, the hint of the same unpleasant odour.

The priest let his eyes survey the room once more; there was nothing surprising. He walked slowly around the confined space then furrowed his brow. Rather than nothing being out of the ordinary, it all was. He recalled the abbess' reception room, which reflected her flustered, confused state. Yet this room, where she lived, was sparse and neat, even following the scuffle. Eadred ran his finger across the bench. Not a speck of dust. He went to the shelf and did the same. The dust was thick, apart from under the candleholder. The room had all the appearance of having been tidied recently and quickly. Whether this was normal practice, or an aberration was something Eadred would need to check. What was clear was that it had not been undertaken by the abbess in her current condition.

Within the hour, she was found. Cold, deathly looking, babbling inanely, Hereburg was pulled out from behind a woodpile. Whether by design or sickness, she struggled to remain upright and was held up by two guards. A cloak was wrapped around her; she was manacled and then constrained in a cell.

"It was not me. I swear on the Holy Book! You must believe me. I murdered no-one." Her demented wailing continued for close to an hour. Slowly, it ebbed then stopped, to the relief of the whole community. She lay exhausted, sobbing, clutching her chest and breathing fitfully.

The young priest felt torn – relieved in some ways but vexed. Unlike many, who had tried to escape the cries of despair by pushing beeswax plugs into their ears, he sat close by, listening to the words she had howled.

The abbess was behaving in the strangest, most suspicious manner; hiding from those around her and making no sense with most of what she cried. Yet with monotonous repetition there had been one claim amidst the ranting gibberish. The words altered somewhat but before she collapsed, exhausted, the abbess repeated the same declaration five or six times.

"My God will judge me for the murderous intentions of my heart, but I am innocent in the world of men. Others tricked me."

It was infuriatingly confusing, for Eadred was certain that she had some involvement in the murders, at least of the princess and the ealdorman, but she could not have acted alone. And she must know who had done the killings. There were a dozen questions he wanted to ask her but that would have to wait until her trial, and he would only have some involvement if Aelfric allowed it.

It was Bishop Aethelbert who worried Eadred further, after he demanded to know the priest's progress.

"The abbess' behaviour has condemned her; not what she says but what she has done. She could not have acted alone, that is certain. Four are now dead, if we include the unfortunate slave. Whoever did this has no fear of killing. They must have much to lose and they will not take kindly to your involvement. Be careful, dear boy. I could not bear to lose you. Bolt your door at night and do not go alone to any lonely place. Now, return to your cell and try to get some rest. Daylight is but a few hours away and you will need all your wits."

It was a watchful priest who returned to his cell, cold but with his mind far from frozen, as ideas advanced, retreated, fought against each other, and were often butchered. He bolted his door, checking it carefully, and prepared for bed. What now? The abbess would face trial, but it was acknowledged that she alone could not have perpetrated these horrors.

Eadred may have had a hand in precipitating her undoing and had persuaded Aelfric to leave the hole in the perimeter wall open, where perhaps the perpetrators had come and gone and may make use of it again, but that was little comfort with the time allotted to him due to expire in the afternoon.

Eadred's mind struggled to turn to its routine of prayer. It was not helped by needing to seek forgiveness for an outright lie. When the bishop looked Eadred straight in the eye and demanded assurance that the priest had not spoken to anyone about his progress and thoughts, Eadred solemnly affirmed that he had kept his pledge. It troubled him that he had lied so readily and that he could not keep his vow. The truth was that God had given him a friend to share the cares of his task but Eadred doubted that the bishop would approve of God's choice.

SIXTEEN

Ambush

Within a few hours, the priest was knocking – not so gently – on Tatwine's door. He was greeted with a smile.

"Come, Brother Tatwine, there will be a way through this. The next step awaits us and with God's help, we will find it. Let me talk with you and let us see what happens."

The hermit moved two stools to face each other.

"Gladly, my friend. My mind is clear and I have prayed for insight. How should we begin?"

Eadred sat and stared at the ground. He opened a linen bag and took out its contents.

"These are the balls of woollen yarn that were forced into the mouths of Cuthburg and Ceolfrith. Smell them, if you would."

"It is unpleasant." Tatwine stared at Eadred then breathed deeply once more. "I know this smell. It is dwale,

121

perhaps mixed with some herbs to disguise it. A poison that can kill if much is taken at once or if smaller quantities are taken over many days. Yet, it can heal certain ailments if used carefully. I have made and used it myself for this purpose. But only the small ball smells; the other seems free of it."

"Now, answer me this. Why only poison the small ball and why put it in the ealdorman's mouth?" Eadred held up the other, which was close to twice the size. "And why was this pushed with such force into Cuthburg's mouth that it has deformed her face in death?"

The hermit folded his arms and sat quietly for a few seconds.

"Could it be that the murderers had little time or were surprised? In their haste, they pushed the ball into the wrong mouth."

"It could be so," Eadred replied. "It makes me wonder what the balls were for, and also the dwale. It can subdue a man?"

"Assuredly, but it would take a while. He would suffer from shortness of breath, weakened strength and faintness – but not immediately. A man of the ealdorman's power would need to be given enough of the potion an hour or two before he was weakened sufficiently to be overpowered." The priest looked displeased at Tatwine's response. The hermit continued, "I cannot imagine the ealdorman allowing a ball soaked in dwale to be pushed into his mouth, unless he were already subdued."

"Then the balls were to keep them quiet while they were hanged. The feast would have finished and although many were drunk, the noise of the effort to overcome the ealdorman and the princess would have been heard by someone." As he mulled his words, Eadred looked more uncertain and forlorn. "I must go. There is little time."

"Where are you going?"

"The small gap in the outside wall that I told you about. I have Lord Aelfric's permission to talk to the group of guards who watch over it. They have not reported anything, but I will question them. I have no other ideas. I will go alone – we need to keep our knowledge of the place secret, so I will approach quietly. Pray, if you will, for some sign of the truth."

The sky was clear and the morning fresh. The sun's orange light beamed low across the courtyard, filtering through the smoke of many fires, igniting the walls and giving colour to the pale faces that he passed. Crisp frost made it impossible to proceed quietly but fortunately once Eadred had left the open spaces to travel through the narrow passages, his steps made little sound.

The king's men were arriving with the wagon containing the instruments for the ordeals to be administered on all those who were at the minster at the time of the murders, unless the culprits could be found first. Although innocent and despite his faith, Eadred dreaded the uncertainty and the pain ahead. Bishop Aethelbert had pleaded with Aelfric for his priest to be spared but to no avail. There was a cold determination in the ealdorman's son. But there was also a hope that one of the murderers had been found and would soon identify her accomplices and there would be no need for painful ordeals.

Eadred thought carefully as he went, to remind himself of the way along the final twists and turns through the warren of passages, but after correcting one mistake, and after checking that he was not being followed, he came upon the pigpen. It stood before him and slightly to the right, alone against the outside wall with a passageway before it. Two sows had been recently moved to the pen and lay beneath a precarious lean-to at the back, disinterested in the priest's presence. To the right of the sows, also beneath the lean-to, were several stands of green firewood. Eadred looked to his left, where there were two storage huts for grain. He walked towards the furthermost hut, looked around once more, and tapped on the door three times. A small crack appeared.

"I am Father Eadred."

The door opened and closed behind him.

"I know. I am Aethelric, who commands this post, and this is Edmund, one of my charge. I have recently joined my lord's hearth group," the warrior whispered.

Edmund nodded indifferently and returned to the small window from where he viewed the pigpen. The priest and warrior spent a few seconds evaluating each other. Eadred saw a man of similar age to him, well-built but lean. He hoped he recognised in Aethelric's expression a sharp and serious approach to his duty. Happily, his instinct was soon reinforced.

"My lord asked my opinion of your plan to watch the gap behind the pigpen. I was there when you spoke to him. He also asked others – older, more experienced warriors. I told him that I thought you spoke well, and the plan was good, for I also believe that the traitors remain in this minster. A few of his closest men agreed; some did not. It is impossible that the abbess committed these crimes alone – she is a weak and old woman. Not only weak in body but also mind. Yet, she knows the murderers.

"The traitors will try to kill her before the trial. At my urging, Lord Aelfric has placed a strong guard on her cell at all times. And I agree with you that the young nun, Verca, was murdered because she harboured some knowledge of the murders and the traitors needed to know whom the nun had told; but she took it with her to the Lord God. If all they wanted was her silence then a knife would be sufficient, not the torture of such a frail body."

Eadred's chest rose when he heard this affirmation.

"We face traitors who would destroy the kingdom for ends that I cannot understand but I will do my utmost for my lord, with my body and my wits, to discover the killers. The noble ring-giver has entrusted me with this task – my first in command – and I will not fail him."

"It is good for me to hear this, Aethelric, for we have thoughts and ideas but we do not know if we are on the right path until we are far along it, and it may be then that we discover it is wrong. Your faith is encouraging. Now, what has happened here?"

"Nothing, as yet, but I remain hopeful. Many men and holy Sisters have passed this way; some have looked towards the pigs that I put here for I thought they would stir and alert us." Aethelric smiled. "The sows do not seem to accept my commands, but I am vigilant and as the trial nears, this place will become more important. You should leave us to our watch.

"Oh, before you go, I should tell you that I was not one of those who jeered you on the night of the feast. It was not a manly act and brought no glory to those who joined in. You should know that none of my lord's hearth companions agreed with your mistreatment."

Eadred thanked Aethelric for his words and with no-one in the passageways nearby, he quietly left to return the way he had come. He offered up a short prayer for he felt encouraged by his meeting with the young warrior. Not only from his parting words but also because another thoughtful being had vindicated his own belief that it was worthwhile to watch the only apparently unguarded exit to the wider world.

Eadred's silent prayer was shorter than he had anticipated. As was often his way, brief, solitary prayers in the course of his working day, did not take him far from the sights and sounds around him or his routine concerns. So, the sound of a single footfall by one who sought concealment caused him to turn suddenly.

The figure swore and lunged forward. Eadred saw the long, thin blade in his raised hand. A yelp of fear and he slipped sideways, away from the wall. The knife flashed close to Eadred's right ear, as the attacker lost balance and thudded into the wall. The priest's life had never been threatened. He had never needed to defend his own body, but instinct drove him to kick his assailant in the side; sufficient to wind him and to elicit a groan. Eadred stepped back into a gap between two buildings. He wished he had made a better choice; a large pile of wickerwork hurdles barred his escape.

Eadred seemed frozen to the spot. The attacker – an older man, wiry, of no greater apparent strength than the priest, wore a scar across his bald head and a savage expression. He scrambled to his feet. Whether from his fall or an earlier injury, he limped as he moved forward, smiling.

"Come, my young friend, make this easy for both of

us. This is my skill. One thrust to the heart and your trial is over in an instant. There is no escape, and you are destined for the joys of Heaven. Struggle and you will still die but in agony."

The attacker's intent to kill was stronger than Eadred's to live and the priest simply stared as his assailant closed on him. Eadred could not bring himself to scream, imagining that it might accelerate his death. The killer made a rapid movement, shifting his impending attack from a downward stab at the neck to an upward thrust into the priest's heart. His free hand readied to grab Eadred's cloak by the shoulder, to pull the body closer to the knife thrust.

Eadred let loose an ear-piercing shriek. The man moved quickly, pulling his arm back then thrusting his knife forward towards Eadred's body. The priest swung his hand towards the man's exposed wrist as it came towards him and the blade, that Tatwine had insisted he carry in his pocket, disappeared into the flesh, ripping through to the other side.

The man's eyes bulged in surprise then he screamed with pain, leaving his own knife to hang limply from Eadred's stomach. Despite the disabling of his right arm, Eadred's attacker collected his wits, pulled the blade from his wrist and advanced unsteadily towards Eadred with the weapon in his other hand.

The priest had used the opportunity well and had moved away from his debilitating position. He turned to run. The way was barred by Aethelric.

The warrior, with sword drawn, reached for Eadred's cloak and pulled him to the ground. He walked over the sprawling body and brought his blade down on the attacker's wounded hand. Flesh and blood exploded, and fingers fell to the ground. The man dropped the knife and he fell, this time with unabated howling.

"Take him and have his wound bound. He must not die." The injured man was dragged away by two warriors. Amidst the wails of pain, he shouted the foulest abuse that Eadred had ever heard. Aethelric ripped off some of the man's tunic and shoved it into his mouth. "And you, Father Eadred, you should go to the infirmary."

Eadred stood shaking, pulling away his torn tunic, staring at the gash where the knife had pierced his flesh. He examined himself intently.

"The Lord God was watching over me. The cut is small and shallow." The priest looked up with a fragile smile.

"You defended yourself well. Go now, so you may join us when we question your assailant. The quicker, the better. His injury is severe. He will weaken quickly and draw faint. He could be dead within a few days, but I have good news. My Lord Aelfric has granted more time for your work to discover the murderers. The date for the ordeals has been delayed and they will not take place until after Abbess Hereburg's trial. It has been convened quickly by Bishop Aethelbert and is set to start tomorrow under the auspices of the bishop and Lord Aelfric.

"You are not a fighting man by calling. I suggest that after your wound is bound you return to your cell and lie down. Take this with you. It is a special balm to spread on the wound. I have always used it. My mother makes it. It is good."

Eadred took it gratefully. He had warmed to the young warrior and Aethelric's next words increased his admiration.

"Take a few cups of ale or wine if you wish. You will

feel the better for it later." However, the warrior's parting remarks made Eadred shiver. "Someone wants to return you to the Lord God before your natural time. We are closing on the murderers; I doubt this man acted alone. Be careful. Lock your door. Keep that blade with you."

Eadred vomited several times when his mind returned to the attack he had endured and that his own life remained at risk. He did take a few cups of wine, but the best remedy was a visit from Tatwine, who had heard of the vicious encounter. The hermit shed some tears when Eadred recounted what had occurred. They prayed together, thanking God for his protection, and that the attack had unearthed someone else who must be implicated in the murders.

Tatwine grabbed Eadred's forearm and gasped when the priest carelessly mentioned the limp the assassin possessed.

"On the night of Eanswith's murder, I remember that one of the figures that ran towards Elmstow had a limp. I pray to God that we have found one of the foul animals and that he is now suffering."

SEVENTEEN

The Limping Man

The insistent words and the pounding were not a dream. "Father Eadred, are you within? Aethelric demands your presence. The limping man is to be questioned."

The priest had slept for no more than five minutes, but it had been a deep repose. He blinked and groaned, struggling to control his limbs and to keep up with the warrior who took him to the room where Aethelric and several of his men stood around the prisoner. On the way, the soldier informed Eadred that he was expected to lead the questioning. This expectation woke Eadred and his flustered mind began to organise some of the ideas and questions he had been considering. The door closed behind him. The priest froze.

A single, small window had been covered with a wicker frame, so despite the midday hour, the light was subdued, and several candles bordered the prisoner, bathing him in a sombre glow. He lay stretched out on the ground, bound to four stakes. The man's face displayed the struggle to control his fear. The priest had himself felt the intimidation of the warriors and he harboured some sympathy for his would-be murderer, thanking God that he was not in his position. Once his eyes had adjusted to the gloom, Eadred saw to his surprise that Tatwine was also in the room, standing back against the far wall.

"The questioning of this man has been approved by Lord Aelfric, who has been given lawful control of the armed men at Elmstow by the king. The man's trial will follow that of Abbess Hereburg." Aethelric spoke forcefully as one who wanted all to know that whatever transpired in this room had been sanctioned properly. Eadred wondered if the bishop, who had joint authority over the trial of the abbess, had also agreed to this examination. To the priest's mind, this was part of the same legal action. However, he decided not to press the point. "Father Eadred." Aethelric prompted him to commence. Eadred breathed deeply and started.

"What is your name, your lineage and your village?"

The woeful prisoner cast his eyes at the warriors looming over him and decided to speak.

"Godric and my father was of the same name. I am from Hildericstow."

"It is a small settlement not far to the west, in bog country, close to the border with Mercia," Aethelric added, staring hard at Godric. "A poor and unrewarding place. Those who wish to evade the king's justice seek its refuge. Lord Ceolfrith sent a troop there in summer and brought two men and a woman back for trial. They were executed."

"How long have you been here in Elmstow?" Eadred continued.

"A week or so."

"And why are you here?"

"I beg for food and seek shelter in one of the animal pens."

"You came before the feast when the princess and the ealdorman were murdered?"

"I arrived the same day."

"Are you certain?"

"Yes. I remember the ealdorman and his men arriving. I came in after them."

"Why did you try to kill me?"

"I wanted to rob you."

"There are many rich nuns here, who are weaker than I. Why choose me to rob?"

"You were on your own and I took my chance."

"Your knife; it is not the weapon of a poor beggar. It is a rich man's blade – long and with a jewelled handle."

"I stole it."

"Here, in the minster?"

Aethelric stared at one of the warriors, who had started to tap his thigh in frustration.

"No. I brought it with me."

"That is not possible." Eadred became more spirited. "All those who entered on the day of the feast were searched carefully."

"I hid it well."

One of the warriors ran his sword over Godric's body.

"Where?" He mocked the prisoner's slight form. "The search was thorough."

"Unless one of the guards let you pass undetected?"

Aethelric bristled at Eadred's question but said nothing.

"Answer my question. Either a guard allowed you in or you have an accomplice in Elmstow who gave you the dagger."

Godric said nothing but he did scream. The warrior, who stamped on the prisoner's bandaged stump at Aethelric's order, smiled. The screaming continued, blood spurting from the wound. Godric writhed like a fish pulled from the river, his limbs struggling against the bonds that held them.

"Leave if you have to." Aethelric turned to Eadred, who had turned a ghastly white.

"No. No. I'll stay." The priest coughed and spat out some bile. "You were sent to murder me by another. Who?"

"Answer!" Aethelric yelled. "Or you lose your other hand. Who ordered this?"

"I cannot," Godric blubbered, "or he will kill my son."

"Who will kill your son?"

The prisoner continued to cry.

"Ah, cut off his ears."

A warrior took out his knife and sat across Godric's chest. The prisoner continued to wail and to plead. He twisted and rolled his head to avoid the knife, but his right ear was pulled hard and the knife sawed it from his head.

"Did you kill the princess and the ealdorman? Answer and we stop. Do not and we continue."

"I cannot." His other ear was sliced away. Godric's head soaked in an expanding pool of blood but still he refused to answer.

"Remove his privies."

"Oh, God, no! Have mercy."

Eadred raised his hand for Aethelric to stay the order.

"Godric, listen to me. Your life will soon come to an

end but then you face all of eternity, either in the company of the Lord God or in the torments of hell. What you are going through now is like a grain of sand compared to the fullness of the earth.

"The sacred word of God says that each of the dead, great and small, will stand before his throne and each will be judged, as their deeds deserve. Anyone whose name cannot then be found written in the book of life will be hurled into the burning lake.

"Godric, our Lord is a merciful God. Tell me the truth and I will pray earnestly for your soul. Seek redemption. If your son has committed no crime, then Lord Aelfric will protect him. Now, unburden your heart. Tell me all or your sins will weigh you down to hell."

Godric wept, his tears flowing down his bloodied cheeks. His eyes glanced down to the warrior standing between his legs with knife in hand.

"Father, there is a man and he alone talked to me. There are others but I do not know them." Godric's voice was weak. The priest raised his hand to ensure silence around him. "He told me to kill you. He gave me the knife."

"Why want me dead?"

"He fears you will find the truth."

"Who is he?"

Godric breathed deeply several times and he stared upwards.

"His name is unknown to me. He is a slave here, in the minster."

"A slave! We want the truth."

"I swear, it is the truth. I am done with lying," Godric replied to Aethelric. "My eyes look to the journey of my soul. He does the bidding of others. He is a slave but seems more; perhaps a warrior."

Godric's voice was now difficult to hear, his breathing shallow. He coughed. Aethelric ordered that he be given water. He took a few sips and coughed again. Eadred needed more before Godric was beyond speaking.

"Were you involved in the killing of the princess and the ealdorman?"

"Not the princess, I swear."

"The ealdorman?"

"He was drunk; slumped against the wall. We carried and dragged him then put a rope around his neck."

"You hanged him?"

Godric nodded.

"Why?"

"Gold – but I swear I did not know it was to be him."

"And the abbess, what did she do?"

"The abbess? I do not know." Godric appeared confused.

"Godric, listen. Have you taken other lives?"

The dying man looked into Eadred's eyes and nodded.

"A young woman on the hill south of this minster – the same night as the murder of the ealdorman?"

Godric groaned. A slight movement of his head acknowledged his guilt.

"Why?" Tatwine yelled, his voice faltering. He rushed forward, pushed Eadred aside and lowered his head so his ear was close to Godric's mouth.

"Alone, young, at night... calling out. Such firm flesh. It was easy."

"But why kill her?"

"She could have talked."

EIGHTEEN

Before the Trial

"Come, sit, my boy."

Bishop Aethelbert ushered Eadred to the bench where he sat with Aelfric. The bishop was smiling – a good sign for the priest. Aelfric sat, stone-faced, which did not bode so well.

"Tomorrow is the trial of the abbess. We have chosen you to inquire into her truthfulness on our behalf before the whole community. It is a great trust we place in you, as you know. Never has one so young and without status been given such an honour. We—"

"All those involved must be rooted out," the ealdorman's son interrupted. "The ordeals have been delayed. Bishop Aethelbert has persuaded me that your approach could bear some fruit. I am doubtful but let us see. It is not sufficient that the abbess be tried but that all the guilty be found and their purpose uncovered. It is fortunate that you were attacked."

"And fortunate that he survived," Aethelbert replied.

"And I will have a guard with him at all times to make sure he survives until the killers have been taken," Aelfric retorted.

"Now, Eadred, tell us what you know."

The bishop had given Eadred some warning that he would have to recount what he had discovered, so he started boldly.

"The criminal, Godric, and one he calls a slave owned by the minster, killed your father. Godric's reasons were gold and that his own son might be killed. He said he had no inkling that his victim was to be so great a person as the ealdorman of the kingdom and he denied killing the princess. I do not think he lied, for men so close to death choose Heaven over hell if they can.

"Godric was a common thief and murderer but the so-called slave seemed to him to be more than what he appeared. Two of the greatest people in the kingdom were not slaughtered for gold. There is a vile and treacherous spirit to these deaths and the so-called slave, and the abbess, hold the key."

"I have had all the slaves taken. The numbers tally with those the minster owns. You will question each of them after the trial."

"I will, Lord Aelfric. When we find the right man, we will know who killed your father and why."

"What of the princess?"

Aelfric sat almost in prayer. He looked up and Eadred felt the pain in his eyes as he had on the day he helped him with Cuthburg's body.

"The so-called slave is responsible for the princess'

murder and did the deed himself. He would have the strength on his own to overpower and to hang her without Godric's help.

"I have learnt more that helps me understand what happened. Of the two balls of wool that were found in their mouths, that of the ealdorman smelt of dwale but not that of the Lady Cuthburg. I think that he was weakened by the dwale, so that he could be more easily overpowered."

The bishop nodded but Aelfric narrowed his eyes and pondered Eadred's words.

"How so? Even strong dwale takes an hour or more to weaken a man – and my father was a fierce warrior. He would not allow a ball soaked with dwale to be forced into his mouth for an hour. He would need to be subdued first."

Eadred nodded.

"The dwale had already been given to your father, disguised in other drink. He had been weakened enough that his hands did not need to be tied; neither were the Lady Cuthburg's. Did your father seem confused or unsteady at the feast?"

"I did not talk to my father at the feast. My mind was elsewhere but I will find out." The ealdorman's son shouted to a guard to fetch Aethelric, who arrived quickly.

"He did stagger and did stumble over his words, my lord. His face was red. He had drunk much but your father could take his drink well," Aethelric replied.

"He was served dwale with the taste obscured by strong wine then the woollen balls were used to keep the ealdorman and princess quiet, while they were hanged. The stink of dwale on the wool in your father's mouth came from his breath," Eadred added.

"Who served him wine at the feast?"

"It was Leoba, the postulant," Eadred responded to the bishop.

"She served many warriors from the same jug. None had the same illness," the ealdorman's son countered. "It must have been administered in some other way. Now, is there any more need for us to talk?"

"No, my lord. The abbess' behaviour has been strange, and she acts as though guilty of some crime. I am ready for tomorrow."

When Eadred returned to his cell with a guard beside him, he was happy to see Tatwine sitting in the passageway beside his door.

"I have some stew and a jug of wine."

"Then you are doubly welcome," Eadred smiled. "Come. Enter."

Some short time later, the hermit returned with two further jugs of wine.

"I should become maudlin if I think overmuch of the dead. Thank you for sharing this drink with me. Eanswith did suffer. She was searching for me, I am certain, on the night of her lonely death, hoping I could help her with some unknown problem. At least, one of her murderers has received justice." Tatwine covered his face to hide the tears.

"Dear friend, if I possessed any words that could comfort you now, I would give them gladly. She is with God and is safe for eternity. You will see her again when time passes no more, and her wounds will be gone, and she will smile at you. And I make a solemn vow that the other man who perpetrated this atrocity will be found and will face the justice of God and man."

"Eadred, do not pray for that vile creature, Godric. He held the life of others so cheaply."

"Tatwine, I gave my word, and I must. It is for the Lord God to balance justice and mercy. Now, leave it be for I need your counsel. I am troubled by what I have heard today. Here, take a cup with me, and listen."

Eadred recounted his meeting with Aelfric and Bishop Aethelbert and how he had ventured the opinion that the ealdorman could have been weakened by drinking dwale put in the wine at the feast. The woollen ball in his mouth had not been drenched with the poison but had been pushed into his mouth after he had drunk to stop him crying out when the murderers set upon him.

"Now, when it was asked who had served wine to the ealdorman, I reminded him that it was Leoba, the postulant. The moment her name was mentioned, Aelfric said that she had served many warriors from the same jug and drew our time together to a sudden end. Even the bishop was surprised and offended. I remember clearly that Aelfric spoke harshly to Leoba at the feast and the wine jug fell when he grabbed her. Is that not strange?"

The hermit rubbed the tears from his eyes and face.

"It is strange that he should defend her, rather than demand that she be questioned. Did Aelfric grasp Leoba before or after she gave wine to the ealdorman?"

"After but it is true that many warriors drank from that jug. Yet, she could have served from another jug earlier – one just for the ealdorman. I have questioned Leoba once; I must do so again."

"Did she seek to explain why Lord Aelfric had grabbed her at the feast?"

"She said that he wanted her to bring Edith to him – for fornication! I hope that is not true. I saw how Aelfric became distressed when he saw the dead body of the princess and he touched the body in intimate ways. I cannot believe what Leoba told me, that the ealdorman's son has had many women, and may do so still. Or am I so green in the ways of the world that I imagine our princes and lords all to be honourable?"

"In my experience, they are the least honourable," the monk replied. "They have power to do as they wish and little to curb their lust and greed. Many in the Church have stopped trying to change them, and many have come to adopt the same sins. That is why I avoid this place.

"I know of Leoba's sister, Edith. Her beauty marks her out. I hear that she tries to avoid men's demands but often fails. For she has no power against them or against those here who would provide her to entertain rich and powerful men who are drawn to this shithole. Yet I cannot believe that Leoba poisoned the ealdorman and his son knew of it. Even in this place of unnatural behaviour, it would be beyond countenance. When the trial is over, question her once more.

"Now, thank you, my dear friend, for your company this evening. If a man has one good and trusted friend to share his heart, his troubles and his joys, he is fortunate. You are that friend to me. Sleep now. Tomorrow is a day when you will combat darkness once again, and you will prevail with God's help."

"You are a friend indeed and we will prevail. Bless you, good monk."

Eadred fell face down onto his bed. At least the bell to

bring the Sisters to prayer would not be rung and wake him. With the abbess to face trial, all communal services had been suspended – a sign that the world was disintegrating.

He woke with a start when the three o'clock service would have been.

"Eadred, Eadred," he chastised himself. "This was not the night to seek wine so eagerly." He sat on the side of his bed, holding his head until the throbbing eased. He managed to piss in the corner of the cell then slumped back onto the hard frame.

He imagined that the guilty had written their deeds upon a page and on the other side, they had written several false stories. Then they had cut the page into many pieces and thrown them across the minster to confuse and to conceal. Some of the pieces had blown over the minster walls and were lost. He had found some of those remaining. As he looked at them, they enticed with their smiles. Eadred felt he could almost grasp how parts of the page connected but the closer he looked, the more the associations evaded him.

How would he ever find enough of the fragments and discern their truth or falsity to piece together the story that the vile beasts had written? The truth was there to be found. The Lord God, who knows all that happens in Heaven and earth, knew the truth.

"Help me find it, my great and merciful Lord. Help me beat this sin."

NINETEEN

The Trial

Bishop Aethelbert and Lord Aelfric, under whose auspices the trial would be held, sat in front of the altar in the minster church. It was midday. Before them, some seated but most standing, the whole community, warriors and the few visitors gathered. The accused sat to one side, guarded by two soldiers. She whimpered and sniffed, her head bowed.

Aelfric rose and announced the charge against Hereburg – that she had murdered the princess and the ealdorman, and later Sister Verca and was concealing the identity of her accomplices.

"Before the Lord God, are you blameless of these charges?" There was sadness in the bishop's voice.

The abbess rose slowly, needing the support of her chair. There were gasps when she lifted her head: her face was ashen, drawn and glassy with sweat, her eyes wide and bloodshot. She stood, shaking.

"My lords, I am muddled by what I know and what I have done. I am guilty of many crimes, I think, and of being foolish, but I killed no-one."

"Come now. The matter is straightforward. Are you blameless?"

The abbess mumbled some words.

"We cannot hear you."

"Yes, before God, I am blameless of committing the act of murder." Hereburg sighed.

"Will any of this community support your oath?"

Her face creased in a sad smile of resignation.

"None of this world will so swear but the Lord God, who is my only judge, knows of what I am innocent and of what I am guilty."

The bishop shook his head, unclear as to what the abbess was saying. He nodded to Eadred and the priest responded by rising and bowing to the bishop and Aelfric.

The young priest did not look well himself. He had been sitting slumped slightly forward, rubbing his face and eyes. He exhaled loudly and commenced.

"Reverend Mother, if not murder, what crimes have you committed?"

The abbess lowered her head and reflected, mumbling to herself, before looking past Eadred to the bishop.

"Reverend Father, forgive me, for I have sinned." She sobbed, raising her hand to still the murmuring. For a few seconds she remained silent, swaying to and fro, pondering her next words.

"I have committed carnal acts and allowed the Sisters-in-Christ in my keeping to do the same. I have also concealed my lineage from you from the time you first knew me. I was not born and raised an East Angle, as I told you, but I am from Mercia – from a noble family."

The bishop, still in a state of bewilderment caused by what he was hearing, raised his hand to calm the noise from the assembly.

"I trusted you and supported you. I raised you up. You lied to me."

Eadred had never seen the bishop as dismayed as this. The hurt was deep.

"You told me – you swore to me – that you were of our country, from the northern shores." Aethelbert shook with anger.

"Reverend Father, if it were my faith alone that decided the outcome, I would have been truthful. But you know that I would not have been allowed to rise within the Church of the East Angles if it were known that I came from Mercian nobility. Not in this age, when the antipathy between our kingdoms has spilt so much blood and continues to do so. To serve God as Abbess of Elmstow was all I yearned for and it led to dishonesty and death. I am sorry for my part."

"And with whom have you committed the vile acts you mentioned?"

Hereburg clutched at her stomach and groaned. The bishop asked again.

The abbess looked skyward, avoiding the many eyes that watched her mouth, waiting for the names that she would speak.

"With Ceolfrith, Ealdorman of the East Angles, and he alone."

"What monstrous lie is this?" Aelfric rose to his feet.

The bishop tried to calm him and was pushed over in the attempt.

"Let me question the abbess." Eadred's plea and the restraining influence of Aelfric's closest comrades were just enough to return the ealdorman's son to his seat. The quivering bishop was also helped back into his seat, but he was sorely shaken. What would Hereburg say next and what effect would it have on Aelfric? Eadred feared the worst.

"Did you lay with the ealdorman on the night of the feast – the night he was murdered?" The uproar of a few seconds earlier turned miraculously into complete silence.

"Forgive me." Hereburg looked to the bishop. "I did and I was tricked into sapping his strength. Yet, he was alive when I left him. This I swear by our Saviour's blood."

Eadred's voice hesitated. The enormity of Hereburg's confession and its impact on Aelfric daunted the young priest but he needed to continue to delve into this profane liaison.

"Have you lain with him before?"

The abbess burst into sobbing. With no answer being offered, Eadred asked again.

"Twenty or more years past, perhaps twenty-five – I cannot count the years – well before I was accepted into Holy Orders; I did." Hereburg held her stomach, screaming in pain. She lifted her hand to forestall more questions. After regaining some composure, she tried to continue.

"What have I done?" She shook her head then doubled over, like a decrepit hag, and tumbled to the floor. She looked up at Aelfric. "At that time, Lord Ceolfrith accompanied a mission to the Mercian court to negotiate an exchange of prisoners of rank. I was there with my father and the ealdorman noticed me. I was a beauty in those days, though I own that it is hard to believe so now.

"We became lovers and I left with him. It destroyed my parents. It could never last. Your father helped me start a new life with a new name and gave me money to establish myself in a nunnery. Then he continued his steps upward in the court. He continued to see me for a year or so then came no more.

"When he arrived here several days ago, it was the first time he had seen me since those times. I had taken another name, so he had no idea it was me until we cast eyes upon each other."

"Return her to her seat." Aelfric gestured to the guards to lift her. "Lady, there is no escape. Why all these lies? Why did you murder my father?"

Despite her frailty, Hereburg shouted her denial, slowly, with precision and anger, staring into Aelfric's eyes.

"Have you not listened? Lord, I would not and did not murder your father, but I hoped to rekindle the passion of our younger years and was sorely used by others who profited from my stupidity. I have lost the beauty I once had and sought to use a magic potion, others gave to me, to lure him. I told your father it was to take away the pain of a recent wound. There was no magic in the liquid, but he saw me still as I was those many years ago. He was full with wine, and drank it without question. I was tricked into sapping his strength and others did then take his life.

"Before God, I wish it were different. I wish I did not attempt to strip away the years and to taste the warmth of carnal pleasure one last time. See how that unnatural desire has poisoned me!"

"If not you then you must know who did the murders? Who made the poisoned cup? Who killed Princess Cuthburg, Ealdorman Ceolfrith and Sister Verca?"

"No, you should not have asked me," Hereburg replied to Eadred, then her legs gave way and only the guards stopped her fall.

"Let me confess to another crime for I am done with the secret. I do not care about the crimes of others, but I can hold this to myself no longer. It is killing me.

"We had planned for many months to end the lives of the king and Princess Cuthburg; both when the king visited the minster."

Eadred sat with his head in his hands while the outcry continued. Slowly, and only with the threat from the warriors who guarded the court, did it subside.

"But she was murdered by others on the night of the feast. Not by me, nor by those I knew."

"Who killed her?" Aelfric shouted at the abbess. There was no reply.

"Lord, there is something wrong with the abbess." The guard sat her down and looked closely at the face. "She is dead!"

TWENTY

The Slave

Eadred watched the troop of the king's guard move through the minster enclave. Their leader, muddied from a clearly arduous journey, had ridden into the minster a few minutes earlier. He barked orders that were obeyed as if he were moving his own limbs. It was past midday, the day after Hereburg's trial, and all the consternation, confusion and suspicion of the proceedings had spilled throughout Elmstow.

The raucous debauchery of the feast had turned to gut-twisting fear. Amongst the highest in the land had met their premature ends and their naked bodies hung up to humiliate and sow discord. A righteous Sister-of-Christ had been tortured, disfigured and her demeaned body also displayed naked. A slave had been murdered on the road just beyond the minster walls. The abbess had helped to shed light on a few aspects of the murders but had died before Eadred had been able to ask her important questions. A door had been closed before the priest had been able to look the other side.

He had had more to do with armed men this past week than at any time in his life and Eadred found himself noticing how this new warrior seemed to differ in bearing and behaviour from either the ealdorman or his son. He was undoubtedly imposing of frame, but there was also purpose and energy in all he did, despite the rigours of his ride. Compared to the arrogance and bullying of the ealdorman and the inexperience and disabling grief of his son, this man seemed to exude genuine and thoughtful confidence. It was a surprise to Eadred when this seasoned warrior looked across the courtyard and gestured to him to follow.

The guard closed the door behind Eadred.

"I am Hygelac of Dommoc, who commands the king's guard." Eadred's eyes followed a man who seemed to find standing still a difficult task. He continued to walk around the hall while he talked, checking the benches, the large pot of stew that bubbled over the fire, and the firmness of the bolt that locked the door. Without looking at the priest, he continued, "Sit." The brisk leader of the king's guard pointed to a stool.

As with many in the minster, Eadred felt confused about the arrival of so many of the king's own men days after the murders. There was something odd going on and it worried Eadred. Were there suspicions about the innocence of the ealdorman's son?

"Bishop Aethelbert has spoken highly of your abilities to the king and our lord granted you time to use your skills in finding the pigs who committed the murders. You have had some success, but it has not been fast enough.

"I now control this minster and all within it in the king's name. Evil has touched the king's own family and he is saddened beyond measure. His borders are weakened and his heart weeps for his people. He will purge this place with righteous anger. I am here to smoke out the last of the vermin and to bring them to justice – quickly.

"Because King Athelstan is a Christian king, who strives to preserve peace in his kingdom and to win God's favour, he still accepts the bishop's faith in you. However, it will take more than talk. Your mind is still useful but so is this." Hygelac tapped his sword hilt.

Eadred had no option but to accept the inevitable.

"What would you have me do?"

"I love the king above all men. He ordered that I take heed of what you have uncovered. Time is short. I am listening." It was an offer that the priest accepted with both hands.

Eadred recounted the events of the previous days in as few words as he believed were needed. Hygelac listened with intent and in silence. When informed of the gap in the outside wall, Hygelac replied that Aelfric had been at pains to tell him about the cleft and that it continued to be well-guarded and with secrecy.

Eadred left nothing out, other than the odd behaviour of the ealdorman's son towards Leoba. The priest had initially considered that Leoba might have had a hand in poisoning the ealdorman and with Aelfric's involvement. It was a thought that had dismayed Eadred. However, Abbess Hereburg had admitted being duped by an un-named man into giving the ealdorman poison. His vehement accusation of Hereburg at the trial suggested that Aelfric was as alarmed by the abbess' admission as was Eadred.

"The rumour stoking the fires of fear in Elmstow is that the abbess was silenced to stop her naming her accomplices. There is much truth in this. I went close to her body when she was announced as dead and smelt dwale. It was the same smell as on the ealdorman's breath. Both were poisoned. With the ealdorman, it weakened him so he could be overpowered. With Hereburg, it killed her. The same person or people killed both the ealdorman and the abbess.

"The time is drawing near when the last of the killers will be uncovered. He or they wanted to ensure the abbess was dead and that she took their names and their purpose with her – but there is a sinister reason why they chose not to escape once the princess and ealdorman had been killed."

Before Eadred had a chance to continue, Hygelac spoke.

"Their killing has not yet finished."

"Yes." Eadred felt encouraged by the quickness of the warrior's mind. "Their purpose is still incomplete. Unfortunately, Hereburg died before she could tell us the reason for the murders.

"The Lord God has put other questions into my mind to help uncover the culprits. Have the murderers been here for long? The abbess said that they had been planning to kill the king and princess for many months. The so-called slave, whom I consider is the murderer of the princess, ealdorman and the abbess, must have been in Elmstow since then. I think that the paid killer, Godric, was brought from Hildericstow recently by this slave to help with the killing, as he feared that Ceolfrith could overpower him in a struggle. To make certain of the killing, a draft of dwale was also employed.

"My mind has also been led to ask what is different about the princess and the ealdorman, as well as what is similar? As I sat at the trial, waiting for peace to return, it came to me. The princess had been at the minster for a year or more, yet it was but a few weeks ago that the king decided to send the ealdorman to Elmstow. Perhaps the original plan was to kill the king and princess; but the ealdorman's arrival changed this."

"You have insight and wisdom, Father Eadred. I can see that. But what of the strange words of the abbess that she slept with the ealdorman; are they to be believed? The ealdorman hated this place. Never had a good word for it. And the abbess was past her youth – well past it."

"It is such a strange story that I think it true. I found threads from the ealdorman's cloak in the room set aside for spinning and weaving – and woollen strands of the colour of the ball pushed into his mouth and the smell of dwale – and oddly, there was also a bed. Could they have met there? It is not far from Princess Cuthburg's chamber. If the ealdorman were killed separately from the princess, it could have been in that room and he was then carried or dragged to the princess' chamber. So, I think her words were true."

"So much is still hidden but the hour has come when the fog must clear. The king is unharmed but if there are traitors who wish him dead and they are still free then his life remains in danger."

It was then that Eadred realised why Hygelac had arrived. Hereburg had revealed the plot to kill King Athelstan. A rider had been immediately despatched to the court and the best warrior had returned at haste with orders to root out whoever remained alive of the traitors. Eadred felt unsure about his own role but it would not be long before he would be tested.

"Now, it is time to question the slaves. My men will go with you, as will Aethelric. They are skilled in extracting information quickly if your methods fail."

Eadred nodded. Theirs was a method he could not administer and would not wish to, but he was glad that those who could perform such work would be with him. He prayed silently that the false slave would be found quickly and that most of the others would not have to face the grim treatment that Hygelac's men were ready to deliver.

"The work the slaves perform is needed. If you must be harsh with them, leave them able-bodied."

"My men know many methods. They will not harm their value to the minster. You will have your opportunity first and if that fails then we will use another way."

*

Some had been bought, some had been given, and one had been provided in lieu of payment for the burial of two sisters by a priest from Elmstow. The minster owned fourteen slaves, who worked the fields, tended to the livestock and their butchering, caught fish and eels, worked the mill, did repairs in wood, thatch and stone, cooked, and prepared hides and cloth. Mostly they performed the heavy, onerous and disagreeable tasks, but also some skilled work, when a slave possessed a particular aptitude. Eleven were men and three were women. The youngest was fifteen and the eldest was close to thirty. All were now locked inside two stone outbuildings. Eadred had asked for a list and his questioning would start with the men and of those, firstly, the most recent arrivals.

A slave called Wistan was brought by two warriors into the room where Eadred and Aethelric stood. His hands were bound behind him and his feet fettered in iron manacles. He was strong and young – younger than Eadred. Fear possessed him and his words were confused. Eadred sighed. This was not going to be as straightforward as he had hoped.

"This is not the way," Aethelric expressed his annoyance. "They will all lie, and we will know no better than we do now. Let us bring all the men here and look carefully at them and question them together. If Godric saw and heard that one seemed more than a slave, then we also will."

Eadred seemed resigned to the change of plan.

"Bring all the male slaves," Aethelric ordered. They filed through the door and Eadred moved forward to start questioning the first one.

"Father, you misunderstood. Let me question them. I am a warrior and will pick a warrior quicker than you. I know the signs." Aethelric's smile was unpleasant.

Unfortunately, the priest knew that Aethelric was right. Most of the men in front of him were muscled from hard toil. He looked at them and virtually all could be warriors. The priest nodded.

Aethelric stood in front of Wistan and asked where he was from. With no warning, a warrior punched him in the stomach with enough force to send him flying back into those behind him. Eadred shouted out, in shock. Aethelric gestured for a guard to put his hand across the priest's mouth.

"Do not interfere! It would be best if you left. I will have you called when we have finished."

Eadred flushed red. He turned and left.

Wistan floundered with the effort to raise himself. A warrior's boot hit him in the face then he was pulled up and dragged before Aethelric, blood pouring from his lips and nose.

"You are lower than a pig and will die as one." Aethelric drew his sword.

Wistan cried and pleaded for mercy. A kick in the back sent him crashing into the wall.

"Hang him later."

Aethelric stood in front of the next slave. He cried out his name before a fist into the face sent him crashing backwards. He screamed for mercy but was dragged to his feet and kicked between the legs.

"Worthless shit! Hang him and let their bodies rot on the rope."

The third fell to his knees when his name was demanded, and he was treated as the others. The fourth pleaded that he had done no wrong and was left a blubbering, bloody mess. The fifth was treated likewise.

"Name?" Aethelric shouted into the face of the next slave. "Answer!" None came. The kick into his stomach doubled him but he did not fall.

"Make him kneel. Pull his head back."

Aethelric held his blade against the slave's throat.

"Then die like an animal."

The slave stared into his killer's eyes. The dim candle flame glowed on his sweaty face, yet he remained silent.

"Tear his tunic away."

With a few rips by strong hands, the threadbare tunic was gone, and the sinewy body exposed. The slave groaned and toppled against the wall.

"This is the one. Take him back. Tie him to the wall and guard the door. Keep these others locked up here for now. Do not free them until this one has told us what he knows."

TWENTY-ONE

No Peace

Impassive faces lined one side of the road, while despondency gripped the other. The heavy-wheeled wagon splintered and crushed the ice, groaning in its misery, rising and falling over the rutted surface. Cuthburg and Ceolfrith were starting their journey to the kingdom's capital. The bishop stood, head bowed, supported by Eadred. From the minster's gate to the point where the road to the capital left the southern route to circle back to the north-east, tear-soaked warriors watched their lord depart. Memories of battles, of campfires, of gifts given by the great man, of laughter, sadness, pain and joy, lived once more. Many had known no other leader. Aelfric waited at the junction, increasingly unable to control his misery. The line of cloistered women, there by order not by heart, shivering, suppressing yawns or staring into the distance, hoping that soon they would be free to return to the warmth of the minster.

An hour later, Eadred conducted the services for Sister Verca and Eanswith. A small cemetery had been consecrated some five months earlier, attached to the outside of the minster wall. Three bodies rested there thus far waiting for judgement – an old nun, a farmer and a child. The dead from the surrounding settlements and farms had for countless generations been interred in a burial ground a few miles distant. Christian and pagan alike had been welcomed there to rest alongside their kin and neighbours, as in life. Since the minster had been established, Bishop Aethelbert had sought to encourage those living nearby, when their time came, to rest alongside the community of the minster faithful, rather than casting an eye back to their dead kin, some of whom had cleaved to beliefs that the Church had condemned. It seemed, though, that it would take a greater effort to change the people's customs. At least two more souls were now to be welcomed.

A gentle breeze blew in from the meres, bringing the scent of rich, damp earth. It was a smell that Eadred loved, always reminding him of his country and his childhood. And the vastness of the sky imparted to his heart the immeasurable love and mercy of his God and Saviour. It was a small group of Sister Tetta, two other nuns, Leoba, Edith and Tatwine, who watched the bodies, wrapped in their winding sheets, lowered into the fragrant earth.

Eadred spoke of the heavenly bliss awaiting both women. Sister Verca had embraced the cloistered life with all her heart, mind and body. No task was too menial for her, no-one was beyond her prayers and care, no opportunity to praise, to listen and to talk to her God was wasted.

"For some unknown reason, our Sister was taken from

159

us violently. Yet, I saw her face in death. Even through the torments she endured, she stayed smiling. The flesh alone would have screamed with pain, but God's spirit was with our Sister and she died in his peaceful arms. I shall never forget that wondrous smile.

"Eanswith was a slave who was journeying to the minster. We do not why she wished to come here and although her death was cruel, her soul is for God. I know from Brother Tatwine that Eanswith was a baptised Christian, so she will rest here in sacred ground until the last day."

Eadred looked back at the end of the service to the two mounds of black earth and to Tatwine, who was kneeling, convulsed with tears, praying for the slave who had tried to seek him out and who died a harsh and lonely death. How was such anguish possible to bear?

*

It was a day of many struggles for the priest; his final task was the hardest. The wagon stopped at the end of a seldom-used track.

"We walk from here, Father." The two slaves were ordered to lift their burden. A guard led the way, followed by Eadred, the slaves, then three more warriors followed. The pathway edged gradually downhill between increasingly dense walls of woodland that trespassed onto the muddy strip, ripping at clothing and catching feet. The air darkened and grew colder and damper.

"Is it far from here?"

"Not far now, I hope." The warrior's voice carried no conviction. Eadred wished for a better response. Daylight was retreating to the upper reaches of the naked canopy and drawing the priest's spirits with it.

Soon after, the wood gave way to a clearing and the slaves were ordered to rest their load on the wet meadow grass and to start digging. There was a strange silence – no birds, no wind and no peace. Towards one end of the dismal opening, an earthen platform had been constructed, now partly covered with undergrowth and crowned with a decaying gibbet. To either side, short stakes had been hammered into the ground. Ever curious, Eadred walked amongst them, noticing they mostly came in pairs. Some had clearly been there for many years. The leading warrior came and stood by the priest.

"This was the execution place in days gone by. I saw a few here. It is no longer used – too difficult to keep the path open. Punishment must be seen to be done, so a place closer to the capital is now favoured. The bodies, limbs, heads were buried around here." He pointed to the stakes. "And those who could harm us – witches and the like – are also under this ground; their bodies butchered and pinned with rocks."

"The abbess is to be buried amongst such people?"

"On the king's order," the warrior replied to Eadred.

"It seems very harsh."

"H'm. I thought it too generous. She aimed to kill the king and princess. Her body should be hung on a gibbet outside the king's hall, but she will end up here, in cursed soil."

"To be separated from God forever, in hell. It is a terrible fate."

"She made that choice when she set herself on the path of treason."

161

"Yes, but she was abandoned by the Church in life – and now in death."

"Anyway, the hole is ready. Put her in and cover it well. Say your words, Father, and we will be off – quickly."

*

Laughter was returning. The fear, the doubt, the seclusion, at last could ease. Holy Sisters and warriors who had eyed each other or newcomers suspiciously, began to talk and smile together once more. The buds of lust swelled, pushing aside any remnant concerns that Elmstow still harboured killers. The doubts that rested still in Eadred's mind that there may be another dark soul lurking with a blade or poison did not enter the thoughts of a community desperate to put aside fear and to embrace the warmth of another body, rather than fear it.

Two murderers were dead and the final captured, or so it seemed. The daily cycle of communal prayer was to start at midnight on the following day – but tonight there was to be feasting. Intimacy that had been torn apart after its first consummation was ready to burn hot once more.

The chuckling of young nuns running along the corridor with their bawdy banter hurt Eadred's ears. He pushed hard against both sides of his head; it subdued but did not end his torment. What bruised him more; the violence of yesterday or his timid response to Aethelric? As was often his way, when he felt he had failed, his thoughts were consumed by self-recrimination. He became as if paralysed, unable to move forward. Occasionally, in these times of doubt, he might gain an insight into how he could avoid such failure

162

but mostly his mistakes returned over and over and sat as a rotting carcass in his thoughts. This was such a time.

It was violence that caught the traitor who sought to deceive by the pretence of being a slave. The best service that Eadred had given had been as a lure for Godric to murder. What had happened to the hope he had gained from Tatwine's vision? The ordeals by hot iron would have been best. And what did the future hold? Eadred could see no task for himself in the interrogation of the so-called slave the following day or in any part of the cleansing of this debauched place.

The priest struggled to lift himself and he sat on the side of his bed staring at the earthen floor of his tiny cell. His mind was exhausted with the whirr of images of death, laughing as it duped and dragged unsuspecting souls, intent on pleasure and power, from the light and into the darkness.

Had all the murderers been dealt with? His mind struggled to think about the crime. Hereburg had said that 'we' planned to kill the princess, but they found that the task had already been undertaken. Who else was in that group? Certainly, Godric and the so-called slave. How many more remained free? One, two or none?

Should Eadred remind Hygelac that death might still stalk Elmstow and that this was not the time to turn from vigilance? Or was Eadred's imagination creating false meanings from the signs he had seen and the words he had heard?

Hereburg's death cast a shadow over the young priest. She would have been filled with the spirit of the Lord God at one time. Her life would have had a great purpose. How could her maker have treated her so poorly? She did not deserve such a painful and desolate end – on earth and for eternity. Eadred felt the weight of his calling. It would be better to live a simple life with no great expectation of the days ahead.

He rose, listening to the sounds of joy outside, and fell again upon his bed. Eadred reached for his cup, drank then closed his eyes. The face of death, not ugly and terrifying but attractive and appealing, smiled at him. He was clothed richly and spoke words of comfort, not of judgement – of understanding, not of expectation.

Eadred woke with a gasp, his chest rising and falling, aching. He was alone. He rubbed his face hard and filled his cup. He returned it to the bench, its contents unemptied, and he left his cell.

Flaming torches lit the way. Eadred shivered; it would be a cold night. There was not to be one communal feast; there had been no time and no office charged with its organisation. Spontaneous joy had replaced fear and desperation. Groups congregated around a handful of outside fires, where victuals carried from the storerooms and the minster kitchens were being cooked. Warriors carried vats of wine and ale and armfuls of wood to feed the fires. It was a scene of exuberant chaos.

The slaves who would normally have performed most of the preparation were still locked away. Thus, holy Sisters with severely limited experience of roasting, stewing and other skills required to turn raw and salted meat, vegetables and herbs into edible delights, struggled with their ingredients and preparation. A few fingers were burned but nothing that the attentions of a muscled warrior could not remedy.

Unlike those he passed, the scene caused Eadred anxiety.

It was like the night of the murdering feast but worse. A killer could still be free amongst them, ready to pounce. Eadred looked into the eyes of those he passed, intoxicated by happiness and anticipation. The unions that had formed at Ceolfrith's feast now reformed and, relieved of fear, were rushing towards gratification without restraint. No-one would heed Eadred's warning, so he voiced none.

One feast was underway within the stone walls and Eadred headed towards it. Four or five benches encircled the fire in the hall. It burned gloriously, throwing light and shadows across the room. Around the benches sat Aelfric, Hygelac, Aethelric, half a dozen or so warriors and a handful of cloistered women, all young.

"Father Eadred, you are welcome. Tomorrow we will see what the man who feigns to be a slave has to say – and you must be there. Aethelric thinks he has the bearing of a warrior, a man familiar with pain and proud of his courage. He would have the strength to kill a powerful man and drag his body a distance. He is our man."

Hygelac, who spoke, possessed the arrogance of quick success. It annoyed the priest that it should come so easily to him. Eadred cast his eye around the other participants; none hid their admiration for Aethelric's robust method of threshing the slaves for the culprit. This was not a place where Eadred felt at home.

"I thank you. I shall not remain long for I would dampen this scene of happiness. I come only to raise a warning. I have thought carefully about the last few days and about the words that the abbess and Godric said. I may be repeating thoughts that you also possess but…"

"We may not yet have them all."

"Yes," Eadred replied.

"They are in our minds. You may be assured that they will not escape. We are not fools. Some of the men I brought are missing from the feasting. I have them guarding the minster and its occupants. We will make the false slave talk and I am confident that he will identify who else was involved. Now, eat, drink, if you will."

Eadred took some meat and wine at a bench but was far from comfortable. He left quietly – few noticing his departure – avoiding as best he could, the sounds and sights around the fires that sickened him. This was a bawdy army camp, not a house of God. When this was over, never again would such indulgence be permitted.

The noise of celebration faded behind him and, turning a corner, the priest found himself facing the passageway that led to the pigpen that hid the gash in the outside wall. He felt himself shiver at its memory. If Eadred wished to avoid retracing his steps through the flesh-pits, he had to proceed along that route. Several flaming torches encouraged him and slowly he advanced into the darker quarter of the minster with its animal pens, older storehouses and musty smells.

He came to the final turn before, if his recollection were correct, the pigpen should stand. Eadred felt menaced. His disposition was not improved when he peered around the corner to see a solitary torch, flickering low in the last minute of its life. A cold breeze whistled and, if there were pigs still in the shadowed pen, then they were taking their rest. The storehouse door was closed, and the priest hoped that Hygelac's men were there, inside, watching the approaches to the pen and its secret door to the outside world. He moved into the sombre light and with heart in mouth, scampered past the pen, past the sad flame and into darkness.

Under the veil of clouds pressing down on him, Eadred hurried forward in complete blackness, guided only by the wall, against which his right hand brushed. Somewhere ahead was the door that led back through the wall of stone and to his own cell. Fear quickened the priest's pace. Suddenly, the wall disappeared, and he fell.

Eadred turned over and lay on his back, clutching his right knee. He pulled up his tunic and tried to subdue a cry. His hands became sticky with blood. With his other foot, Eadred felt the remains of a low wall, probably part of a ruined storehouse. He had rushed straight into it. Struggling to regain his feet, he shuffled forward and found the wall once more. He limped on, hoping his right leg would not give way, and bumped into a solid door. Thank the Lord God it was not locked. Eadred laboured with the massive obstacle but slowly it moved. A blade of light cut through the darkness. He pushed harder.

"Stand still; there in the light. Do not move!"

The axe head quivered.

"Wait, I am Father Eadred. The king himself has given me a mission in this place. I fell in the darkness. I do not threaten." The priest held his hands high. "Hygelac, your commander, told me that his men guarded the minster tonight."

The warrior eyed Eadred cautiously.

"Close the door then move forward."

Eadred would not argue with a bear, so chose to obey.

"I have seen you in his company. Move off. Your face is smeared in blood – for your own protection, clean it."

Fortunately, his knee began to move fairly freely, though it bled still, and he navigated the corridors back towards his own cell. Preoccupied as he was with his own discomfort, it took longer than usual for Eadred to realise the sounds ahead of him.

Weeping. It was a woman weeping. Eadred had witnessed enough sadness and violence over the past days and anxiety took hold in an instant. Biting his lip and wincing, Eadred approached a door on his left. He searched his mind, for he should have known each of the doors by now, although he approached them normally from the opposite direction. It was beyond him.

The cry of one with wounds, insistent but controlled, came again from within the room. Also, a man's voice.

The priest took his knife from his belt and touched the door. It was unbolted. With his heart pumping hard, Eadred readied then pushed the door back with a single hard shove and entered with the knife in his raised right hand. Horror overtook him. He had never seen such a sight.

Lying on a cloak partially hidden by the open door, the bloated, cauldron-shaped, naked body of the moneyer faced away from him. The smile disappeared and his head arched back towards the priest. Sitting astride him, also naked, Edith the postulant, wiped blood from a cut lip. Regenhere's hands gripped her bleeding breasts, pulling her towards him. The moneyer cried out for help. The knife bounced on the floor.

"Foul creature! By all that is sacred, how can you treat a cloistered woman thus?"

Regenhere released his hands and fumbled for his cup. Edith rolled sideways, clutching her chest.

"Get out! Get out!" Screaming obscenities, he picked up the cup to hurl at Eadred, spilling most of the liquid over his face and arm. The throw missed but hit the door. Eadred stood frozen. More obscenities.

"I will have you tried for this crime."

"Interfering priest, you will suffer for this." Regenhere spewed invective.

"Quick!" Edith grabbed Eadred by the tunic and pulled him into the corridor. "Take your knife and hide it." The cries and the noise had brought nearby Sisters to gape at the scene.

"There is no murder. Father Eadred has freed me from misuse and perversion."

Though some of the holy Sisters were used to rough caresses, the sight of Edith, standing unclothed with her blood smeared from cuts to her breasts and lips, was beyond their experience. Heads peered into Regenhere's chamber and beheld his flaccid carcass. They ran quickly from the abuse and disappeared along the corridor, some screaming, some laughing.

"To my cell; not far." Eadred and Edith moved quickly and soon were inside Eadred's cell and the door bolted.

"Lord God, ease this pain!" Eadred turned to the wall, while the postulant rocked backwards and forwards, holding her bruised and bloodied breasts.

"How anyone can treat you thus?" Eadred groaned out his failure. He placed his cloak across her shoulders. "Here, some water and a cloth. It will soothe."

"Have you wine or ale?"

Eadred poured a cup of wine and lit another candle and sat silently against the back wall. Edith faced the door, using the cloth and water to ease her suffering and to wash away the worst of the blood.

"Some more wine?" her voice winced.

"Yes, of course." He refilled her cup.

"Can I fetch a nun to help you?"

The short shake of the head did for words.

"Leoba will care for me once she returns from the feast. She has been ordered to cook."

"My poor Sister. This must come to an end. I promise you. The man has gone too far. It is a crime to attack a religious woman and in her own minster. I will accuse him publicly."

"Father, leave it be – for now. He is not the only one. They are too powerful and can cause great harm. Please. I pray that this place will be cleansed but do not try to fight them alone. You will not win. Let the king close this minster and then the evil will have lost its nest."

The priest shook his head.

"How did you come to be there and with him?"

"I was told by one of the holy Sisters to come to the moneyer tonight and to do what was needed to satisfy him. It is not what you expect in God's house, is it?

"He had served me badly and worse was to come. He has strange and violent desires. I took his whipping, his slaps and whatever else he felt like doing. I managed to unlatch the door, hoping someone would come. You saved me from more of that treatment. But beware, he will not take kindly to what happened. You have spoilt his pleasure and humiliated him – and made for yourself an enemy."

"If a man becomes my enemy because I stopped him from committing evil then so be it. This treatment is monstrous. Could you not refuse?"

"And my sister and I will be thrown from the minster with nothing. This, we have already been told. What would happen then to us?"

"The woman who gave you this order; who is she?"

"Sister Moira."

"And is it she who has given you these orders before?"

"Yes, always her."

"I have seen this woman. I remember her well from the night of the ealdorman's feast – richly dressed, enjoying my plight. She laughed more than anyone at my distress. She almost fell from her stool." Eadred's face grew pallid at the memory. "She is, I was told, the youngest daughter of a rich family. What is happening to our great families?"

"There is a sickness that comes from wealth and privilege without fear of the Lord. It is all around us."

"Edith, who else in the minster have you been ordered to serve like this? Tell me their names."

The postulant gave the names of two of the minster's priests.

"Are there any others? Please, trust me with their names."

"I am offered to many who visit but I will not name them. That knowledge is dangerous."

Eadred creased his brow.

"Your sister said that Lord Aelfric spoke of his desire for you."

"He may have said that to Leoba but nothing happened. This is the truth. I swear, it is the truth.

"Father, I will go now. Can I keep your cloak? I will return it once I am clothed."

"Of course. And I promise you, Edith, I will stop this foul treatment that you suffer, one way or another."

"Be careful, Father Eadred. You are too good for this place." Edith rested her hand on the priest's shoulder. "I am worried for you. Take good care. With God's help we will survive this horror."

Eadred willed himself not to look but it was beyond him. He raised his head and beheld Edith's eyes looking at him. He felt her breath on his cheek.

Eadred lay down in his bed a short while later. He could not pray. The worst of things and the best of things had happened to him that day. He would remind Hygelac of the undertaking he had given to have a guard placed always with him – it seemed to have been forgotten. Perhaps Eadred's value had fallen? It was not a pleasant thought.

His distracted mind turned to Tatwine, who could never forget Eanswith but was never able to put into words why she had affected him so much. At least Eadred understood some of his attraction to Edith. A woman struggling to live her faith but with a searching soul housed within flesh that men craved and mistreated. The priest thought of her now. He knew he should pray to be released from the image that filled his mind, but he wanted to hold it for as long as he could.

TWENTY-TWO

Last Chance

Eadred fell asleep in the early hours, confused and distressed. He woke several times and on each occasion, the same concerns came upon him. Now, he awoke for another day and felt burdened by so much in his life.

It was the men with power with gold and with muscle who ruled. How could he stand against them? When mercy and care and the king's law were boiled away – and it took little to do so – then the result was the sin and filth of Elmstow. And sin fought sin to see who would rule.

The sounds of rain splashing heavily on the mud outside his window intensified. The day would be cold and damp. He could not get too wet and succumb to illness, as he had some winters back. His body had shaken and ached. He could not eat and he could not warm himself. His father had sent for a priest, but he never came – the flood consumed every track. The faith of his parents saved Eadred but it would not happen again. He rose to face the day with no enthusiasm.

Eadred opened the door of his cell and found his cloak wrapped neatly, lying on the ground. His heart began to beat wildly. He raised the cloth to his face and smelt her. Eadred was doubly happy to draw his cloak closely around him – it was warm and intoxicating. An object fell from one of the folds – a small crucifix on a chain. A gift. The priest kissed it.

Eadred scurried across the mud towards the door of the hut where the false slave had been imprisoned and where his questioning was to take place. Sheets of wind-crazed rain drove Eadred forward. A warrior appeared suddenly from the door and ran into the deluge. The priest bolted through the same opening. The scene inside was not what he expected.

Hygelac and Aethelric stood together with their backs to the wall. Eadred's dramatic entrance encouraged two guards to raise their swords. Aethelric calmed them. A figure lay collapsed against the opposite wall, his hands still tied together, raised above him by a rope attached to a metal ring. The rope had impeded the body from reaching the ground and the head slumped sideways. Eadred glanced at the two leaders then stooped to examine the man.

"He was dead when the door was opened this morning."

"And the overnight guard?"

"I have spoken to him," Aethelric replied. "He is a good man. He said nothing unusual happened. These men guard their brothers while they sleep. I trust him."

Eadred moved closer, so he was only a few inches from the man's staring, bloodshot eyes.

"I smell dwale, yet again."

Hygelac mumbled a cheerless agreement.

"It would have been given before he was questioned yesterday. I would have been able to see the signs if I had been given the chance."

"He would have died anyway by this poison. I picked the right man. You would have taken all day. The result is the same." Aethelric turned to his superior. "We needed to move quickly, and we now have them all. His death proves his guilt."

Eadred's response in such a contest would normally have been to avoid a dispute with the stronger man but today was different. He sensed well enough that the warrior had already been lashed by Hygelac's tongue and Eadred had learnt a valuable lesson from Aethelric's usual air of confidence. It was not enough to speak the truth softly; it had to be championed strongly if it were to prevail against a bold lie. The priest shook his head.

"The result is not the same. I know the effects of dwale. I would have seen amongst the faces of the slaves, one that was glassy with sweat with eyes that were unnatural. Godric killed for gold and knew little but this so-called slave killed for another reason. The purpose of his treachery remains unknown because of his death. We have lost the chance to question him. If another hand did poison him or if he killed himself to protect his fellow murderers, the truth remains the same – we have not unearthed all of them."

"He took his own life, as would a warrior, rather than face the shame of a rope."

"If he were the last of those who killed the princess and the ealdorman, a warrior would want to tell the reason for his actions. He died to protect the names of those who remain and who might still sink their knives into our bodies. I do not say it would be easy, but a fevered man might have given away some clue or secret if we could have questioned him."

Aethelric fought to keep his mouth shut but let out a grunt of anger. Hygelac looked troubled.

"It is indeed unfortunate. We must find the last of the murderers or the king will not be kind to us." He looked at Aethelric.

"Not all lessons are learned in battle. Remember what has happened; what has been said. Think, both of you, as will I, what you remember from the moment you arrived here. There may still be a way for us to uncover the last of the murderers. Watch the gap in the outside wall. There is glory enough for us all if we succeed and misery and shame for all our lifetimes if we do not. And work as one."

Both the warrior and the priest appeared to accept Hygelac's order and acknowledged each other, not extravagantly, while he looked on. They ran in different directions, into the roar of the downpour; Aethelric towards the outside wall and Eadred back to his cell to get dry clothing.

The splashing bearing down behind him caused Eadred to turn in fear. He fumbled for his knife. A figure had sped from another door. He was instantly recognisable despite the deluge.

"Tatwine, quickly!"

A short while later, they were both standing inside the door of a small hut, used to store tools and implements employed in the fields and to fish. Both had dry clothes provided by one of the holy Sisters who undertook repairs for the community. They watched the rain sweeping in arcs across the courtyard, blurring the outline of the buildings and with such sound that they were obliged to shout.

Tatwine pushed the door closed and secured it with a log. They resumed their seats, warming themselves around a makeshift fire with a pot of gruel and a cup of wine.

"Nothing can withstand the cleansing rain sent by God. It will purify this place and wash away the evil that has lived here for too long." Eadred could tell from Tatwine's words and how they came like a chant from his mouth that the Spirit of God was with him and it pleased Eadred, because he needed to feel that strength now.

"We should never doubt the Lord's word," Tatwine continued, "even if our experience appears to deny it, for what is given in the Spirit will come to pass in the world of men. The evil here will be defeated, and you will play the part that the Lord God has ordered for you. It is almost done so do not despair.

"Now, tell me, what does your mind tell you about this last murderer?"

"My dear friend, unfortunately, there may be one; there may be more. I have thought much about how I can uncover whom they are. Hereburg said at her trial that the plan was to kill both the king and the princess but Cuthburg had already been murdered. To my mind then, if we are to believe Abbess Hereburg, there are two groups of murderers. It may be that neither group knew of the intentions of the other. I have no idea who took Cuthburg's life or the reason.

"As to the ealdorman's death, he was killed by Godric, the false slave and maybe others. I think that the ealdorman may have discovered the plot to kill the king and his daughter and was killed by these butchers. The plot was the highest treason possible but who would have been so bitter and dishonourable?

"No-one seems to have attempted to escape Elmstow so far. So, are we to think that both groups of killers have further deeds to undertake? It is a terrible thought that the murderers may not be finished – but it is also our only hope of catching the rest of the nest."

The hermit smiled and punched Eadred's arm playfully.

"What your mind can do! I can see you sifting through all manner of possibilities. You are distilling what is true from the dregs. Do not stop. Keep going and it will become clear. And let me join you. Is it not possible that if the princess' murderers are not of the band that killed the ealdorman that they do not know of the gap in the outside wall and believe themselves imprisoned here for the moment?"

Eadred smiled in return.

"You are right. We have several paths to explore.

"Now, we must return to the problem we have talked about before because I am sure that it contains a clue for us. Why was the small ball of wool pushed into the ealdorman's mouth and the larger – twice the size if not more – pushed hard into Cuthburg's smaller, more delicate mouth?"

Tatwine rubbed his ear.

"In the confusion of the attacks, the murderers picked up whatever was to hand and made a mistake?"

Eadred gazed into the fire.

"I smelt dwale in the room set aside for spinning and weaving and on strands of cloth belonging to the ealdorman. I believe that was the room where the ealdorman was subdued. Now, let me imagine what could have happened.

"The abbess serves the ealdorman with a cup – maybe more – that unknown to her had the dwale secreted within. He is already drunk. They have illicit relations in the weaving room; the abbess leaves and following this he is overwhelmed by the false slave and Godric, knocked out, the woollen ball forced into his mouth, and carried or dragged across to Cuthburg's cell, where he is hanged.

"The killers had probably already waited for Lord Aelfric to leave the princess and they entered her room intent on murder but found her already beaten and dead. The black-hearted killers removed her clothing and hanged her beside the ealdorman."

"But does that mean that Lord Aelfric killed her?" Tatwine sounded sceptical.

"No, neither can I believe it. He is tormented by her death. Others entered her cell after Lord Aelfric left. They attacked her from behind and she fell into the wall, so both the back and front of her head were injured.

"The wound to the back of her head was severe. I think it would have killed her. So, what point was there to the huge ball of wool in her mouth if not to stop her crying out?"

Eadred took another sip and sat with a mystified expression. Tatwine spoke to him but he did not hear. Was it possible that what he was thinking now was the truth of what had happened?

TWENTY-THREE

Aelfric's Lament

Under coffin-lid skies, night came prematurely. It was early afternoon and still it poured. The nearby river had muscled from its path to flow through the water meadows. The slaves, now freed from prison but never from toil, worked to shore up the earthen ramparts around the minster.

Aelfric lit another candle. Though the gloom outside had little bearing on the light within the hall where he sat, he was in need of something brighter. The timid glow did nothing to change his spirits and he threw it to the floor. Only the ordeal of hot iron administered to all who were within the minster on the night of the feast carried the possibility of unearthing the remaining murderers. The bishop would undertake the ordeals as the Lord God wished but Aelfric knew that they would sweep up all manner of sins. There was no lack of evil in Elmstow and the sole crime that he needed to uncover could go undetected in the torrent.

Riders had arrived earlier with news that Aelfric had been elevated by King Athelstan and was now the new ealdorman. Once Elmstow's isolation was over, there would be a formal ceremony in the capital with the king and his great noblemen, but the Lord God had been gracious to the new ealdorman and for now he was nurtured by the unquestioning support and love of his own hearth group. For he knew that nothing in his experience or spirit was adequate for such an immense responsibility. His great father looked down on him and condemned. Aelfric could not even perform the only role he wanted for himself.

Every stone and stick in Elmstow reminded the new ealdorman of his wretchedness. He had tried to overcome his melancholy by throwing himself into the task of finding the remaining murderers, but this was now in others' hands. Each murderer had died before he could undertake the task he had pledged before God to fulfil – discovery and capture of the vile soul who had ripped his beloved from him, who had defiled and demeaned her body.

There was a knock, and a guard announced the expected visitor. At least, he could be of some help to someone.

"Lord Aelfric."

"Mildred, you are welcome here. I am sorry that I have not been to see you. How have you been, now we are all imprisoned? Here, sit down."

"I have lost my mistress. I still cannot believe what happened. And for you, the loss of your father and your betrothed. I know from the intimate time the princess and I shared, how she loved you."

Aelfric struggled to compose himself and stared upwards.

"It is done, and I must go on. In battle, the dearest

friends can be cut down mercilessly before your eyes but, after a time of mourning, the days must be faced again. And so it is with me. You have heard that I am made the new ealdorman?"

"I have indeed. The news has been welcomed by everyone. The kingdom will be a safer place for it. The king has chosen well."

"There are many things now that must concern me, but still I will do my utmost to find her killers. It is my duty. My father trained me well. Soon, the bishop will administer the ordeals and the killers will be found.

"And what of your future? Most of the Sisters will go where they are told once the minster is closed but you were the Lady Cuthburg's companion. I know that the queen chose you, though I doubt it was your life's choice to enter this community."

Mildred bit her lip.

"Lord Aelfric, I believe I am ruined. My father is dead, and my mother can barely survive. The princess promised that she would care for me and find me a worthy husband, but that hope is gone. I am still of marriageable age and the princess was gracious enough to say that I was the most beautiful woman she knew, apart from herself. I am at a loss, lord. I will entreat the bishop to send me to a good house, where I might grow old in service of Holy Church."

Aelfric reached out and placed his hand on Mildred's shoulder. He smiled but without conviction.

"Mildred, the Lord God has given me an esteemed position in this kingdom, and I will use this blessing to reward those who serve me and who served the woman I loved. The princess spoke very highly of you and it is my duty to see that her companion is cared for." Aelfric stared into her eyes and spoke with care. "You must tell me now, what is your greatest desire? If it is your wish to enter the cloister, I will speak to the bishop but if you desire to be married, I will find you a good husband from amongst the warriors I command. I will safeguard your future. This I promise."

"You are beyond kindness, my lord. To be truthful, from the time I have spent here, I have learnt that I am not suited to the cloistered life. I love the Lord, my God, but I have not the discipline to live as a cloistered woman. But I would be a good wife. I was brought up learning how to be a companion and support to a great man. How to manage a family and a household. How to host feasts."

"The man we find for you, Mildred, will be indeed fortunate. Not only all the virtues you mention but I believe the princess was right, you are the most beautiful woman in the kingdom after her. You have an elegance about you. It is a skill I admire in a fine lady to wear clothes that give prominence to that beauty."

Mildred smiled, gazing down to the fine white linen dress she was wearing.

"My lord, I am pleased that you noticed. I chose to wear this dress today to honour you. I pray that the man you choose for me matches my beauty with his strength and his rank. We would be the envy of the kingdom."

"I will do my best." Aelfric smiled faintly then his face changed. "Without my love beside me, I find it hard to think about the joy of others. Forgive me, Mildred, but the loneliness is hard to bear. I dreamt of the days and nights Princess Cuthburg and I would spend together but now, it is not to be."

"Forgive me, lord, for thinking only of myself." Mildred dropped to her knees in front of Aelfric's chair. "I too am lonely, for my mistress is gone and through service to her, I am unmarried. Please, lord, do not think that I am being bold, but may I think that perhaps I could soothe your nights?"

The new ealdorman looked troubled and confused.

"I am warm and have a heart and body that are eager to give. I do not give them lightly, but I will give them deeply to the one I admire and cherish. I can support a great man and give him all he desires."

The man's expression softened.

"Dear Mildred, life has dealt us both severe blows. I wonder how I will ever live up to my father's reputation. Such thoughts consume me, and I have little room in my mind or heart to think of tenderness. But we should not let happiness pass us by. I need to be married, as should you." He reached out and held her shoulders. Mildred took his hand and kissed it; Aelfric responded likewise then moved close to her ear and whispered, "Could you come to my chamber tonight? My bed has been cold and lonely."

"Gladly but why not now? It is dark as night and let me comfort you in a special way."

Mildred moved closer to Aelfric, clasping her hands behind her back; arching her body, so her breasts brushed the backs of his hands.

Aelfric's eyes scanned the woman kneeling before him. The imp within him nodded.

"There are no rivals to your body." Aelfric bent forward once more and spoke closely. "Even the Lady Cuthburg was envious when she saw you once, naked."

"Come then and I will show you what she saw."

"She was jealous of these." Aelfric squeezed Mildred's taut breasts. She purred.

"They are yours, lord, for comfort or pleasure."

"But the princess told me that you craved to have a face as wondrous as hers."

"That is not true, my lord. Her face was indeed pretty but I have such fine features."

The new ealdorman's expression teased, and he ran his finger along Mildred's nose.

"She told me that once she made fun of this, saying it was too long, and your lips were thinner than hers."

Mildred pulled away.

"Do not laugh at my expense, lord; it is hurtful. She had drunk too much wine when she said that. It was not meant."

"It is in the past but there is another, more important, matter I need to know before we draw closer." Aelfric reached out and wrapped his hands around Mildred's breasts once more. "I have been told that you bedded the moneyer's son, Raedwulf, on the night of the feast. I would be thought a fool if I took you for my wife if that were true. The boy is an idler and lecher."

"She made me do it, my lord," Mildred pleaded. "I had no desire to please that awful man. She threatened that she would have me cast from the minster if I did not do her bidding. You must believe me."

"I want to, dear Mildred. I want a life of happiness with you, but we would be blighted by the Lord God if it were known that I married a woman who sought the beds of other men. Raedwulf has sworn before me that you did say to him you would be a good marriage partner. I could not believe it, but he offered to bring forward many men who would swear that his oath was good."

"Cuthburg ordered me to bed him. I swear it is true." Mildred began crying.

"Lady, when I was with the princess that night, she told me that she had seen you whispering to the moneyer's son at the feast and pressing your body immodestly into his. She laughed that with so many warriors to choose from, who were eager for a woman's body, you chose a limp idler because that was your worth. Did she tell you that when you saw her after the feast?" Aelfric sat back in his chair.

"She laughed in my face! She said I was as ugly as a sow and Raedwulf was a good choice for me! But that was before the feast. I never saw her after."

"Raedwulf has sworn that he did not spend all of the night with you. You let him into your room, then after your desires were satisfied you said you felt ill with wine and disappeared, to return later. I remember well when I left the princess' room, for I had a duty to check the guard around the hall. I never returned for I was searching for my father. If I questioned Raedwulf now, I wonder if your absence from your bed would match with mine from the princess' chamber?"

"I did not see her again after the feast. I swear." Mildred grabbed her hair in her hands and pulled at it.

"Lady, I will question everyone who was in the minster that night and if anyone casts a doubt on your word, I will find out. If anyone saw you, I will know.

"Guard!" The door opened. "Take this woman to her chamber and make sure that she does not leave. Tomorrow morning, she will face the ordeal of hot iron and God will be her judge."

"No, lord. No!" Mildred screamed, struggling as she was pulled to the door. "Not that. My hands are soft and clear of blemish. It will ruin them.

"I did not mean to harm her. I swear. I was addled with wine and felt strange, and when I saw you with your men, I did go to her chamber, to laugh together as friends. She asked and I told her that I was bedding the moneyer's son and she burst into such mocking laughter and scorned me. Whenever she ridiculed me, she would call me ugly. When she turned around, just laughing at me, I found a piece of wood and hit her. I never realised how hard but I was beyond anger. She fell into the wall. When I knelt beside her, I saw that she was dead." Mildred stared at the wall, her voice tailing away.

"Why then did you push the woollen ball into her mouth?"

Mildred struggled to speak through her sobs and cries.

"She would laugh about my face, when the mood took her, as she did that night. She called me sow-faced. My anger was more than I could control. I picked the largest ball and thrust it as deep as I could into her mouth. Evil gripped me. I hoped that her body would stiffen in death and her face would remain misshapen and hideous as a pig.

"She was not the woman you thought, my lord. She was evil and vain. She used her body to bewitch you."

"Take her away, bind her and guard her carefully."

The noise from the forlorn woman disappeared. From behind a tapestry walked Eadred.

"It was as you said." Aelfric held his head in his hands.

"It is hard for anyone to accept what that woman did, my lord. When I thought more about the murders and that the killers of your father and the princess could be different people then the murders were committed for different reasons. The woollen balls might then have served different purposes. The ball used on your father was to keep him from crying out while he was overcome. It had to be pushed quickly into his mouth. The princess was already dead and the enormous size of the woollen ball unnecessary, except to disfigure. Then I believed it was a woman's work, aroused by the jealousy of one who was close to her and who knew her thoughts.

"But it took a lie to break her lie. At your father's feast, I saw her enticing Raedwulf but I paid it no heed until now. When I came to suspect Mildred, that memory put in my mind the hope that if we devised some imagined words that the princess said about her companion then we might break through her mask."

"It was a risk worth taking, though I almost rejected your plan. I am sorry for the venom in the words I threw at you. The woman is a temptress; I soon saw it in her eyes and in her conduct, when she knelt before me. I am grateful for your wisdom but that the princess should create such enmity and that such evil repay it. I will convene the trial quickly. I want that vile woman executed."

Whilst Eadred understood Aelfric's disgust for Mildred, it was still difficult for him to hear the clamour for a woman's blood.

"I will send a rider to the court. It will be hard for them. The queen chose Mildred to be companion to their daughter."

"I had forgotten," Eadred groaned. "The poor woman. I will pray for the king and queen that their hearts may heal."

"They will be grateful to you, Father, as am I. More than you can know. Mildred will be the only one of the murderers not to escape lawful execution. The king and queen will have their revenge. They will want her taken to the capital to face their fury."

TWENTY-FOUR

Trials

Aelfric was not alone in wanting Mildred's trial to be over quickly. The murders and the stillborn sense of release from fear and isolation had left the community fragile. Cuthburg's companion had never been liked and now the holy Sisters wished and prayed for a swift, uncomplicated trial and the removal of the final murderer. God would surely then say that penance had been made and he would forgive the survivors and let the gates open.

Bishop Aethelbert and Ealdorman Aelfric conversed quietly; both with nods and smiles. Not so, Mildred, who stood with tear stains on her cheeks, manacled, in a simple, coarse tunic.

"Were you alone in committing this vile act or were you part of the band of criminals, who included the Abbess Hereburg, Godric and the nameless slave, who murdered Ealdorman Ceolfrith and Sister Verca?" Eadred commenced.

"I was not part of the killing of the ealdorman or Sister Verca and those people were not involved in the end of the princess. But there was one other who helped me."

A moan arose from the assembly. The bishop buried his head in his hands. Eadred looked doubtful.

"You gave no other names when you spoke to Lord Aelfric?"

"A dog that expects a bone acts cheerfully but if it is kicked instead, it slinks away, confused. My time with Lord Aelfric was not as I expected. I spoke of myself only because of what I faced, and I forgot to mention the other person."

"Then who?"

"Raedwulf, son of Regenhere the moneyer, was with me when we went to the princess' chamber."

"That is a lie! I never went to the princess' room with her." Raedwulf leapt to his feet, as did his father. A wave of disbelief crossed the hall. A few voices rose, throwing insults at the woman. Raedwulf continued to object, until two guards grabbed him, and Bishop Aethelbert ordered him to be silent. His father continued with his raging objections with guards descending upon him.

While the proceedings were being disrupted, Eadred sat perplexed and worried. He had been certain that Mildred had acted alone. The blow to Cuthburg's head and disfigurement of her face were an outburst of jealousy and spite, a spur of the moment action. The priest could not see another person being in the room and when Raedwulf had been questioned by Lord Aelfric, Eadred felt certain that he was being truthful about Mildred's solitary absence – but he had lied before. Eadred began to doubt his own intuition.

Was it possible that Mildred and Raedwulf had gone to Cuthburg's chamber together and that he had also felt the sharp ridicule of the princess' tongue? Or that Raedwulf had helped Mildred, through his desire for her? Suddenly, Eadred felt an enormous sense of tiredness. This procession of human bile was never to end. With order restored, Eadred was still unsure.

"Why would a young man, with the prospect of a rich, privileged life, give it up and risk everything? There is no sense to it."

"I am to be executed. There is no way out for me. Why would I lie now? If I am to face cruel justice, then so should he who is also guilty. Raedwulf came with me to the princess' chamber to petition her to help him, and when she laughed at both of us, I hit her but, in his fury, he helped me push the woollen ball deep into her mouth. My hands and arms are weak – see." She held up her delicate limbs. "I would not have the strength to hold her head and push such a bulk into her mouth. And while we were treating her thus, Cuthburg opened her eyes and struggled but her breath gave out."

The bishop raised his hand to quell the shouting and threatened Regenhere and his son with huge fines unless they stayed quiet. Mildred also raised her arms once more, responding to cries to see their proportions. They did, indeed, look slight.

Eadred struggled with what next he should do or say. What was transpiring was beyond anyone's experience. He looked to the bishop, who was as confused as he and offered nothing.

"What was so important that Raedwulf should petition

the princess at that hour and in her chamber? You have no oath-helpers to vouch that your word is good, so why should this strange behaviour, that you say happened, be believed?"

Mildred's smile was wicked.

"Money, of course. Money and rank. Although he may deny it, Regenhere is anxious that his son be accepted by the king as the new moneyer when he dies. He is entreating powerful people to support his desire and to plead his case. And he is promising gold to those who help him. Raedwulf saw that he could petition the princess on his own behalf, as I was her companion. He did not want to waste time."

"Why do you say such shameful things?" the bishop scowled.

"Because that is what I was told by Raedwulf." The moneyer's son managed a few words of objection before a guard slapped him hard on the ear. The bishop followed by imposing a stiff fine.

"Men feel a need to boast when they are in my bed – and in the morning they often regret how much they had said to me. Raedwulf told me that he would be the new moneyer once his father died."

The bishop threw his hands up in dismay at the outrage to his ears.

"I know the name of a man here today, whom Raedwulf said would speak to the king on his behalf, and that man accepted money from Regenhere."

"You will say no more!" the bishop thundered.

"I am to die, anyway. I thought you wanted the truth?"

"There are rules. This is your trial. Death through execution comes in many ways. Now, be quiet and there will be some leniency." The bishop gestured for Eadred to come to his chair. They spoke briefly then Eadred resumed his position.

"Mildred, companion to Princess Cuthburg, is found guilty through her own words of murdering the princess. Raedwulf, son of Regenhere the moneyer, has been implicated and will face ordeal by hot iron to determine his innocence or otherwise."

"But I can bring many oath-helpers to support my son's good character. Give me time and when we are free to leave Elmstow, I will gather them. He should not have to face the ordeal. He is innocent. Who can believe this woman?"

"We are beyond that. Your son will face the ordeal to determine his innocence. We must leave it to the Lord God to decide."

"No! Lord Bishop, please listen to me." Raedwulf rose, despite the risk of being cudgelled or fined. "Let me face questions from Father Eadred instead of the ordeal. We all know that although God speaks through the ordeals, men are fallible in discerning God's decisions. If this woman was allowed to be questioned by one of the clergy then let me also face such examination. I am innocent and it will be shown."

An agitated Bishop Aethelbert gestured once more to Eadred and they spoke quietly with Ealdorman Aelfric. Then the bishop addressed the court.

"Raedwulf, son of Regenhere the chief moneyer, you have been accused by Mildred of helping her murder Princess Cuthburg. You will face trial by examination to determine your guilt or innocence.

"Take this woman to a cell and shackle her."

*

Eadred sat alone in his cell. Outside, the birds of the fens boomed and shrieked their twilight calls of foreboding. Vapour seeped from the ground and the monsters of hell stirred amongst it. Though pleased to have the thick walls of the minster separating him from the terrors of the meres, those stones had also harboured a spirit that was as evil. Please God that its reign was closing.

Mildred had lived a life of little purpose and her death would be unmourned. Yet, Eadred determined he would pray for her in her final hours for they would be full of more misery than she had faced in the rest of her short life. He had never witnessed the torture of a woman and prayed that he would be spared from such a spectacle.

Around a small fire he had made, Eadred sat on a stool supping a thick vegetable and marrow soup. A cup of wine – his unfailing companion – rested on the ground. It cheered or dulled but never judged. The priest's eyes stared at the comforting flames and his face felt their gentle warmth.

Eadred loved the stable routines of life, looking forward to a familiar pattern for each day. He wanted it to last until his dying breath. He could cope with some diversity, for the life of a priest was never entirely predictable. Yet his dream was to soak himself in the word and presence of his maker; not for the world to distract and tire him with uncertainty. But apparently, it was not what God wanted for him.

Not only had many of his anchors been cut away but the tiny vessel of his life on earth had been set on a voyage of discovery – and Eadred was scared. Those who had committed crimes were uncovered by a tried and true system. Many admitted their guilt without any need to accuse them or to uncover their actions for they feared the judgement of the Lord God. It was much harder to expose the guilty when they sought to hide it.

Accordingly, thieves were feared and despised, for they sowed dissent within a community, as neighbour suspected neighbour. And the same for those who stole the lives of others and sought to cloak their guilt. If an accused man were of good standing, his denial of a crime would likely be accepted if he could furnish the required number of oath-helpers, who would each swear that his word was good. But if he were of bad repute, this avenue was closed and he would be forced to undergo at least one ordeal, such as carrying a hot iron for a prescribed distance.

The affected hand was wrapped and sealed to be opened on the third day. If the wound were clean, God had shown the man's innocence. If foul and festered, God had uncovered his guilt and punishment followed. Yet, discerning God's will was difficult, and often uncertainty plagued the outcome.

What if the greatest in the land had been murdered and the culprits and their reasons remain hidden? Even if a man were found guilty of the crime, he was unwilling to identify his accomplices. He could deceive and spread falsehoods about others to disguise the true killers and their reasons, and to spread fear.

Eadred's approach of searching for the truth, of querying those who might be involved, was bold and new – and this terrified the young priest. He wanted to be anonymous, to go quietly and with meekness through life, but it was not to be. He rejoiced in a simple, mundane life but his mind burst into colour and travelled in strange, unpredictable directions when he confronted murder.

In the cold air of a winter's evening, when contemplating

how to take the next step, with hundreds of eyes watching him and as many ears listening to him, with life and death decisions resting on how well his mind worked, Eadred wished he was a simple priest with no gifts at all. Even more disconcerting was the knowledge that rich and powerful people were involved and they would have scant regard to the king's law if their lives and livelihoods were at stake. It was a point that the bishop had made earlier that day.

"Listen, my boy. You are to question the moneyer's son tomorrow. He is a fool and a braggart, but I very much doubt he is a murderer or Mildred's accomplice. He has not got the boldness or malice. I suspect what Mildred said about Regenhere offering gold to great men to support his case to the king is true. It happens but it does not need to be proclaimed in my court. The moneyer has a rival and if it were known that men of influence had taken gold to support Regenhere's cause to the king then there will be trouble – and we have enough of that. So, tread carefully my boy. The fates of Mildred and Raedwulf do not depend upon airing the moneyer's bribery.

"You have the gratitude of the new ealdorman; he has witnessed and benefitted from the fruits of your gifts. He will grow in strength and power and become in truth what he is now in name – the second most powerful man in the kingdom. If you are wise, you will try to serve him well and he will protect you from wicked lords and he will watch over you and your calling. Aelfric fears the Lord and is a good man. Cleave to him, Eadred, and you will be rewarded throughout your life."

The court reconvened in the church at Elmstow. Even now, no-one who was present on the night of the murders had been allowed to leave, other than a few riders to the king's court.

"Raedwulf, son of Regenhere the moneyer, you are accused by Mildred, companion to Princess Cuthburg, that you assisted with the murder and disfigurement of the princess and the veiling of the crime from the eyes of others. How do you swear?"

"By the Lord God, I am guiltless, both in deed and counsel, of the charge of which that woman accuses me."

"Very well. We are agreed that you will face trial by examination. Father Eadred has been selected to question your actions and conduct."

Eadred rose.

"Why would Mildred say that you were with her when she murdered the princess?"

"It is spite. When we were together in her chamber after the feast, she asked that I wed her and promised all manner of delights. She was jealous of the princess and doubtless thought marriage to the new moneyer would give her a life of luxury. I said I did not want to marry yet and she became angry. Then she left, saying she felt overwrought with wine, and did go to the princess' chamber without my knowledge and returned later, saying she was better. I know no more."

Eadred was distracted by voices behind him. Two guards had barged unceremoniously into the court and pushed their way between the tightly packed and irritated assembly, making for Aelfric. The guards around Aelfric drew their swords, such was the atmosphere of distrust within the minster. The intruders raised their hands to show that they did not hold weapons. One of the newcomers bent and spoke in Aelfric's ear. Aelfric's expression hardened and he asked something of the guard, who turned to the other. The latter nodded. Aelfric turned to the bishop. Eadred saw how the blood drained from Aethelbert's face and the old churchman struggled to his feet.

"This court is over. Elmstow is about to be attacked."

TWENTY-FIVE

Preparing the Defences

"You did well." Aelfric scanned the road heading south over the slight hill where Tatwine had come to live as a hermit. Over the summit, only just visible by the cold, pale sun reflecting on their metal, came the Mercian vanguard. "At least we have some time to prepare. How many do you think?"

"The road bends not long beyond that summit," Hygelac replied. "The men I placed to give us warning of any unfamiliar movements on the road could not see to the end of their line. At least a hundred; possibly double."

Beyond the perimeter wall, the slaves were herding the remaining cattle and sheep back within the minster. Fortunately, many had already been slaughtered before the onset of winter's bleakness. The storehouses were being checked for joints of beef, mutton and pork, and hams and cheeses. Salted fish, eels and vegetables in earthenware crocks. Two pits contained corn. There were jars of honey and dried herbs but not enough supplies to withstand a siege.

The feast for Ceolfrith had depleted the minster's stores. The older, more practical nuns thus waded through the fish ponds, snatching for the silvered bodies that darted beneath them. The pious women scurried through the vegetable gardens, pulling what leeks, parsnips, onions and cabbages of whatever quality remained, throwing them into carts. There were cries of fear and tears from the younger nuns, who sought the comfort of the older Sisters.

"Get those women back inside. I do not want this wailing or distraction!" Aelfric rubbed the back of his neck.

"We have a hundred warriors, at best. Should we arm the churchmen and the moneyer's son?"

"We should, lord."

"And the slaves?"

"No, they have no allegiance. Lock them up each night, as we do now."

Aelfric pulled Hygelac closer.

"There is something else I want done. Quietly."

*

Eadred was ordered from his cell. A soldier whispered the priest's task into his ear. Eadred shivered and sighed.

The warrior led the way, and another followed him. They set a vigorous pace across the courtyard towards the dormitory, refraining from responding to the priest's objections. If he slowed, the warrior behind his back nudged Eadred along. Into the building and along the dimly lit corridor, until they came to a cell. The first warrior tapped on the door. They entered and the bolt shut softly.

Two small candles failed to banish the gloom. The air was cold, damp but above all, it smelt foul. Human waste, sweat, blood. Eadred's stomach heaved and he blinked his stubborn eyes. He wished they had stayed idle. If this is what Christians did to a body, God knows what a pagan was capable of. Eadred turned away.

"This is not right, in the sight of God or man." He cleared his mouth of the bile. "We are in God's house and we have done this!"

"The court's decision was correct and just. Pray for her, if you will, although she deserves nothing other than her sentence."

Mildred – for it could be no other – stood on a stool, her hands tied behind her back. Her jealousy and anger had condemned her. She was always going to die badly, yet when she told that Cuthburg was alive when the woollen ball was pushed with design and hatred into every space within the princess' mouth, Mildred sealed an awful fate. When the companion owned that awful crime in court, Eadred watched Aelfric's expression; at first bursting with sadness then twisting into an avenging angel.

A ball of cloth filled Mildred's mouth. Her cheeks were pierced by wooden barbs that had been embedded into the material. Her eyes were all that she had left to testify to her terror. They darted across those figures in front of her and settled upon Eadred. She emitted a frantic, pitiful groan and her eyes pleaded for some crumb of mercy. She had been given none thus far.

Her lips, ears and nose had been sliced from her body.

The blood oozing through her stained and spattered tunic and dripping to the ground showed she had suffered further, terrible mutilation. Eadred knelt, without looking up, and prayed for the once proud and arrogant woman.

The stool was pushed away and slowly she ended her life.

"The bitch is dead. She showed no respect or mercy to the princess and she received none. Go now, Father, and leave the rest to us."

"And the poor creature, she cannot speak now. Whatever she knew has gone with her." Had powerful voices spoken that she must die sooner rather than later? But for now, his mind was filled with apprehension about what was to come. The axe he had been given for the forthcoming fight lay in his cell. The sight of it was enough to bring him to a sweat.

*

As the day's light faded, the extent of the Mercian force became more visible. The vanguard was entering the minster's fields, while the flaming torches of the rear now flickered down the northern slopes of the hill.

"Close to two hundred, perhaps."

"Why now?" Aelfric replied to Hygelac. "They have not chanced any more than small raids for a year or more. Do they seek to invade?"

"We have sent riders to the king. This is more than a raid."

"When the false slave brought Godric from Hildericstow to help murder my father, it is possible that the Mercians learned of an opportunity to strike. Is it not perverse that we hoped to keep the murders secret but that the plot was already known in Mercia!"

"This is not lost, lord. Elmstow was built for defence. Your father knew the value of this place and he was right. The bowmen are ready. We can make the Mercian arrival uncomfortable, while we still have light. They are struggling in the mud to make their camp and are careless of their defence."

"Then fire upon them."

The sharp iron points fell silently but their effect was far from muted. They pierced deeply into flesh and shattered bone. Twice, the East Angles let loose their bows before the recipients found and positioned their shields.

"Now, further back," Hygelac ordered.

The next volley fell upon those who were still arriving in the minster clearing. Their weapons and camp supplies weighed them down, and they suffered for it, but the next burst was blunted by a shield wall.

"No more. Save your arrows. We start well, lord. There is no better sound for a warrior than to hear the misery of an enemy."

Aelfric nodded and took Hygelac by the shoulder, ushering him away from the earshot of others.

"I am not yet my father – far from it – though he taught me well. You are the best warrior here; I would be a fool not to admit it. I know my father would tell me to take heed of your experience and judgement. If we survive this, I will see you rewarded well. If we lose then our homeland is at risk.

"I have been burdened by the loss of someone dear to my heart. I look to an empty future, but I will heal in time – that is God's promise to me. She cannot be restored but the double affliction of her killer escaping without penalty has been remedied – and it is such a weight lifted from me. I thank you for seeing to her execution and disposal."

"Lord, I serve you gladly. That odious woman had time to regret her crime and learned that there is a just payment for such an atrocity. It was a deed I undertook with joy. I remember the desolate faces of the king and queen, God bless them, when they heard of their daughter's murder and the untold grief when the defilement suffered by the princess was reported. They will feel some relief, I hope, when I tell them the manner of the torture and death of their daughter's killer. It is another reason why we must win this fight.

"I served your great father and grew close to him. He lost his dear wife and your sweet mother too early. Many men who go through their days without the gentle support of the woman they chose as their life-partner become hardened and harsh.

"Duty became everything to your father; it was the anvil on which his nature was shaped. He spoke few words about his family but when we were together campaigning in Mercia, he told me one night, when we were sharing brotherhood around the campfire, that you reminded him of how he was at your age. He said that he grew slowly in judgement about war and people and had made many mistakes. But much more would be expected of you and you would have less time to learn. He wanted you to become the next ealdorman and to defend your king and his kingdom with valour and perception. I have no doubt that you will."

Most words that are said or heard create shallow ripples that fade soon after they are voiced but not these. Some continue to wound and bind us to misery but not these. The new ealdorman smiled.

"I did not know that he said those words. They are a great comfort to me. I will do my utmost to defend my king and country, to bring honour on my family, and if it is God's will, we shall prevail."

Aelfric surveyed the scene unfolding before him. The last of the Mercians were arriving and taking possession of the flat, treeless fields, gardens and water meadows around the minster. They had kept their distance, beyond the worst that arrows could inflict, but while this eased one discomfort, it had created another. Their camp fires flickered but most were stillborn and much of the Mercian force was destined to spend a cheerless night with their feet washed in the shallow pools.

The new ealdorman had a hundred thoughts weaving chaotically through his mind. It was beyond his experience to know whether the minster could be defended. His father had certainly railed against the minster's current use, saying it was the most defensible point in the south-west of the kingdom and could withstand a siege of many months – but it had to be prepared and well-led. And a traitor might still conceal themselves within the walls and their black purpose not yet be complete.

"Lord, we should keep the walls guarded while others sleep. Twenty warriors should be enough, and they should fire shafts once in a while overnight to vex the Mercians and disrupt their rest. They will fire back, so our men should sleep under cover."

"Very well. See it is done and that the gap in our wall has been repaired and protected; then come to my chamber later with our leading men and we will talk further about our defence. I will talk now to Bishop Aethelbert. He has asked to see me."

*

"You know Sister Tetta?" The bishop ushered her into Aelfric's chamber. "I have known Sister Tetta for many years and her eyes have seen much beyond the cloister. I pray that you would listen to what she says."

"Welcome, both. I do not have much time, but I will listen."

The bishop looked to the nun.

"Lord Aelfric, there are some twenty cloistered women and two postulants within these walls. I and three others of my age have witnessed fighting at close range before and have learnt how to make balms, ointments and potions that can help heal wounds and calm fevers. We can also set broken bones if the injury is not beyond care. A few of the younger Sisters and our postulants come from poor families and, like me, are used to hard work and famine. They can cook to make what food we have last longer. Their backs are strong. They can fetch and carry.

"But as you have witnessed, the other Sisters are delicate and used to being served. Many come from rich and powerful families. They will not be of much use now but can pray for our success. Leave it to me, if you will, to allocate their food. They will complain, of course, at the small amount but so long as you will support me and not give in to their demands, it will go well. They will follow my orders or face a beating from me."

"I ask that you do as Sister Tetta bids," the bishop spoke. "What food we have should strengthen those who need to face our enemies in fierce combat. Without their victory, we will not survive. And it is time that we – the Church of the East Angles – fight the devil's forces, whether within or outside of this community, with our bodies, as well as our hearts and voices."

"Gladly. Sister Tetta, do as you must, and I will support you. Bishop Aethelbert will watch over you. I will leave the women, in every aspect of their activity, in faith and in other matters, in the hands of both of you.

"Now, if you would leave me, for I must think about our defences."

*

Eadred, as was his way when his mind was vexed and full of concerns, had sought out Tatwine, and the two friends sat around a small fire in Eadred's cell. Their axes rested against a wall. The priest was in need of some flicker of consolation about the approaching battle but Tatwine's mood was uncommonly and disagreeably dark.

"Surely, we are defending God's house and he will see us through this?"

"I do not think so. You know the filth in this place. The Lord God is rightfully angered at how his people and his Church have wallowed in corruption. The Scriptures tell us – warn us – that he will bring plagues and afflictions down on those who anger him. Our king has already been punished grievously for allowing sin to multiply. We should not be surprised that the punishment continues. The Mercians are God's blade." Tatwine rubbed the tears from his eyes. "We will not survive this fight now our God has turned against us. Many men will die. The women who have desecrated the cloister will face untold misery and the kingdom will crumble."

This was not what Eadred expected to hear but he knew that the hermit was close to the heart of the Lord God. It was an uneasy priest who questioned Tatwine.

"My friend, you have been granted a prophecy that we are to be slaughtered for our failures?"

"We do not need a prophecy for it is clear. First, the demonic murders and now our greatest enemy is at our gates when we are weakened. Battles are won or lost in the world of the spirit before being fought in the world of men. The outcome is clear."

"But what of your prophecy about me? You said that you are not granted such visions other than for great purposes. You told me that I was God's weapon to root out the evil in Elmstow. Either you lied or God gave me hope and purpose, only to destroy it. Our God is not a pagan trickster. I swear I do not feel that this force outside our walls is destined to destroy us. It is part of the evil that we must weather but it is not from God."

Eadred expected a sharp reply from Tatwine but the hermit stared at Eadred and did not speak. Instead, the priest continued, "Do not believe that the Lord God has abandoned us, but we must pray for victory. We must see it in our mind's eye and have faith that the Lord will deliver us from our enemies. We must pray now, and we must establish constant prayers by the community for our victory."

Tatwine followed Eadred and knelt and the priest began to speak an earnest, fearsome prayer for their victory. As the words formed, Eadred shivered and his muscles tightened. His voice rose and fell, and the images filled the room. How the Lord God guided King David in war. The priest's eyes followed the thousands of chariots, horsemen and soldiers, stretching into the distance, advancing and gathering speed against God's enemies, who were scattered and slaughtered and rivers of blood ran through the desert. Eadred saw himself standing on a nearby hill, witnessing the king subduing all who stood against him and giving thanks to God.

"How did you conjure such an image?"

"I conjured nothing. I am as astounded as you. It was the Lord God, leader of the armies of Heaven, who talked to me with a message of hope."

The two men returned to their stools and sat silently absorbing what had just occurred. Eadred shook his head and smiled.

"I came to see you because I fear the battle. I have never needed to use force against those who sought my death but now I remember, Godric was a practiced killer and I did not fail to defend myself. Yet, I still have had no battle practice with weapons. It is a skill I lack. What would I do with this?" Eadred picked up the axe only to feel it topple from his hand.

"It will be well, my friend. Forgive me. I feel weak in faith that I doubted my own vision. I have just witnessed its truth – you have indeed been chosen to be God's weapon in this challenge. He calls us to do our utmost in this fight, for victory is never assured, but he has promised he will be at our arm. I doubt that we will need to wield these weapons but early tomorrow I will teach you what I know about their use. I have had need a few times to fight off thieves and others, who sought to attack my home. You will be ready in body, as well as mind. And I think that of those who sit beyond these walls, not all are battle-hardened. Whilst here in Elmstow, we have the closest battle companions of Ealdorman Ceolfrith and his son and some of the best of the king's guard – and we are well led."

"Then I am more than happy to be in their company."

TWENTY-SIX

The Attack

" I am Osgar, leader of this army from the Kingdom of
Mercia. Whom do I address?"

"I am Aelfric, Ealdorman of the East Angles."

"Ah, we thought you had left but are pleased you
remain. Your father is dead then and we rejoice. Never was
there a more hateful name from your kingdom, other than
Athelstan, your petty king. Listen, Ealdorman Aelfric, while
we besiege you, stopping you from returning to your king,
our noble King Wiglaf marches with a great army on your
capital.

"Your kingdom will be crushed and Athelstan executed
as he deserves. Your women will be taken into slavery or as
concubines, and your great estates will be given to our noble
families.

"You cannot escape and will perish slowly as your food
stores are used but I give you one chance for the men and

women within your walls to survive. Ealdorman of the East Angles, come out from your prison alone, and give yourself up to us. I give my word that if you give up your life then your countrymen will be spared. They will be allowed to leave safely, without their weapons but with the minster's treasury."

"This was not expected." Hygelac spoke to Aelfric. "It is assuredly a trap. The Mercians know that they cannot defeat us while we are protected within these walls. If we leave, it will not be to safety. They will attack us when we are drawn out along the road with our women to protect and with no spear or shield."

"And what if I refuse?" Aelfric shouted.

"Then your men all perish – starved then their throats slit like pigs. The holy Sisters will be at the mercy of my men." Some of the younger nuns had been drawn to the walls by the shouting and cried out on hearing Osgar's words.

"Get them inside!" Hygelac thundered.

Aelfric crouched low behind the wall he was resting against and spoke to Hygelac.

"You knew my father better than I. What would he have done? I surely know of no better warrior than he was."

"Lord, your father knew that aside from the king himself, he was the one who rallied the men and led them. His presence and life were worth much. His duty was to lead, not to throw his life away and leave a dispirited army to disintegrate."

"But how can we stay here with many of the kingdom's best warriors, while the king, whom we love and serve, is in peril? We would face eternal shame."

"What is your answer, Ealdorman of the East Angles?" Osgar bellowed. "I will not stay here waiting for you."

"Reject the Mercians' demand, lord, and let us think more about our actions."

Aelfric stood and faced out towards the Mercian leader.

"I have no trust in your word, Osgar the Mercian. I stay with my people and will see you damned!"

"Let the arrows fly!" Hygelac barked the order and a torrent of killing points flew from the wall towards the Mercian army. This time they were well prepared, and many shields took the shock. It was the turn of the East Angles to be disturbed.

Shouts and the clash of metal came from the other side of the minster complex. It was impossible for Aelfric to see what was happening with the sombre presence of the church obscuring his vision.

"Go!" Hygelac waved some of the king's guard towards the sounds, which now included cattle and sheep bellowing with confusion and fear. A dozen or so warriors ran across the courtyard and into the narrow passageways. "They never meant to besiege but to attack us. They have already climbed the walls." Hygelac swore at his own negligence.

Atop the wall, which spanned that far section of the perimeter where storehouses and animal pens had been built, Aethelric and a handful of warriors battled Mercians who were streaming from several ladders. While some of the attackers engaged with Aethelric and his men, others had already taken their ladders, using them to descend into the minster. There they joined more of their countrymen, who had broken through the small hole in the wall, and together they had set about the animals.

Sharp axe blades smashed into the legs of screaming cows. The animals writhed helplessly with more blows cutting into their ribcages, skulls and backs. Sheep were butchered; the ground littered with bloody lumps of meat. The men Hygelac had sent ran from the passageways and attacked.

Osgar had planned well and soon Elmstow was under attack on three sides. Arrows and heavy flint rocks rained down on warriors advancing into the ditch, wading through the ice-skinned, waist-deep water, and clambering up the other side. Some shouldered the ladders, while others sought to protect them with a roof of shields. They suffered a heavy toll. When a rock unbalanced a shield, in an instant, one or two points sped through the gap, plunging into unprotected faces, necks and shoulders. Even the thick leather helmets were of little protection and many men died with arrow points thrust deep into their heads. The Mercians fired their weapons up into the faces of the defenders and little by little they gained ground. Precarious ladders were thrown against the walls, some pushed back by long poles but others succeeded and attackers surmounted the walls and clambered down into the minster.

"We do not have the men to push them back everywhere." Aelfric stared at the chaos around the walls to his left and right. He moaned aloud.

"But we know the buildings and passageways, lord. I will take my chosen warriors and fight those coming from the west if you go to the east."

The ealdorman did not answer.

"The buildings are defensible, and we can make unexpected attacks from the passages. We can hold the Mercians. Lord, do you hear me? There is no time." Hygelac stared into Aelfric's terror-blinded eyes and shouted once more.

215

"I hear you. Go and I will go to the eastern wall."

Hygelac hesitated.

"Go. My mind is strong now."

Hygelac called for his own hearth companions and what remained of the king's men to follow him. These were battle-hardened and trusted warriors and much depended on them, for the main Mercian attack was concentrated to the west.

They came across a sight approaching Mercian victory. The remainder of the East Angles were pinned against the perimeter wall and surrounded. More attackers were clearing the wall and descending several ladders. Hygelac's force fell upon them, firstly with arrows then with axe and sword. The deluge from their bows found the unprotected backs of many attackers and quickly cleared the ladders of men. While some of the hearth companions climbed the ladders to secure the top of the wall, the others took on those who were now themselves pressed against the stone perimeter. The fighting was fierce but soon all the Mercians had been despatched and the wall secured from further danger.

Aelfric found the eastern wall awash with attackers and his own countrymen retreating towards him. It was impossible to fire arrows into the enemy on the ground, shielded as they were by East Angles. Yet, the arrows found useful work buried in the backs of Mercians descending the ladders.

With a roar, Aelfric's men ran forward to engage the attackers. The shock of new warriors slamming into them halted the Mercian advance. The small space between the wall and the advancing East Angles soon teemed with contending bodies, so that a warrior found it almost impossible to wield his axe. Those with swords and knives thrust them forward to be met by a hard shield if the opposing warrior were skilled and fortunate, or by flesh if he were not.

Inevitably, the initial charge began to lose its impetus under the weight of numbers. Preoccupied with the risk of being encircled, the new ealdorman was caught when a Mercian warrior cut into the edge of his shield.

The protecting wooden guard, covered with tough leather and studded metal, spun from Aelfric's hand. The Mercian warrior lifted his own shield to protect his body, while he raised his arm to bring his axe down. Aelfric jumped backwards, the blade whistling close to his ear. Whether close or far mattered little to the ealdorman – it caused no damage. The Mercian's right shoulder was now exposed until he could bring his arm back from its downward sweep and raise his shield. Aelfric thrust his sword into the man's shoulder. The speed of the injury caught the Mercian by surprise. Aelfric took the opportunity to sweep his sword back low across the man's knee. It sliced into bone. The shield fell and the next blow smashed into the side of the man's head.

"To the door behind me. No-one turn their backs." Slowly, the East Angles withdrew towards the dormitory door; the Mercians pouring ever greater numbers against them. Then the door opened from the inside and, a few at a time, Aelfric's diminishing band entered the building. A cry was heard from behind the Mercians.

Hygelac with around fifteen of his men appeared from a passageway. After firing their arrows into the enemy climbing down from the wall and at those who attacked the ealdorman, they destroyed the ladders and advanced with blade. Though a welcome diversion, it was quickly clear that the numbers were not enough to stem the weight of the attack on Aelfric.

"There is Aelfric, ealdorman and son of Ceolfrith. Capture him! Lord Osgar offers gold to those who take him alive."

The Mercian effort surged but the ealdorman's closest companions stood around him, giving and receiving blows, edging him closer to the open door and then through it.

Bodies and butchered body parts collected around the door. As hard as the East Angles tried, they could not close it. Then the decision was taken from their hands. A huge warrior with tree trunks for arms and thighs appeared and with a few axe blows smashed the door from its hinges. A roar of success greeted his achievement, and the splintered wood was thrown aside.

"On, on! Take Aelfric and the battle is won. Gold to those who capture him!"

The giant saw his chance to win treasure. He barraged his way through the opening, smashing heads and limbs with a smile of easy success. It was a look of surprise that met the arrow that pierced deeply into his forehead. He grasped the shaft and pulled it out. Juices flowed into his face. He held the arrow high, laughing, then collapsed.

The Mercians flooded through the doorway but after the initial open area, they were constrained by the corridor with its cells leading from both sides. Only two warriors could engage with two others. Individual contests played out in the cells with neither side gaining the ascendancy. Then the battle took a turn for the worse for the East Angles.

The fighting at the most isolated wall was going against

the defenders. Aethelric, who commanded them, lay dead, hacked to pieces and stripped of his armour, but others fought on. Some of the attackers had run on through the passageways and came upon the door at the other end of the dormitory building.

It was secluded and seldom used. A flurry of unexpected arrows felled all but two of the defenders, who tried but failed to secure the door and were pushed back into the building.

"Help! The Mercians overpower us." The pair of defenders fought hard but succumbed to sword thrusts. They had held up the Mercian advance long enough for some of the ealdorman's men to run along the corridor and to engage the attackers. Aelfric found himself cut off with the doors at either end of the building under attack.

Perversely, six of the younger nuns appeared from the church and ran across the courtyard. Immediately they were in the open, they began screaming, drawing attention to themselves. Hands grabbed for this unexpected boon. The Sisters kicked and thrashed against their captors but punches to their faces and stomachs brought a swift end to their defence. They were roped, hand and foot, and dragged to a wall, where they lay on the ground terrified and crying, while the conflict raged around and above them.

While the ealdorman's position, barricaded within the dormitory building, obscured any understanding of what was occurring within the wider minster, Hygelac was not so limited.

"You are not trained warriors, but you are young and keen to defend our Christian kingdom." Hygelac addressed half a dozen men – Eadred, Tatwine, Raedwulf and three priests. Each now had a leather helmet, shield and axe. "It is time for you to join my warriors. Three must join the band to fight at the far-most wall and three will stay and fight here."

"I have some experience with weapons and fighting. I will take Father Eadred and one other to the back wall."

"Take the moneyer's son and join those warriors running towards the passageway. Go!" Hygelac replied to Tatwine.

Hygelac had a few moments to determine where he and his best warriors should next engage. There was no sign of the Mercian leader. While Hygelac knew that the East Angles had suffered, he could also see that the Mercian force was much depleted. There were many men slighter of build, not familiar with defence and attack, and who had been fairly easy to cut down. This was a force that had been put together quickly. The best Mercian warriors would be on their way further north to attack the king. There was hope yet for Elmstow but Hygelac knew his place was with King Athelstan. It lay heavily on his heart.

*

"Stay close to me and remember what I taught you," Tatwine yelled while running down a passageway. "The Lord God has much for you to do in your days. Today is not the day of your death."

Eadred's heart was pounding hard and not only from running. He was rushing towards a fight and preparing to defend his life. He glanced at Raedwulf, who looked similarly alarmed. They turned a corner; Raedwulf cried out and vomited.

Eadred's boots sank into blood-soaked mud. Raedwulf slipped. The ground before the wall was worse than a slaughterhouse floor. Limbs, heads, burst torsos – from beasts and men – lay in confused profusion. A few men lay wounded beyond recovery, some howling with pain, others moaning quietly while their last moments of life drained from them.

To one side of the carnage sat a group of Mercians, seeing to their wounds or recovering their breath and strength. Others were stripping the dead East Angles of anything valuable – weapons, armour, armbands, rings, belts, boots. On the other side, three Mercians were executing prisoners, spreading them face down in the mud and hacking at their necks until decapitated. Several had been so despatched.

The fresh East Angles burst upon them. Desperate men, tired or wounded, struggled to grab their weapons and stand to defend themselves. Tatwine launched himself at a man who held his shield before him, while he pushed himself from the ground. The shield splintered and another of the East Angle warriors caught the man full in the face with a blow from his axe blade.

Urged on by his countrymen to slaughter the Mercians before they re-armed, Eadred swung his axe at a shield raised before him. The blade lodged fast in the wood and leather. Instant panic consumed the young priest. He pulled at his axe, while the Mercian stretched for his weapon and tried to stand on a wounded leg. Perversely, Eadred's action was a helping hand to his enemy, drawing him upright.

"Remember what I told you!" Tatwine screamed out.

Eadred raised his right leg and kicked it hard against his opponent's shield. His axe dislodged and the man tripped backwards against the wall. Eadred swung his axe again, this time at the side of the shield and it buckled. The priest gripped his own shield and axe hard, readying himself for the Mercian's response. A spear point flew into the man's eye. Eadred turned to see Tatwine pushing the point hard into the skull.

"This is not the cloister!" The monk stared at Eadred with such venom, he wondered that it was the man he had prayed with the evening before. "You have one chance to learn. Do not wait for your enemy to prepare. Attack first!"

Eadred trembled. Tatwine's mouth moved but the words were unheard. The monk reinforced them by hitting Eadred hard on the shoulder. Then he struck again, repeating his rebuke and swearing at the priest.

"When you fight killers for your life, you cannot be as yourself. You must become a killer."

There was a cry for help, shrill as a captured chicken before its neck is wrung. Raedwulf was recoiling before the blows of a Mercian warrior. One slashing stroke jarred the shield from his hand. Eadred ran at the attacker. The Mercian turned to face the priest and the axe blow that smashed into his shield, splintering the wood. With most of his countrymen now dead, the Mercian turned and ran. The spear point tore into his calf and he fell. Tatwine shouted out his victory.

No Mercian escaped and two had been captured. Eadred looked away. The captives were made to kneel and held up by their outstretched arms. An East Angle turned his axe-head and hit the first with a furious blow to the back of his skull. It shattered. The other man struggled, and the first blow pounded into his upper back. The second hit him in the skull, taking most of the head from the body.

"To the battle. There is more to be done."

"Do not think less of me, Eadred." It was a fervent wish from Tatwine. "When in battle, you must be merciless to survive. You do not face gentleness but brutality. We are fighting for our lives now and if we fail there is no minster and no kingdom."

Eadred grunted and looked around.

"Where is Raedwulf? He was not killed or wounded."

"He must have run. Forget him for now."

*

For over two hours, the battle had raged. Hygelac climbed upon the eastern wall and sent men to check other sections of the perimeter. There were no more Mercians surrounding the minster – all were engaged in battle – and that battle was being fought in and around the dormitory building. Hygelac had no idea of the condition of Aelfric and his men, caught within the stone building.

At one of its two doors, the Mercians had become frustrated by the limited access to the interior. While several clashes were underway not far within its walls, many of the attackers were constrained in the courtyard outside, repairing their weapons and seeing to their wounds. At the other door, the Mercians also struggled to make headway and were troubled by the East Angles attacking them from behind. Exhaustion and stalemate were taking hold.

Then, as Hygelac had ordered earlier, his men from the furthest wall arrived. He thundered above the cries of battle, "Companions, let us continue to fight bravely. We have started well with the slaughter. Our lord expects us to attack once more. Let no man be kind-hearted with these invaders. They do not have the fire or guts we expect of Mercian warriors. They have been pulled from their farms. You have their measure. Bring glory to your names and families. On!"

With a sign from Hygelac, they launched themselves with a roar into the Mercians. Eadred stood beside Tatwine. The monk seemed like a demon, slashing his blade like a monstrous clawed bear. Over and over, it cut and tore into soft flesh. If Eadred had not known the hermit to be a human, he would have thought him a beast from the underworld. He was as ferocious as the great warriors who attacked around him and seemingly as unconcerned with his own survival. He flew at one Mercian after another. Did he know where they would try to strike or to hold their shield? Did he know where his axe was needed next to smash a limb, to meet a blow or to break a skull? Surely, he did.

"Strike!" The hermit's voice was like a bolt of lightning. Eadred brought his axe down on the shield in front of him. It shattered. Before his opponent could respond, Eadred had pounced forward, knocking the man backwards, and had sunk his knife into the throat. The priest picked up his axe, leaving the knife to hang from the thong around his neck. He climbed over the dying man and aimed his axe at the next Mercian to face him.

The trembling to his body and in his mind had long passed. His limbs now throbbed with power; his eyes saw like those of eagles and he hunted as a wolf.

From where Hygelac stood, he could see the impact of the new arrivals. The existing East Angles had been fortified and together they hemmed the Mercians before them. In several places, warriors were making inroads into the invaders. Like a shoal of fish, the trapped Mercians attempted to avoid those who would attack them but for many, escape was impossible. A faint smile appeared on Hygelac's face. Another voice barked orders.

Somewhere, in the middle of the Mercian horde, was Osgar. Here was a chance to end the matter once and for all. But no sooner had the thought been born than it was answered by the Mercian leader. With shouts of defiance from the heart of the Mercian force, it struck out in two directions. Stirred by a fear of total annihilation, its ferocity was boundless.

Eadred, the priest of the Lord God, now bloodied and bruised, moving from one opponent to another, looked to his next attack. The East Angle ahead of him was felled by an axe blow and the body thrown backwards by a boot in the chest. The Mercian leapt forward at Eadred. The priest toppled. The axe shattered his shield and cut into his arm. Eadred gasped in pain, lying pegged by the fallen body. The warrior raised his axe to strike the helpless priest. Eadred closed his eyes and gritted his teeth.

"Lord God, take my soul."

"He does not want it yet." Tatwine swung his axe at the Mercian, who blocked the blow. The monk readied his axe for another attack. The tide of men caught both the Mercian and the monk unprepared and both toppled.

"Stop them! Keep them penned in!" The struggle to hold the Mercians from breaking through the East Anglian line was proving too much and Hygelac's order went unmet. The barrier broke.

Murderous chaos overtook the courtyard.

"To the wall. To the ladders." Osgar and his chief men

shouted their intention. Hygelac, and now Aelfric, who had broken through the Mercian blockade, bellowed to the East Angles to stop their enemy from escaping.

Around the remaining ladders a deadly exchange ensued. Men began climbing to escape the carnage, while their opponents attempted to tear the ladders down. Mercians, whose wounds hindered their escape, were hacked down, sometimes by their own countrymen, desperate to mount the rungs to safety.

"They are taking the Sisters. Stop them!"

Eadred sat against the church wall, away from the fighting, wrapping a length of cloth around his bleeding forearm and a similarly cut thigh.

"No! In the Lord's name, no." Eadred could see two nuns, who must have been knocked senseless, being carried over the shoulders of warriors climbing the ladders. Three others were being dragged, screaming, to the wall. If the Mercians managed to escape with them, they faced a certain and appalling fate. "Save the holy Sisters. They must not be carried off."

A captive nun bit hard into one of the arms pulling her along. The man – surprised then furious – rested his axe shaft momentarily against his leg while he punched her full in the face. He turned to continue to drag her towards a ladder. He suffered a second shock – the determined face of Sister Tetta – so close that he felt her breath. The kitchen knife, whose sharpness was her pride, slashed across his cheek and up into his eye. He dropped the nun and his axe, held his head, staggering before falling to his knees. His screams were short-lived. The blade slid into the side of his neck and sliced open the throat.

"Come on, my dear, stop all that noise. All will be well. It is just a nasty bruise." The formidable nun helped the Sister away from the fighting.

The Mercians were determined to take the other holy women, fighting off several attempts to free them then carrying them to the wall. Men continued to fight around the base of the ladders. They turned to watch their sole means of escape being hauled up behind them. Seeing they had been abandoned, they threw down their weapons and screamed for mercy.

Tatwine, who had fought to exhaustion to keep the Sisters from capture, knew from the smaller frames and inferior weapons of the remaining attackers that they were farmers, not warriors, and had been sacrificed.

"Show us mercy! In the name of the Lord God, who reigns over us all. This is not our fight. We were dragged from our homes."

Their pleas and tears were pointless. In a flurry of axe blows, the screams died. One man knelt, pleading, before Tatwine, seeing the tonsured head of a monk. The hermit swung his axe into the body.

"We must follow the Mercians and free our Sisters," Tatwine appealed to Aelfric and Hygelac. "While they are close to the minster. It is disgrace to lose them."

"What do you see, monk?" Hygelac looked around him. The fading sun sent its golden fingers across a scene of unmatched butchery. Barely any of the minster courtyard had escaped its share of blood and gore, the dead and dying, hacked meat that had a few hours or minutes earlier breathed. Even the walls were spattered and stained in red like a slaughterhouse. "How many brave East Angles live? I fear but half of those who woke this morning. We have no strength to do more."

The monk issued a howl of misery.

"They are holy women."

Aelfric rested his hand on Tatwine's shoulder.

"We must look to our wounded now. The king is attacked, and our duty is to go to him. If the women come from wealthy families, they will be ransomed."

"Or persuade the bishop to part with some of his treasure for their return." Hygelac spat the words.

Tatwine groaned. It was the sad truth.

"But I know some of them."

"They still have life and hope. Many here have lost that." Then the ealdorman addressed those who could hear.

"You have all brought glory to your names. We have won the day. Now rest and food will be brought to you. There are holy women who are skilled in mending injuries. Be patient and they will attend you."

Several of Aelfric's hearth group raised their weapons and shouted his name. Others – some resting on the ground or against a wall – found the strength to stand and joined in the salute. Soon, all the survivors who could speak were calling the ealdorman's name. He raised his hand in response. Aelfric turned to Hygelac and embraced him, weeping.

"I prayed for victory and the Lord God has been gracious to us." The ealdorman wiped his eyes. "You are a mighty warrior, Hygelac of Dommoc. I will see your name raised amongst our people. Find the men to secure the walls, in case of further attack. See, if you will, what can be done for our wounded. Finish off the Mercian wounded. Do it mercifully.

Tomorrow, when we know more of our condition, most of those who can, will ride with us to the king. God willing, the Mercians are being held at bay. Choose your best warrior to command Elmstow while we are gone."

"Lord, you have won a great victory. You are your father's son in many good ways. The Mercians may return, although I doubt it. I will keep my eye on the horizon and send some arrow points to speed them off. The fault is mine that the Mercians escaped. I should have made a greater effort to destroy the ladders that gave them freedom."

"All our force was engaged in battle. There was no opportunity to do more. Look around us; few of them escaped. I see no fault."

Tatwine climbed a ladder and started to push the dead from the wall. He watched the Mercian survivors – few as they were – hurry, as best they could, along the path they had taken the day before. He was glad that Eadred was not there with him. The captured nuns were already being stripped, beaten and mistreated in foul ways as they ran. They cried back to Elmstow for protection, but none would come. He was helpless to do anything.

Sister Tetta and several of the older holy Sisters were soon helping the wounded where they could – giving water, wiping wounds, applying her ointments and balms, and wrapping cloth tightly around gaping flesh. The holy Sisters had spent the battle in the church with the bishop, in broken, fearful prayer, while the grim sounds of killing continued beyond its walls. They had expected the worst but somehow no-one entered. Tetta organised the younger nuns, who wailed as ghosts at the sights they saw on leaving the church, to bring out food and, in pairs, bear the weight of wounded men as they limped into the hall, where they would spend the night out of the freezing cold air.

Eadred watched Tetta quietly and methodically go about her work with skill and compassion. When she came upon a wounded Mercian, she prayed for him then gave a sign to one of the East Anglian warriors to do his work. The other nuns, young and old, asked her for direction in what they were doing. The priest's heart lifted for, despite the day's anguish, he saw the order and love she brought, despite the horror her eyes and hands witnessed.

"Sister, you are as an angel to us."

"Father Eadred, I do what I can. I am praying that many of our wounded will survive. And your cuts, how are they?"

"Mercifully, not deep. I will assuredly survive, thanks to the Lord God. But some of the holy Sisters were captured. I will never forgive myself that we could not keep them safe."

Tetta shook her head.

"They put themselves in danger. I cannot understand them. We were all scared but together in the church, when suddenly some of them, who knelt together, rose and ran from the door without purpose. I ran after them and managed to save one, but I fear for the others.

"I will send a nun to you soon to see to your wounds."

Before long, a Sister came and asked about Eadred's wounds. He showed the cuts he had sustained, and she saw to them diligently, then moved on.

"Father Eadred, here, have this." Edith handed him a bowl of thick, hot soup. "Bless you for fighting bravely for us. I think we are saved." She looked at the desolation around her. "There are many East Anglian dead but, I think, far more Mercians."

"Thank you, Edith." Eadred took the warming bowl and sipped. "The Lord God has been merciful to me. If not for his protection, I would be broken like these poor souls."

"I prayed that you, by name, would survive this battle. You have been the only man who cared for my sister and me." Then Edith burst into tears.

"Pray, do not be distressed. We are alive and safe."

Edith was inconsolable and stared at the ground.

"Father, I cannot find Leoba!"

"Edith, no."

"I do not know if she is alive or dead. I have searched – but nothing." Edith buried her head in her hands. "I am alone without her. I pray she is not dead."

"I will pray the same. Oh, Edith, some of the holy Sisters were taken by the Mercians; your sister could be amongst them. I wish it were different. I have heard that we are too weak to leave Elmstow to rescue them, but the bishop might offer gold for their return."

"What do I care for the others? I am glad they were taken. They cared nothing for us. We were slaves to them; now they face what we faced."

"Edith, you have suffered and are suffering much, I know, but God would not want you to wish evil on these Sisters."

Edith hardened her face.

"You have suffered humiliation at the hands of men. I thought you would understand. I remember many a day, here in God's house, when my hands were tied hard with rope and drunken men stripped me bare when I was defenceless, and I bled from their treatment. And women who had taken Holy Orders laughed.

231

"It is God's will they suffer now. You came to cleanse Elmstow – and are well rid of them. God willing, Leoba is alive. Now, I must serve others." Edith rose, saying she would bring more food to Eadred in the morning and left, smiling briefly through moistened eyes.

A little later, Eadred's legs, after straining against pain and exhaustion, brought him back to his cell. The door of the dormitory building lay smashed. The priest threaded through the wreckage of war, the motionless flesh; but his cell had remained locked and undamaged. He asked a Sister if she knew anything about Brother Tatwine and she replied that he was safe with only cuts and bruises. Then he asked for a jug of water to clean his body, another bowl of soup and some wine, which were brought.

Exhaustion and the wine gave him sleep, despite the pains that tormented his body and the cries of the wounded, but it was not long before he awoke. He throbbed and ached but worse, his mind was tortured by the sights of the day; how men sought to kill him and that he had to kill them to live, how good Christian souls, like Tatwine and Edith, could hate so much.

TWENTY-SEVEN

Sombre Days

"I thought I should come and see how you are. Your wounds? And here, take this – good soup. You have slept through the morning."

The creaking door had woken him. Eadred let Tatwine limp into his cell. He fell backwards onto a stool with a groan, rested his back against the wall and commented on some colourful bruises and a few cuts. His smile was awkward.

"This soup is good, but I could eat like a wolf. My wounds are not too bad, and, thanks be to God, you are safe."

The hermit monk nodded and the words he had been stewing for many hours were delivered in measured speech.

"I am sorry about some of what I said yesterday. My dear friend, I did not want you to die or face the rest of your life deformed by injury. You have a great God-given purpose, and you must live if you are to meet God's plan for your life. The Lord God accorded to me the prophecy about your gifts and that made me your protector. I wanted you to become angry and fierce, so you would survive. When we no longer face blade and point that aim to send us from this life, then we can again become men of God and show mercy. We did not choose to fight but had to defend. I am unsure whether I made the right decision but that is what I did and why I did it."

Eadred struggled to smile and it never appeared.

"Good monk, I know. Through the night, I have thought over many things. I am unsettled by the last few days. I had never taken another's life. I know you did what was needed so I might survive – and I thank you." Eadred began to sob. "But I am troubled by what I saw and what I did."

Tatwine reached out and the two clasped hands.

"I doubt that I will ever be the same."

"It is understandable – violence is one of the devil's best weapons. It unleashes evil. When I was younger, I found that there was a darkness in me that could be murderous. My sin is indeed great. I have fought it ever since and prayed to our Lord to help me. He answered my prayers. He showed me that I needed to live alone, outside of the company of men, until I could master my own sinful nature, but it is still there, as you saw yesterday.

"We fight and kill those who are intent on killing us, as we did. It is natural but it caused such evil to rise in me. It burned like a furnace, without boundary. Soon after the fighting finished, I went to my cell and prayed that light might return and see off the darkness that had flared like a fever. And I prayed for the poor soul that I might have saved but for my fury. We are all sinful, Eadred, and need God's grace and mercy. Without it we are doomed."

Eadred sat up and rubbed his eyes.

"I dare not leave this cell for what I might see."

"The slaves have been collecting the bodies. I spoke to some of the warriors. They say the earth is frozen and almost impossible to dig. Fires will be lit as soon as wood is gathered. The flames will consume the Mercians and other fires will heat the soil, so pits can be dug and our countrymen can be buried properly. The bishop has allowed our beloved dead to lie in the church for now, where their bodies are being prepared.

"Bishop Aethelbert stayed with our wounded throughout the night and is with them still. More have died and he prayed for each of them."

Eadred looked puzzled.

"All the Elmstow priests were killed in the battle, so he alone prays for the dying."

"I should be there."

"No," Tatwine replied. "The bishop wants you to rest. He is very proud of you. We lost many brave men, but I have heard that the Mercians lost twice as many. God gave us a great victory."

"The victory will be great only if it brings peace."

"God willing," Tatwine replied. "There is some good news. Riders came from the king not long ago. There has been no other attack. This was the only one. The remnants of our force can now rest and restore their bodies and there will be fresh warriors here tomorrow to ensure that the minster is safe."

Eadred creased his brow.

"Is it not strange that only Elmstow was attacked and that the Mercian leader wanted Lord Aelfric alone if he could?"

"The Mercians were raiders. It was a raid that Osgar thought would be successful because he had discovered the plot to kill Ealdorman Ceolfrith and believed Lord Aelfric inexperienced. He gathered all manner of folk; many were not warriors, but all were bought by the promise of easy gold. He thought the minster's jewel-chest lay open and that he could win it by guile, but he was wrong."

"Perhaps. And what of the Sisters who were taken? When the king's men arrive, they will surely follow the Mercians and free them?"

"When I spoke to our warriors earlier, some thought the holy Sisters were taken to shame us. Others thought that they would be held hostage in case we captured some of the Mercian leaders but Osgar escaped.

"They doubted that we would try to free the Sisters, at least not now. Even when the king's men arrive, we will not be strong enough to raid into Mercia. The king will avenge the attack but it will not be soon."

"But poor Edith; her sister was taken."

"I know," Tatwine replied. "I doubt many will concern themselves with Leoba. The others have rich families and will petition the king to raise a force to free the captives. They will promise gold for his war-chest – but it will not happen soon.

"At least those guilty of the murders have now all been caught, and justice meted out, either by Lord Aelfric or God."

"How so?"

"I saw Regenhere the moneyer in the church, kneeling by his son's body. He was beyond consolation. I have no liking for the man, but I have rarely seen such sadness. He cried out that his life was over.

"I see the Lord's hand at work. When I last saw Raedwulf, he was alive and did not return with us to the battle. At least he will not have to face the rope."

Eadred rubbed his nose, while searching for the right words.

"I am not sure it is over."

These were the last words the monk wished to hear.

"Oh, come now! Mildred confessed to Cuthburg's murder and Raedwulf is dead. Ealdorman Ceolfrith's killers are all dead. You will have us all murderers."

Eadred murmured his uncertainty.

"Why did Osgar offer safe passage to us all and with the minster's wealth, on condition that Lord Aelfric sacrifice himself? It makes no sense if he were only after the minster's riches."

"Because it was a lie. He would have attacked us and taken our lives, gold and jewels."

"I am still uneasy. Anyway, I cannot sit here all day. Come with me, Brother Tatwine, and let us see where we might bring the comfort of God."

The two friends managed to stand and stumbled from Eadred's cell. The dead had been removed from the dormitory and from around the door to the building. Slaves were still transporting bodies from the courtyard. Those recognisable as Mercian were stripped and their belongings separated into two piles – useful weapons, armour, jewellery, clothing and boots, and useless, torn clothing and broken weaponry. Two warriors kept a watchful eye over the process. The unneeded pile, together with the separated limbs and heads, formed a hellish assemblage to be loaded onto a couple of carts.

The priest and hermit watched one of the loads head towards the minster gate. Once outside, it would journey along a track until far enough from the minster so the smoke would not foul the air of Elmstow. There it would be added to several pyres, ready for burning.

Eadred breathed long and deeply before Tatwine and he entered the minster church.

The priest held his head in his hand. He gave the sign of the cross and wept. The entire floor from west door to chancel, other than a small area surrounding the altar and several narrow walkways, was burdened with the dead. Each body had been wrapped in a cloth of some description, which thankfully masked the worst of the horror, but the fluids that had escaped from vicious cuts formed dreadful patterns on this sorrowful clothing. The bishop knelt to one side of the altar.

"My dear boy," the bishop stretched out his arms. Eadred found a path to the altar and helped the old man onto his feet and the two men embraced. "Our God weeps today, as do all who crave peace and love. But to see you, it is the only joy I have had." Aethelbert held onto Eadred's hands and broke into sobbing.

"Come, Holy Father, the Lord God will bless those who died to preserve his house."

The bishop tapped the back of Eadred's hand.

"He will." Aethelbert struggled to say more but his lips quivered. He rubbed his eyes and nose on his sleeve.

"And I see hope for the future. Look." Eadred turned

to see one of the older Sisters and Edith wrapping a corpse. "This is Sister Tetta's work. She brings the light and love of Jesus to this minster. There is a chance now for a new beginning, not just the death of what went before."

"Bought by blood."

"Indeed," Eadred replied to Tatwine. "But was it not our own dear Saviour who showed that goodness, hope and eternal life spring from sacrifice if the cause is acceptable to God. He is blessing this sacrifice. The riches of this minster will no longer be gold and jewels but hearts that beat to bring Christ's love to his people."

"I think you are right, Eadred." The hermit smiled.

*

Two days later, the wind blew away from the minster and the pyres were lit. Bishop Aethelbert said a prayer for the Mercian dead and the flames began their work. For a while, they struggled and seemed too timid to attack the enormous stands of wood. Slowly, the fingers of fire gained their courage and crept upwards and grasped the army of the dead. Gases heated, the houses of flesh and bone burst and fat dripped into the molten hearts of the pyres. Soon, five great torches blazed and continued so for many hours, with extra wood thrown in by fast-moving slaves, eager to avoid the heat, the stench and the burning, fat-soaked earth. The following morning, the ashes were raked and the burnt bone buried in a pit. So, were over one hundred and fifty Mercians taken from the world of men.

Every East Angle, man and woman of all stations, attended the funeral of their dead countrymen. Fires had burned for many hours to thaw the stone-frozen soil and three trenches were dug and the bodies laid out. In a single day, the population of the cemetery exploded and here they would wait until Christ called them to judgement.

Bishop Aethelbert conducted the service, Father Eadred read from the Holy Bible and some of the Sisters sang psalms. No eye remained free of tears.

TWENTY-EIGHT

Discovery

"Is it time?"

"Good friend, I have spent more days than I expected at Elmstow and such days that I wish had never happened. But there has been a blessing – or two." Tatwine smiled. "I have made a good friend. My only friend with whom I can share my deepest thoughts. And not just an ordinary man for you have gifts that are rare.

"I cannot hide this from you, dear Eadred, but you will suffer sometimes because of your gifts. The evil one hates what you can do, and he will use all his power to attack you when you are closest to victory. But do not lose hope and do not turn back. Remember, if you have faith, he cannot harm you. You will have times when it seems that your gifts have failed and you are accomplishing nothing. These are the very times when the sword you wield for the Lord is about to cause great harm to the devil.

"Your weapon is not shaped from sharp metal. The strength to give it life is not from your arm. The skill that enables it to overcome an enemy is not that of a warrior. But no less than a warrior, you are at war. You will inflict wounds and you will receive them. You will take the lives of evil men and if you falter, your own life will be at risk. So, fight hard, bravely and skilfully, and call on the Lord God to cloak you with his protection for he has promised never to abandon you to your enemies.

"And remember always that your skill is a gift from God. Do not become proud from the praise of the world. Pride was the first sin. All the evil that has happened here has come from men's sinfulness – pride, jealousy, lust, anger, indolence, deception." The hermit's impassioned speech brought colour to Eadred's face.

"There is a second blessing and one I never thought would happen. Elmstow is to remain a minster under Sister Tetta. If she had been made abbess at its establishment, instead of Sister Hereburg, all of this evil may not have happened. She would have taken that famous kitchen knife of hers to anyone who would do wrong to the minster or its inmates."

Both men laughed.

"This is the first time I have laughed since I arrived here. I have a vision of her in my mind's eye; it scares me. Her ferocity and piety are wondrous in equal measure. Elmstow will soon be as it should but there are still things that I cannot make sense of."

Tatwine squeezed Eadred's shoulder.

"Enough! Those who committed the murders are dead and will face God's justice. Leave it now, Eadred. It is in God's hands."

"Come then, let me walk with you to the gate."

"Gladly, and when you return to your own church, remember that I am never that far away. You must visit me. I have missed my simple abode. While Elmstow is grand and will become a crown for our faith, my dark and simple cave helps remove agitation, so the eye of my soul can rest in Christ's presence."

The mid-morning light burst into a jewelled blanket covering the land as far as the eye could see; so radiant that Eadred shielded his eyes on issuing from the dark building. The glory of God's creation would normally give the priest a lightness of heart but not today. He stood outside the gate with his hand raised and Tatwine did so in return, although the gesture was increasingly hard to see.

Already, the hermit was closer to his simple home atop the hill than to the minster. Eadred realised that he had stood on the same spot, occasionally waving, until his feet had numbed. Still, he could not leave; not while Tatwine continued to turn and throw his arm into the air. Some cattle crossed onto the track and Eadred lost sight of his friend. When the beasts moved away, Tatwine was nowhere to be seen.

The bell chimed. Eadred was grateful for the call to the midday service. It was a sign that the normal cycle of praise and prayer was returning. The priest had missed the sacred routine, but he also knew that something in him would soon feel diminished until again he could use his skill to assail evil. He took his place alongside the depleted gathering of the faithful, receiving welcoming smiles from Abbess Tetta and Bishop Aethelbert. It was also a joy to see Edith accepted at the service. She stood, serious-faced, singing loudly.

"Thank you for your help in restoring Christ to the centre of this minster."

"It was my duty but thank you, Abbess Tetta," Eadred responded at the end of the service.

The new abbess was already making some wonderful changes. The Sisters had each to renew their vows and make a formal and public submission to her authority; the day was ordered around communal and private prayer; all Sisters had to perform useful manual labour and to allocate time to reading holy works. All but six of the slaves were freed and their work was allocated among the cloistered women. Those Sisters who found they could not live thus were told they could leave.

"I am a strong believer in the Rule of Saint Benedict, Father. That is how I was brought up as a nun. With the bishop's help, a prayerful, disciplined life will be restored here. The king, the queen and the new ealdorman have all learned powerful lessons of the costs of sin and have pledged they will support me in strengthening Elmstow."

The church had emptied, and Eadred was about to follow the abbess out into the courtyard, when he heard some clothing rustle. It brought a smile to see Edith still kneeling in prayer.

"Forgive me, I should not interrupt your conversation with our Lord, but it is a joy to see you are now allowed to join the community in prayer. And no more will you suffer from the sinful ravages of men. The abbess told me of her dismay when she heard how you had been mistreated. Sister Moira was one of the nuns carried off by the Mercians. She will have opportunity to regret the way she treated you."

Edith nodded and gave Eadred a brief smile.

"You do not interrupt, Father. I am happy to see you, and also to thank you that my future here, in a God-fearing community, should be assured. My journey has not been easy." She began to sob.

"Edith, I know these are tears of joy. Your life can now be given to Christ."

"Father, I still carry a burden that stands between my soul and my Redeemer."

"Well, then confess. He is a merciful God."

"I cannot. There can be no forgiveness, no mercy, for what I have done." Edith rose from her knees and ran from the church.

"Come back. Talk to me. Please." The postulant had gone. The young priest returned to his cell, confused and concerned. Edith had had more than her share of misery in life and now, with so much that had been lifted from her, she was still burdened.

*

He sat alone in his cell. Eadred had prayed and thought for hours about Edith's words but nothing became clear. The jug on the bench beside him was almost empty, his eyes reflecting the addled state of his mind. There was another jug beside him, full of water, and this he poured over his head. He groaned, his head throbbed, the bell for the midnight service pounded in his ears.

"I cannot miss this. Father, forgive me." He stumbled into the corridor and edged his way to the church.

"Sister Hilda." Eadred managed to remember the nun's name. "Your energy is impressive indeed. No-one could fail to rise after your call." Hilda held the bell that called the holy Sisters to communal prayer. She chuckled but then her expression grew serious.

"I will not make the same mistake again."

"I am sure you have made none."

"You are generous, Father, but I failed you once and ask for your forgiveness."

Eadred was anxious not to be the last arrival at the service but duty required a quick response.

"Come, Sister, how have you failed me?"

"I had indulged myself at the feast for Ealdorman Ceolfrith and was late ringing the bell for the three o'clock service. So, I undertook to the Lord God never to fail in my duty again and to ring loudly and on time. Will I be forgiven, Father?"

"You rang the bell?" Eadred clasped his pounding head. The nun nodded.

"You were late in ringing?"

"Yes, Father, by a good while."

"Who asked you to perform that task?"

"The postulant, Leoba. She told me she had undertaken to you to ring the bell, but she was not able to, for she had another office to perform. She asked me to do it in her stead."

"Why did you not tell me this when I questioned you after the murders?"

"Leoba asked that I keep the secret, for she had promised to ring the bell and you would be upset with her if she did not keep her word. I am sorry, Father, that I did not tell you. Will you forgive me?"

The question went unanswered. Eadred clasped his head

in his hands and gazed to the heavens, moaning. He ran to the midnight service, for he needed to talk to Edith. If he were right, then two murderers remained free.

Hilda collapsed to the ground, weeping. Eadred's anger told that she had made a grave mistake, although she had no understanding of it.

TWENTY-NINE

Hot Iron

Ealdorman Aelfric and Bishop Aethelbert presided at the trial. Many strange things had happened at Elmstow over the past fortnight or so and this was another. Never had anyone voluntarily offered themselves to face trial for something so serious.

"Edith the postulant, you are accused by Father Eadred of joining others in the murder of Ealdorman Ceolfrith, Abbess Hereburg and Sister Verca. How do you swear?"

"By the Lord God, I confess openly that I was involved in a dark plot, but I did not carry out my part of the crime. I was called by Christ to turn from this wickedness, to repent, and to face justice. I wish to unburden my soul and to tell all I know about these immoral acts. I am prepared to face whatever lies before me."

"Do not attempt to lay the blame for your actions on others who are no longer able to speak for themselves. If you had a part in these murders, you shall pay the penalty."

"I have no desire to escape the price of my crime, Lord Aelfric, but only to confess what I know and to seek the forgiveness of my Father in Heaven."

"Then do you have any oath-helpers to support the truth of your confession?"

"None, my lord."

The bishop turned to Eadred but before he could ask a question, Aelfric intervened.

"Why should we listen more to this woman? She has openly confessed her involvement in the murderous plot and the court should pass sentence."

"Lord Aelfric, Holy Father, shocking crimes have been committed here in Elmstow. We do not yet know the reason or whether all the culprits have been caught. Surely, it is important that we know why your father was murdered and why Abbess Hereburg and Sister Verca were killed to keep the knowledge from us?

"Edith the postulant came to me to confess her part for it was laying heavily on her heart – and she wishes to declare what she knows and what she has done. She could have walked free but chose not to. It is not our usual practice, but terrible things have happened. Our kingdom has never faced such crime and evil and our traditional ways to uncover the culprits and their purposes struggle. If we can know more, should we not try? Let us listen to what she has to say and then the court can pass sentence."

The bishop spoke quietly to the ealdorman. Eadred could see a tiredness in both men's expressions. Like many, they wanted the past dead and buried and to look to the future. The priest had already spoken to the bishop, pleading for Edith to be given the chance to confess publicly – and not just for her own redemption. Eadred still harboured a concern that all had not been unearthed and here was the chance to question perhaps the final voice that could impart some knowledge about the series of killings. The bishop was fortunately sufficiently persuasive.

"Very well. Edith the postulant, you may speak."

"Over two years past, just across the border from Elmstow, there was a fearful battle between East Angle and Mercian armies. The kings of both countries led their nobles and men in a vicious fight. The Lord God gave victory to the East Angles that day.

"The young son of King Wiglaf of the Mercians was captured. He was but ten years old and innocent of crime. Yet even though the battle had ended and against the accepted practice of ransoming those of quality who had been captured, the aetheling was brutally executed. This killing has been recognised in both countries as an evil act. King Athelstan founded Elmstow as atonement.

"King Wiglaf planned to avenge his son."

"Wait!" Aelfric shouted. "How do you presume to know the mind of the King of Mercia?"

"Because I am a noblewoman of Mercia and my father is a leading thegn."

The court erupted in disbelief; in confusion; in anger.

"You are a viper! How could you murder Abbess Hereburg? She bought your freedom and brought you here to save your soul." Abbess Tetta jumped to her feet and joined the furious noise of condemnation.

"I had no part in Abbess Hereburg's murder or anyone's. Let me continue, please!"

It was only when Aelfric rose and slammed his sword on the bench that finally peace was restored.

"My sister is Leoba and my brother, Edwin. He shammed at being a slave in the fields. You uncovered him and he took his own life with poison.

"When it was heard that Hereburg was named abbess, we three were sent to try to join this community. Hereburg was known to us because of her Mercian lineage. She welcomed us but not as murderers. We did not tell our purpose to start with but that we had been exiled from our country because of a misdeed by our father. Hereburg had no intention of doing evil at that time."

"What was your purpose?" Eadred asked.

"To gain the trust of the abbess, so she might help when we avenged the murder of the aetheling."

The gasps and shouts of treachery stopped the moment Edith began to speak once more. Her revelations were too astonishing to miss one word.

"As days passed, Abbess Hereburg became increasingly ill-treated by the powerful lords who endowed this minster and ridiculed by the women they had brought here to become cloistered Sisters. We could not believe our good fortune. As she suffered more, her heart became more willing to consider revenge on those who were taking everything from her that she held precious.

"As darkness took hold of the abbess, I swear to you all that the Lord God convinced me of the evil I was doing."

Edith shouted back at the cries of derision.

"I swear this is true and will undertake whatever is needed to prove what I am saying. I have more to say."

"Continue!" Aelfric barked.

"I told my brother and sister that I wanted no more to do with their plans – and I did no more and they told me no more."

"Why did you not expose their evil designs to some person of authority?"

The postulant lowered her head and her voice quivered.

"I believed I was within an honourable house but as Abbess Hereburg's authority waned, evil men and women began to look differently at me and then to take their authority over me. I was treated as a plaything for men and sent to their beds by wicked nuns. I was powerless and my anger grew. I despised the nuns and wanted them to suffer – so I said nothing. I am ashamed that I did so, but I was as pained as others when the murders were discovered. Leoba confided in me then what had happened. This is what she said to me.

"As Hereburg's heart blackened, a plan was hatched by the three of them. It was to wait until King Athelstan visited and then to take his life and that of the princess. But when it was known that Ealdorman Ceolfrith and his eldest son were to visit the minster, my brother and sister decided to take their chance and to kill them instead and the princess. For the ealdorman and his son had been involved in the execution of the aetheling."

Many expected Aelfric to shout down Edith's words but he stayed silent, reflecting on them. He raised his hand to stop Edith, then he spoke.

"It is true," he groaned. "This has weighed on my heart ever since and I have feared that God's vengeance would be visited on me – and it has."

"That is why the Mercian army that attacked Elmstow sought first only you," Edith responded.

"I was young and keen to gain my father's favour." Aelfric covered his face with repentant hands. The bishop gestured to Edith and she continued.

"I was told that when my brother and sister went to harm the princess, they found her already dead. Leoba did also say that Abbess Hereburg was duped into weakening the ealdorman by poison and when feeble he was overcome by my brother and Godric. They took him to the princess' chamber and hanged both bodies."

"Why were they stripped and hanged together?"

"Lord, your father was not stripped. He was already unclothed. Abbess Hereburg spoke the truth about them. She never wished harm on your father."

"And Abbess Hereburg; she was poisoned to stop her from telling what she knew?"

"I was never told that they poisoned her but that is what I believe."

"And what of Sister Verca?" the bishop asked.

"She was an open-hearted soul and, as far as I can imagine, helped them without intent but I think, like me, she wanted no more to do with them. Her life was ended because of what she knew and that she might tell others."

"Lady, you try to blame your countrymen for the murders because they did not free you when they attacked. You will not escape justice."

"No, lord, everything I have said is true. Let me face the ordeal of hot iron and let God decide the truth of my words," Edith sobbed. "I have sinned and am repentant. I never knew what my countrymen meant to do. You must know that I speak the truth. I implore you, let me face the ordeal."

The priest watched the faces of Ealdorman Aelfric and Bishop Aethelbert. Their intense speech was continuing for too long; his unease grew. Finally, they faced the court and the bishop spoke.

"Edith the postulant must face justice. We also need to know the truth of her words. If they were not shaped by guile, then the intentions of the Mercian king are known and what happened is known. There will be no more fear that killers lie within the minster. This is needed as we build a pious house. I will administer the ordeal. Let the iron be heated."

*

Two hours later, in the courtyard before the minster church, all was ready. Bishop Aethelbert stood with hands raised and spoke to a rod of hot iron that rested on a bench.

"Let the truth or the lie of Edith the postulant's words, uttered before me in a lawful court, be made manifest in you, through the name of Christ our King and his army of angels and all of his saints. So that what the devil wants to remain hidden from us is made clear."

The bishop made the sign of the cross over the iron. He took sedge leaves and rubbed them slowly along the rod several times. They withered.

"Edith the postulant, you have decided that the Lord God will be your judge of the truth or otherwise of the words you spoke before the court earlier this day. You must pick up this iron rod with your right hand and walk steadily. If you run or go too quickly, you must take the ordeal again. You are to place the rod on that bench. Your hand will then be bound to be opened after three nights when I will see if it is clean or foul. This is how the Lord God will speak his judgement. Now, begin."

Edith crossed herself and rose from her knees. Her sleeve had been tied back to her elbow. She stood still, breathing deeply for a few seconds then lifted the rod in a sudden grasp and turned her hand so it would not fall. She screamed in pain; her legs buckling.

"Do not forsake her, Lord," Eadred whispered, cupping his face; his eyes snapping shut. He heard her skin crackling and smelt it burn.

She did not fall. Walking carefully but crying out with the pain, Edith took nine paces to the bench and dropped the rod upon it. She fell, her face deathly white and glassy.

"Lord Jesus, my Saviour. Do not abandon me."

"Wrap her hand."

Two nuns ran forward and wrapped a cloth tightly around Edith's open hand. Her cries intensified and so did her appeals to God. The cloth was tied. The Sisters dripped hot wax over the knot and the bishop took his seal and marked it.

"Take her to a cell, lock it and have it guarded at all times. No-one is to enter, other than to bring food and water."

Edith's cries continued. She had been given a wooden peg to clench between her jaws, but the loud groaning continued throughout the night and into the next day. Though it softened as the hours passed, whoever went by her door could hear groans and sobs, and once in a while, a scream – but always, her voice was raised in prayer.

*

Eadred knelt within his cell, praying for a miracle. He continued thus, night and day, apart from participating in the cycle of communal prayers – but only one person filled his thoughts. In the early evening before the third night, the priest was summoned to the bishop's room.

"Eadred, sit here, my boy. Tomorrow, following midday, the wrapping is removed from the postulant's hand. I have been praying, as I am sure you have, that what she said to the court is the truth. I have no desire to see a woman hang, because I think she has a good heart for God, but I do not know if that is how the court will see it. Even if God shows her to be telling the truth, she may still hang because she knew of the evil that was hatching and said nothing. If it goes against her, I want you to know that I have done my best."

Eadred felt embarrassed but thankful that the bishop had sensed his concern for Edith. He felt confident to continue to show that interest.

"Thank you, Father. I had never witnessed an ordeal before this one. How does the Lord God show us his mind?"

"Through prayer, my boy, through prayer. I have seen or officiated at eight or nine ordeals of hot iron. Sometimes, the voice of God is clear but often it is subtle. In some, the hand is foul with pus – it is seen and smelt – and guilt is clear." The bishop held up his own hand and examined it. "In others, the skin is burnt and blistered but there is no sign of discharge. God has shown the person's innocence. But in most ordeals, the hand is neither one nor the other and I pray for discernment.

"And God often shows us more than the guilt or innocence for the particular accusation; he shows whether the man or woman has been wholesome or wicked in their life. These should also be accounted for in the sentence. So, a man might steal another's chicken but never have done ill in his past and have been a good man to his family, his community and Holy Church. While another man might also have stolen a chicken and have done many wrong things in his life – beating his wife and harming his neighbour's crops. These differences will be shown in the ordeal but require discernment to understand them. It is not easy and is a daunting responsibility."

It was a troubled priest who returned to his cell to continue to pray for Edith. His heart pleaded for her deliverance, but his mind knew an honest decision would be for her execution. He imagined what she must be going through now; the fear for when the bandage is unwrapped.

Eadred's prayer was interrupted by the harrowing image of what remained of Mildred's face after her disfigurement. If Edith were condemned to die, the ealdorman might exact the same revenge. He needed to speak again to the bishop.

A few hours more and Edith's fate would be known.

THIRTY

Hildericstow

The man sat slumped against a tree trunk, indifferent to Tatwine's approach. A flapping crow perched on his shoulder, pecking at his eye socket. The monk left it to its meal. Tatwine had counted eight so far – the wounded who had succumbed on their road back to Mercia.

He should never have looked from the minster wall. To see the Sisters-in-Christ screaming back to him, pleading for his help. He could do nothing when their tunics were ripped from them; when the cruel blades bruised their bodies and men's violating hands abused them. He had failed Eanswith and it was her memory that pushed him on towards Mercia to free them.

Tatwine walked at pace, with occasional periods of gentle running. He had always moved quickly and the endurance of his lean, strong body pleased him. He would pick out a feature on the horizon that seemed a day's distance and three or four hours later, arrive at the destination with a satisfied grin. At night, the hermit had slept with his cloak wrapped closely around him beside a fire that he replenished regularly. He was accustomed to only a few hours' sleep, broken by prayer and combat with demons.

The road was growing narrower, hemmed by woven branches, and now descended in a gentle curve. It then became unmistakeable; the chill, damp, scent of the forest was increasingly infused by a new trace. When the wooden walls gave way to a clearing, it hung in wraith-like layers; smoke.

A change of smell, of light and of sound brought a sense of menace. A child's cry. The blade slid from its scabbard; he crouched; watched cautiously where his feet fell and crossed the clearing, edging towards the sound. Then other noise; laughs and sobs and crackling wood. Tatwine hid behind a fallen tree trunk, peering to see ahead through the tangle of branches.

Charred bones of several houses cracked and snapped. Hildericstow had been burnt to the ground. The hermit could see two Mercians – one seated on a cloak, eating, and the other limping towards him. The seated man had a tied length of cloth supporting his left shoulder and upper arm. They were two stragglers dragging behind the other survivors.

Moving cautiously to the other end of the trunk, the monk could make out several bodies lying in a pile. Two men hung naked from a branch; their man-hoods cut away. A child – a boy – pulled at the tunic of his dead mother. The only other sound – sobbing – came from a woman who knelt unclothed, shivering beside a tree, her hands bound behind her with a rope that wrapped around the trunk. There was little that Tatwine could do now. He would wait for nightfall.

Gloom descended then thickened. The two Mercians sat warming their hands around a fledgling fire, chewing at some meat and drinking ale. Tatwine had watched them closely for a while and was certain they were alone. The man with the limp had a wound to his thigh that caused him to groan and swear when moving but more importantly, his movements were slow. The other moved freely and his right arm worked as it should, but his left arm and hand seemed useless. These were vital observations for Tatwine's planning. Their weapons rested close beside them. Then the inevitable transpired.

The Mercian with one good arm drew his knife and both men approached the bound woman. Tatwine could not hear what they said but he knew well enough the meaning of their words. She whimpered and pleaded. With the knife pointed at her throat, the limping man undid the rope, and the woman was pulled closer to the fire. A kick to the back of her leg sent her falling onto her knees and another into the shoulder blades sent her sprawling onto her face. The limping man struggled onto his knees, spread her legs and lifted his tunic.

The other Mercian stared into the blackness, suddenly aware of the shining, disembodied blade speeding towards him. An instant later, he was flying backwards, as Tatwine's boot slammed into his chest. He hit the ground hard and as he lifted his head, it met the force of the monk's sword, striking deeply into his face.

Despite his injury, the limping Mercian was an agile

warrior, who instinctively leapt, knife poised, onto Tatwine as he turned to engage him and it was the turn of the monk to be pushed over, his sword spinning from his grip. The Mercian's weight pinned him down and with Tatwine holding onto the man's arm for dear life, the knife point was pushed closer and closer to his throat.

The monk arched his head back when he felt the blade prick the skin under his jaw, but he could not match his attacker's strength and could not stop the quivering point from inching forward. There was no room left to avoid the cold metal and it pierced the skin. The Mercian twisted the blade. Tatwine cried out as his flesh tore and his pain surged. Still, the blade continued to cut into the soft flesh. Then it was gone.

Tatwine's attacker toppled sideways. The monk was as surprised as the Mercian. The woman came running again at the man she had just kicked, and her foot struck the side of his head once more. Tatwine reached for his sword and brought it down on the man's arm, sending the forearm flying. He had little time to scream – the monk's blade swept down again, cutting him from his shoulder into the thorax.

Blood poured freely from Tatwine's throat, running along the fingers he dabbed against the torn flesh. He flinched. Using his blade, he cut a length from the bottom of his tunic and tied it around his neck, holding it firmly.

"You are safe. They are dead. Come here and I will free your hands. I will not hurt you. Come." He spoke to the darkness.

Despite his words of reassurance, Tatwine gripped his sword firmly and his eyes searched the area around the fire. He shouted once again.

He heard steps from the other side of the fire. A young woman crept forward then halted with the fire separating the two figures. The monk picked up the cloak the two Mercians had been sitting on and held it out.

"Come now. I will cut the rope and you take this cloak. You are shivering. I can see you are cold and unwell. You must trust me. I will walk towards you slowly." He took a step forward and the woman retreated a step. "This will not do. You will freeze to death. I swear by Christ's blood that I will not harm you." He took a step then another. The woman tensed but did not move.

"There." Tatwine freed her hands and gave her the cloak. He dragged the two Mercian bodies away to the edge of the clearing and came back to sit on the opposite side of the fire to the woman.

"I have some meat. Here." The monk tossed a mutton bone he had carried in a cloth bag, after tearing off some for himself. "I am Brother Tatwine from Elmstow Minster. I follow the remains of a Mercian force that attacked us – and lost. They took some of our Sisters-in-Christ captive and I seek to free them. The Mercians did this?" Tatwine looked around him.

The woman – younger than the monk by what he had seen of her body but with a face aged by poverty – kept nibbling the bone then scratched at scraps of flesh that still adhered to it. Without speaking, she looked up when he spoke.

"You did well to attack, rather than run away. You saved my life and I am thankful. What is your name? When did they leave here?"

Her tired eyes stared at him, her teeth pulling another strand from the bone.

"They attacked yesterday when the day was fading, killing most who were here. In the morning, they burned the houses and left. The two who stayed were brothers – one to care for the other." She laughed. Tatwine raised his eyebrows at her odd reaction. "And to have me as often as they could get it up. I am Gertie." The woman let loose a string of abuse at the two dead Mercians.

"The two who hang there." Gertie pointed to the two men hanging from the tree. "They were captives from the battle. I pitied them. Their deaths were long and hard – and so was the woman's."

"Which woman?"

"One of those you wanted to save."

"No! Where is she?"

"On a tree on that side of the clearing. Do not look now; you will not sleep. They must have hated her. I have never seen such…" Gertie shook her head.

"And the other cloistered women?"

"It weren't right. They went with the soldiers today. Three were naked. They had been beaten badly and screamed all night with men taking their turn – but one were dressed and she helped defile the ones who were killed."

"She was a nun?"

"Yes, I told you. What else would she be? She knew them all by name and they knew her. She were nasty."

"Do you remember her name?"

"No, I had more to think about than what they were called."

Tatwine rubbed his face in his hands. While Gertie remained preoccupied with the final smell of meat on the bone, the monk sat scouring his memory for a nun who would defile her own Christian Sisters. None that he knew was so barbaric.

"There was a man from here called Godric. He had a son."

"Poor bugger. The son were killed and my husband and my old mother."

"I am sorry. The Lord God will care for their souls. And the child; he is yours?"

"No but I will care for him now. He has no-one."

"Gertie, I will sleep now and leave early. I will catch them, and they will suffer for this. I cannot stay to bury the bodies, but I will return this way, God willing, and take you and the child to Elmstow. They will care for you."

"It would have been my turn today to get the knife. You saved me. If you want me to open my legs, I don't mind."

"No, Gertie, I will sleep. God bless and care for you."

Tatwine stoked the fire and collected more wood. Soon, Gertie and the child fell asleep on one side of the fire and the monk on the other. No-one was spared the visit of demons that night. The pitiful child woke and could not be comforted, and Gertie broke into bouts of tears then abuse. Tatwine doubted whether the child would live long in her company. He also harboured concerns as to whether he could fulfil his mission to free the remaining Sisters. There was only so much one man could do but he would not return to Elmstow without making the attempt; it was a pledge he had made to God.

The child had finally exhausted itself. Tatwine woke with a start, his eyes stinging from the smoke and thick fog, which shrouded the dying embers of the village. He built up the fire and made a torch from dry twigs. Several torments had preoccupied the monk overnight and he could no longer put off the one that was closest. The flame struggled to live and barely lit the way to the other side of the clearing. He held up his light and cried out.

Her feet were not far from the ground, such that her toes would have been able to touch it, while she struggled in vain to stay alive. Tatwine looked straight into her disfigured face. All that had made her human had been removed. What had made her a woman had been mutilated. The monk choked up bile and spat it out. He knew which nuns were missing – and he knew from her hair and the delicacy of her limbs and hands that this had been Sister Moira. Tatwine gasped for air when he cut her down with his shaking hands. There was little more he could do but lay her out. He did the same for the two East Anglian warriors and said a brief prayer for them all. Then he began to run.

Though terror took hold of him many times, he was God's avenging warrior. He did not stop until mid-afternoon; by then he was well into Mercia. Fog still veiled the land. Bald branches reached to each other from either side of the road then faded. Muffled, indistinct sounds loomed ahead. He passed two corpses, both still warm with the memory of life.

The warrior gripped his axe shaft and struggled to rise when his eyes traced the shape that his ears had detected emerging from the fog. The wound in his chest opened as he began to shout a warning. The monk ran onto him and plunged his knife into the man's stomach. Between two heartbeats, Tatwine had drawn his arm around the Mercian's throat to stop him crying out once more and forced the blade through his ear and into the brain. He eased the body to the ground. Another group of Mercians could not be far ahead. The monk prayed that the split second of alarm from his victim had not alerted his countrymen.

With day's candle fading, Tatwine moved along the road as quickly as he dared. He could hear voices ahead – how far was unclear. Then a slight flicker of movement. He crouched and stepped into tree cover.

The glow of camp fires laboured against the damp air. One, two… five strained for life. The talk of companions who had been subdued by loss and wounds was giving way to a lighter mood as the flames of each fire took hold. The smells of roasting meat began to waft on the mist, bringing wisps of laughter and joking. The monk watched the shapes of men eating and drinking. He counted around fifteen figures. A while longer and he would attempt to get closer but for now he closed his eyes.

They were opened by a woman's voice. He knew her well.

The postulant, Leoba, sat with a group of men, talking and laughing. His mind raced through strands of memory to try to comprehend what he was seeing. The Mercians acted with familiarity and talked as though she were one of them. He recalled what Gertie had said – that there was a woman who helped abuse the two East Angle men and the holy Sisters. Leoba was a Mercian or in their pay.

THIRTY-ONE

Justice

The fires glowed, repelling for those who congregated around them the freezing fingers spreading through the fog. Tatwine crouched, beyond the warmth, but close enough that he could make out much of what was happening and being spoken of in the Mercian camp. His body shivered and ached. Far worse, he had not the slightest idea of what he would do next. A shrill cry ended his musing.

The reasons for his mission were manhandled before the fires. Their cloaks were pulled from them and they stood, bound and unclothed – three Sisters-in-Christ. Each night must have brought the same bestial treatment for they wept for mercy. There was none available from Leoba. The monk strained to understand her words.

"Be quiet! You showed us no kindness, so expect none from me."

"But Leoba, we were not like Sister Moira."

"You did not stop her. You all thought you were princesses. And what my sister endured! I will have justice for her."

"Please! We did not know what Moira was doing. Again, we implore you, treat us well and you will become rich. Our fathers are among the richest in our kingdom. They will ransom us."

"I know enough of your lineage. That is why I sought you out and fools that you are, you ran into our arms. And still you do not understand."

"Have you not told them?" one of the men smirked.

"I will then. They deserve to know their fate. Feather-headed fools, you were not captured because you mistreated us, although for that you are now receiving the same delicate care that you once allowed for my sister. You were taken as retribution for what your noble leaders did to one who was helpless and innocent – the execution of the son of our great king."

"But we had nothing to do with that! You must know that?"

"Then you are as innocent as he was and will suffer the same fate. You are going to be executed, dear Sisters. In what manner will be decided by our king."

Tatwine held his head in his hands. The wailing and the pleas from the nuns were terrible to hear but useless.

"Is it not said in many laws that there shall be taken an eye for an eye, a tooth for a tooth, a life for a life? This is just compensation, surely. In the meantime, you have another use."

The three holy Sisters were dragged away. The weeping continued; the grunting and cries of pain soon started.

The monk prayed for the desecrated women then he prayed for guidance and protection, for he would act that night.

*

"Sisters, it is Brother Tatwine from Elmstow. Be quiet! Be still!"

One of the nuns murmured.

"Hush!" The monk covered the woman's mouth with his hand. "Do as I say and you will be freed," he whispered. "One mistake and we will all surely die. Now, not one sound. My blade will cut your ropes. Once cut, do not move. We all leave together or we will be caught." The cautious blade sliced each rope in turn. The distressed nuns stayed motionless and quiet as the grave. Tatwine whispered encouragement.

"Now, listen carefully. Your lives depend on hearing and understanding my words and acting on them. I will touch each of you in turn on the shoulder. When I do, creep slowly on your hands and knees behind me, facing the other way, and do not turn around. When you are all in a line, I will take the lead. I have the way out to the road in my memory. I have cleared twigs from the track we must take but still put each hand and each knee down softly."

Tatwine touched the shoulder of the first nun. She moved away from the stake to which they had been tied and followed the monk's instructions. As she passed by him, Tatwine took her arm to ensure she faced in the right direction then stopped moving. He tapped the second shoulder. She crept away, as instructed.

The monk touched the shoulder of the third nun. There

was no movement, other than a continued shaking. He repeated the action. Still, she remained motionless.

"It is Sister Burghild, is it not?"

She whispered her acknowledgment in a faltering voice.

"Sister Burghild, your Saviour is with you. He sent me to bring you from this torment. Do you believe and trust in his promises?"

"I do." Sister Burghild nodded.

"Then do as I say and move behind me." Tatwine felt her trembling arms take the weight of her body and she wormed back behind the monk. "Keep praying, Sisters, and all will be well." When the three were positioned in a line, he edged past them and took the lead. "Slowly, follow me."

Tatwine faced complete blackness ahead. Behind the strange fellowship, the glow of mostly spent embers ebbed in the murky air. The monk brushed the ground ahead with his palm – to feel his way and to remove any stray twigs. An outlandish smile softened his flint expression, as he prayed and lengthened his distance from the Mercian camp. He felt God's presence as surely as if the path ahead were lit by a thousand candles held by angels. He felt exhilarated. Tears began to fall and his fear melted. Without any impediment, they reached the road.

"The Lord God has been with us, Sisters. I sensed his unseen hand protecting us. Now, this is what you must do for I must return to the camp."

"No, do not leave us, Brother Tatwine." Sister Burghild grabbed his arm. "We are far from safety."

"You will be safe. The Lord God has not taken you this far only to abandon you. That is not our God. Listen to what I say and maintain your prayers – silently. Heaven's candle will soon begin its journey from the east and its glow will begin to lift the gloom of night. Light will still struggle for the fog is thick. You will sense the direction of the road, even now in darkness, by brushing your hand against the tree cover along its sides. Go slowly in a row and you will make good distance. Do not hurry and trip. Your legs have much to do before you are returned to the land of the East Angles.

"When light smears the sky, move more quickly. Rest only when you can go no further. Keep your eye on the road ahead and if you see or hear others moving along the road, seek the cover of the forest immediately. I will follow when my work is done, and the Lord God will see me safely back with you. Now, let us pray together for God's continuing shield over us, then go."

Though they were fearful, Tatwine allowed the Sisters no other option and he was soon back on his hands and knees moving in the direction of the camp. He returned to find only one of the fires still smouldered and the camp silent.

"Almighty Father, protect me now and see me safely through this, if it is your will – but let me bring justice down upon the head of the one who deserves punishment, even if I die."

Tatwine reached out to his right and found the two large flints he had placed there hours before. He crossed himself then bent his body backwards and hurled one of the stones over the heads of the sleepers to the other side of the camp. It crashed into the underwood. The second stone landed close by in quick succession, rebounding off a tree trunk, magnifying the noise.

The camp awoke with shouts of alarm and the clap of

metal. The warrior who yelled orders was not the Mercian leader, Osgar – but he was not whom the monk had returned for. Tatwine watched the obscure shadows moving through the fog. Not long now. He would have one chance.

"They have gone! The captives have gone! Find them; they are my prize." Leoba flung the cut ropes away, swearing.

Tatwine pounced. The air was punched from Leoba's body. She hit the ground, the monk's hands finding her throat, squeezing hard. She tried to shout but his grip held. Her hands moved upward and scratched at his face then her searching fingers found one of his eyes. He muffled a groan, trying to shake her hand way but Leoba's fingers and thumb pushed into the socket and refused to yield. The pain stabbed into his head, but he refused to scream, then brought his forehead down hard onto Leoba's face – then again and again. She moved one hand to shield the blows, as the other forced her fingers into his skull. The monk's hands responded. One pushed Leoba's head back, while the other snatched the knife from his belt and rammed it up through her throat, into her head. She shuddered and twitched in silence with Tatwine's palm over her mouth.

"May God have mercy on your soul."

The monk felt his left eye. It was misshapen, oozing, sightless and burned. Withdrawing his blade from Leoba's head, Tatwine stumbled onto his hands and knees and slunk away. He heard the cries when Leoba's body was found and prayed that he would not be followed.

Soon, he had found the road. Thankfully, the fog had deepened and he disappeared into God's protective shield, his head throbbing with searing pain. The nuns' fear dissipated when they saw him emerge behind them, but they cried and looked away when they beheld the condition of his eye. It would receive no care from them.

Tatwine's injury continued to inflict agony but he pushed the holy Sisters hard with the pace he maintained.

"Quicker, Sisters. The enemy may be after us still and if they catch us, we will face pain and torment that hell itself devises and men cannot imagine." It was a wonder how his words sped them on; faster than they could ever have believed.

Hildericstow was empty with no sign of Gertie or the child. The bodies from the Mercian attack had been ripped to pieces by wolves and their horrific remains scattered far and wide. There was no desire to linger there and they slept on the edge of a forest glade.

*

"It is! It is!" The nuns above the minster gate shielded the glare from their eyes. "Brother Tatwine returns. He has three Sisters with him." Sisters-in-Christ ran to meet them in disbelief. Eadred overtook them. The bishop fell to his knees outside the gate.

"It is a miracle. The Lord God has bestowed a miracle." He wept freely. Sister Burghild and the two other Sisters fell into the arms of their friends and emotions that none of them had experienced since childhood burst from them without constraint.

"My good friend, you have the courage of a lion and have done the impossible." Eadred wrapped his arms around the monk. "There are not enough tears in me for this." Tatwine collapsed into the priest. Eadred sensed the weakness of his friend's body.

"What injuries do you have?"

The monk unwrapped the binding from around his head and peeled away the sticky cloth with a moan. Eadred shuddered. Tatwine's eye socket oozed with pus and juices, surrounded by flesh that flamed as the setting sun and the defiled eye bulged unnaturally.

"I cannot see from this eye. Leoba gouged it with her fingers before I killed her. The pain is terrible. It fills my head and neck. Leoba was involved in the murders here and she killed Sister Moira."

"We know about Leoba. You are safe now."

Abbess Tetta came running from the minster. Whatever horror she may have felt on seeing Tatwine's face, it was disguised well through a sombre, workman-like expression.

"You have done well to wear the pain of this. Come, I will find something to help." She turned to some warriors who were listening closely to the lurid stories of the homecoming nuns. "Do not stand around! Would you help this brave monk to the infirmary?" Once Tatwine was being supported and shuffling away, the abbess opened her arms. "Sisters, come here. This is indeed a miracle." She embraced the weeping nuns. "Let us cleanse and feed you. I can see and hear that you have returned to us from hell, but your wounds will heal.

"My dears, I would spend more time with you but there is a serious obligation on the community today and I must go at once. When over, we will ring the minster bell and rejoice and praise God for his mercy."

THIRTY-TWO

Resolution

The courtyard had filled with folk and expectation. Edith was brought from her cell; her feet manacled and hands tied before her. Eadred looked at her pale, drawn face and empty eyes and struggled to control his tears. She looked as if she had exhausted all hope and was already dead but for the rope.

She stood before Bishop Aethelbert and the bench on which the minster's magnificent psalter lay. Not far away sat Aelfric, with an empty chair beside him, where the bishop would sit once the court reconvened after the outcome of the ordeal was known. All present bowed their heads.

"Edith the postulant has faced the ordeal by hot iron. It was undertaken in conformity with the requirements of the Church and the long-recognised traditions of our people. The iron was blessed in the name of Christ our

King, his army of angels and all of his saints. The hand has been bound for three nights.

"Untie her hands, break the seal and unwrap the cloth."

Aelfric rose and stood with the bishop, while Abbess Tetta cracked the seal and began to unwrap the bandage slowly. With one turn of the cloth remaining, the bishop raised his hand for the process to pause.

"Holy Father in Heaven, we pray that you have made judgement on this woman and that I, your servant, am able to discern your will in the condition of this hand. If the hand is foul and festered, you have revealed that her words were false. If the hand is clean, then you have revealed that the words were truthful.

"Continue."

Eadred stood behind the bishop but eager eyes, to both sides of him, stopped his seeing the last turn of the cloth. He stretched to his left then to the right but to no avail. But he did see Edith's face with her eyes screwed tightly shut and the slight movement of prayer on her lips.

There was a gasp from the abbess. The bishop looked to the ealdorman. He stood silently in thought then nodded. Bishop Aethelbert turned to face the assembly with his hands raised. Too scared to look, Edith continued to pray.

"Nothing is hidden from the Lord God, neither thoughts nor actions. He has revealed to me, his servant, that Edith the postulant did speak truthfully to this court."

Edith's cry rang out louder than the gasps and shouts of the assembly. She put her hands to her face and fell to her knees, weeping and shaking.

"My Saviour! My Blessed Father, thank you for standing with me."

It took a while for silence to be restored. From the gossip to the wise commentary, one issue remained. How cruel it was that despite God's favour and the upsurge of joy it brought to her, Edith might still be condemned to hang as a traitor and that decision was minutes away. The court was reconvened to decide upon the postulant's fate.

"Edith the postulant, the Lord God has shown that the words you spoke to this court were truthful. That matter is settled. Yet, your own words do accuse you of hiding the terrible crimes that took Christian lives. If you had spoken earlier then the guilty would have been caught before committing their sinful acts. I say you are guilty of these deaths, as much as if your hands had murdered them yourself. My own father is dead because of you."

Aelfric's fervent speech was greeted with much affirmation, as Eadred had dreaded. The bishop nodded to the priest.

"I speak for Holy Church. Holy ordeals reveal the truth," Eadred started. "When an ordeal is undertaken, the Lord God declares much about the person. We, his creation, cannot limit what he wishes to tell us. If a man is evil in his heart but speaks the truth on one event, he remains evil and will be shown as such.

"This woman has been shown clearly to be truthful. See her hand." Edith raised it and turned so all could see her palm. It was clearly burnt and blistered but was not tainted by any foul sores or emissions.

"God has attested that this woman has a good, Christian heart. Search your own hearts. If she had spoken of the intentions of her sister and brother, when there was no sign that such a plot existed, would you have listened? They would have denied the charge. Abbess Hereburg would have poured scorn upon her head. Edith was of low rank within the minster; it is likely that she would have been dismissed from Elmstow.

"This postulant could have remained silent and we would never have known why these crimes were committed. We would still be suspicious of each other. She has ended that distrust and ensured her exile from her own country until her last day. The last murderer, Leoba, has been executed by Brother Tatwine, who bravely entered the Mercian camp, and he has also freed our dear Sisters. Surely, God has told us that the guilty have been found and punished.

"Edith has been poorly treated by many here." Eadred could not help his eyes from moving to look at Aelfric, who had instigated her procurement for enjoyment by Regenhere the moneyer.

"Who would hang a woman whom the Lord God has saved? Who would stand before his Saviour on the day of judgement and say I went against you, Lord, and killed one whom you said was innocent? I sought to put myself above you."

Eadred bowed to the bishop and to the ealdorman. If he had looked to Edith, he would have seen a ghost.

"What is your judgement?" The bishop spoke to the line of men before him. They murmured for a few seconds. One of their number stood. He breathed deeply and it seemed an age before he spoke.

"There is much truth in what Lord Aelfric says. If the woman had spoken earlier, Ealdorman Ceolfrith may have lived. Or would she have been silenced by others or ignored? We cannot know and we understand the hurt that Lord

Aelfric feels. It is hard to bear. Yet, who are we as mortal men to question the judgement of God? He has spoken to us and we must obey him."

Bishop Aethelbert looked to Aelfric, who muttered a few words. The bishop then turned to Edith.

"It is God's will and the judgement of this court that you be set free."

The young postulant burst into tears and above the voices around her, she shouted her thanks to all.

"Remove her shackles – and Abbess, see that she is instructed well, so she may enter the minster in good time as a Sister-in-Christ.

"Before the court closes, let me say a few more words." The bishop glanced at Aelfric. The ealdorman seemed consumed by his own thoughts, so the bishop asked once more for leave to speak. A nod sufficed.

"Terrible crimes have been committed here, in a place that should have shone with piety. The Church must bear a share of the guilt for it is our sacred duty to control our own house, as the Lord God would expect. Yet, we are seldom allowed to act as we should. Many have suffered from the sickness we let grow when we let sin find a home here. The sickness has now been purged and the body is healing and with an understanding that we must be more vigilant in keeping it well.

"The Lord God spoke to me when I prayed this morning. Many have paid a price and we have now atoned for the sins that led to such death and misery. The day may come when Mercian and East Angle live in peace but for now it is sufficient to know that in God's eyes, compensation has been paid for the Christian souls who died at each other's hands in that terrible battle a few years past and since that time. Let there be no further blood spilt in this feud by either kingdom. I will send a letter to the Church in Mercia conveying this just settlement. This is the will of God."

*

The evening service was a joyous affair – for the return of the captive holy Sisters and now Edith's release. The voices rose higher and brighter in praise and thanks to God. Sisters-in-Christ, who had been indulged and cossetted all their lives, had now experienced the brutal reality that had been Edith's life in the minster. Her existence had been barely acknowledged but now she was embraced by the Sisters around her. Many who were there said that they felt the presence of Christ among them and that he had finally come to dwell in Elmstow.

"You have served me well, Eadred. This place is finally cleared of vermin and a good Christian soul lives because of you. We have discovered why the murders were perpetrated, the Mercians have been defeated in battle and the kingdom survives!" Bishop Aethelbert held out his cup for Eadred to refill. The priest then filled his own.

"You have a wisdom that many would not attain in their lifetime. To ask me to talk of the blood of the East Angles and Mercians that has been spilt as providing atonement for the wrongs that have been committed – it was a thought that must have come from God the peacemaker himself. I watched Lord Aelfric's face after I had spoken, and a weight seemed to have lifted from him. As any son, he felt that duty and honour obliged him to avenge his father's death at Mercian hands – but, hopefully, that burden has gone. Many lives will be saved.

"Now, my old mind struggles even now to understand how you discovered that Leoba was involved."

"I was not certain, Reverend Father; far from certain. Edith was weighed down by guilt and sin but would not confess to me. Then I found out that her sister had not rung the bell for the night service, although sober and promising to do so, and sought to hide this from me. I then looked differently at my meeting with her and Edith on the night of the murder. I thought she might be hiding some awful truth.

"Yet truly, Father, it was the Holy Spirit who led me to look differently at the pieces of the story and how they were connected.

"Looking back, I realise my dull head made many errors, but I made two serious mistakes. I wandered aimlessly, searching for those corrupted intentions that are caused by illicit relationships or conflicts over land and wealth. I failed to understand quickly enough the importance of the Mercian lineage of Leoba, Edith and Hereburg – and the anger and injury to Mercian honour caused by the senseless murder of their king's young son. When I began to doubt Leoba and knew her sister harboured a great sin then I recalled Hereburg's revelation at her trial that they planned to kill the king and the princess, and much fell into place. For what East Angle would plan to kill their king and his daughter? None! Mildred did not plan to kill Cuthburg; it came from a violent fit of anger and jealousy.

"I needed to confront Edith about the sin she carried. When I did, she finally confessed all to me, as well as her desire to unburden herself before the whole community and to face justice. And from there, as you know, she came before the court. She is a brave woman. I feared the court would hang her, for there was reason – but God spoke.

"I believe that when Edith's brother journeyed to Hildericstow to hire a killer to help with the murders, he found a way to send a message to his countrymen. The deed was at hand and they should prepare an attack, for Elmstow would soon be in disarray.

"And I never thought of questioning the slaves until Godric spoke of one. I never thought them capable of anything but menial work. Yet, I might have discovered that one of their number had been missing for a few days. One was a murderer, but the others are Christian souls and I barely thought of them as human.

"I have one question for you now, Reverend Father. Why would you let no-one from Snailwell Minster accompany me on this mission? I would have welcomed support. It was hard and lonely."

"I am sorry, my son. I could not tell you; it would have made you worry even more. The ealdorman had spies everywhere. There is one in our home minster of Snailwell, I am certain. I have my suspicions but cannot be certain who he is, and he may have poisoned the minds of others. If I sent you to Elmstow with someone in Ceolfrith's pay, you might never have come back. He was always a ruthless, dangerous man. Now the ealdorman is dead, I will see if I can flush out the rat but that is for another day.

"And I have one final question for you, young Eadred. Why do you dismiss Regenhere and his son as possible murderers? I thought they could have been the culprits."

"I did as well for a while. But the more I thought about it, the more I realised that their family's wealth and name were dependent on their links to the royal house. A moneyer has to have close ties to his king and relies on his patronage. Regenhere was desperate for the king to agree to Raedwulf succeeding him as the kingdom's chief moneyer but the son's reputation was so poor, it was unlikely to happen. So, Regenhere sought to bribe Lord Aelfric and probably others to speak to the king on his behalf and he also lied to cover up his son's appalling behaviour. Yet, we will never know the truth now Raedwulf is dead.

"But now Lord Aelfric is ealdorman, I pray that his conduct will come to befit his high rank. As you know, I believed for a while that he was involved in his father's murder. Ceolfrith was known to be cold to his eldest son – unnaturally so. I also saw him with the moneyer, agreeing to something underhand in return for gold. I was still suspicious until I realised the truth about Edith and Leoba.

"What I cannot remove from my mind is how close the plot came to failure. If Sister Hilda had not been late in ringing the bell for the service that morning, it may have disordered the activities of the murderers. As it was, they continued uninterrupted."

The bishop smiled and shook his head.

"I have not had this much wine for many a month – but tonight is special. Let me take a piss then help me to the midnight service. We have much to be grateful for."

THIRTY-THREE

Edith

The wall of cold air took Eadred's breath away. He wrapped his cloak closely around his shoulders and scurried from the church towards the dormitory. The midnight service had finished and there were many tired but relieved souls eager for the warmth and comfort of their beds – but not Eadred the priest.

His mood had veered chaotically over a day that he would not have thought possible a month earlier. Even amongst recent times of war and murder, this soared. He felt joy – indeed pride – that he was now known within Elmstow for the novel way in which he had discovered the truth of the crimes committed there.

"You are destined for great achievements," the bishop had smiled. "Your name will become known and maybe will draw fame as great as that of the renowned warriors of the kingdom, if you use your gifts wisely." But Eadred also dwelt on Tatwine's warning – that as his gifts threatened the guilty, so they would endanger his life.

The priest reflected on his dark hours: ridiculed by the old ealdorman; laughed at by warriors who now acknowledged him with a friendly nod. Young Sisters-in-Christ, who a few weeks earlier would not have even noticed his existence, now looked into his eyes as they would a warrior.

Eadred had been changed by the power and the passion that abided within Tatwine; forces that had driven the hermit to venture alone into Mercia to fight for the lives of women who had become transformed by his audacious faith. Eadred had played his own part in saving the life of a woman who ignited feelings within him that he felt might burn as they will at any moment, without constraint. It was all seductive and dangerous and battled within him.

The same turn of mind that dug deeper and deeper into a crime until he found the truth also persecuted him. Did he now wear a mask that the world celebrated but could so easily be torn or thrown away to reveal the same inadequate boy whom he knew so well? Or had he changed? Had he fought a fight against the evil one and been victorious, so the fame he now experienced was like the golden arm rings given to a brave and loyal warrior by his lord to show his love and gratitude? If the arm rings were given to Eadred by men, then they were fleeting; if by the Lord God then he felt they were truth. But Eadred conceded with a wistful smile that whoever bestowed the rings, he would likely be entranced by their lustre.

The priest needed to talk to Tatwine. The hermit would have drunk and laughed. He would have expressed amazement at how a poor priest of no status or wealth could have seen through such an entangled web of exploits and lies. He would have helped him understand where the eternal truth lay.

"The Lord walks with you; that is obvious. For man alone could not see through this muddy pond," the hermit had said to encourage Eadred. The priest missed the muscled words of his good friend; words that struck home. It was good to talk to Bishop Aethelbert but he was old and Eadred did not feel comfortable in opening his heart to one of such stature in the Church. There was so much that Eadred wanted to talk about.

There would be no warm, mystical communion with his friend around a fire that bewitched. Eadred feared for the monk's life. He lay in a bed groaning with a pain that would not lessen, his dribbling eye covered with a poultice. Here was a real hero in the world of men and in the unseen realm.

With disappointment, Eadred closed the door of the dormitory building behind him. It was solid and an improvement on the former that was smashed in the battle. After the midnight service, the corridor was lit by a couple of torches that flickered gently. The priest was a forlorn traveller on the deserted journey back to his cell. Then he heard a voice chanting a psalm. It was a wondrous sound. He was passing the room set aside for spinning and weaving.

Her voice was a delight that made his skin prickle. It was Edith. Eadred stood still, weighing a thought that refused to wither or to let him walk on. If he could not talk to Tatwine then Edith was almost as close to his heart, although she was unaware of her impact. Perhaps improperly, but Eadred tapped gently on the door. The singing stopped. There was no response. He tapped again.

"Go away. You have no more power over me. In God's name, leave me be!"

"It is Father Eadred."

The bolt slid open.

"Father Eadred!" Edith's perplexed expression eventually turned into a smile.

"I was returning to my cell. I heard your voice and thought I would see if all is right. You have faced momentous days – and your hand?"

"Do you want to come in? I thought I would stay here awhile and give thanks for my deliverance without disturbing the other Sisters."

Eadred nodded and Edith closed the door. The postulant sat on the bed that still looked out of place with the purpose of the room. Eadred took the stool.

"It is healing well." Edith showed her palm. "The abbess has given me a pot of balm to rub over my hand. She says it will speed its healing. She is a wonderful daughter of God and even asked my forgiveness for the charges she shouted at me during my trial."

Eadred nodded.

"It still amazes me how darkness has turned to light in only a few weeks. We serve a great God, indeed. You were brave to confess and bring yourself before the court. Your courage, your faith; they astound and encourage me."

"Father, I could not bear such knowledge on my conscience. I knew that I had done wrong in the world of men, and men had good reason to hang me, but I prayed and God spoke that if I were truthful and had faith then all would be well. He wanted Elmstow purified and for suspicion to be cast out."

"Edith, you may call me Eadred, if you wish."

"I would like that. Although the Lord God showed me what I should do, it was you, Eadred, who was sent by God to walk with me. They were your words that touched the minds and hearts of the court and took the noose from around my neck.

"Elmstow was a cauldron of every sin imaginable and I was here only to please the foulest lusts. The Lord God came to me, as you are now, and showed me that this was the price of my sin. It was a glimpse of hell. But in his mercy, he told me that it need not be so. I had the choice to turn from evil and, with his almighty power strengthening me, I did so."

Edith rested her head in her hand and her eyes moistened.

"I shall never see my family again. I turned from them to follow Christ. My sister and brother are dead and face an eternity of torment. For all her grievous faults, my sister always cared for and protected me. When I told her that I wanted nothing more to do with their plans, she hugged me and said she understood. Abbess Tetta told me that I would need to be ever watchful, for there would be those ready to take their revenge. What happened to Ealdorman Ceolfrith, Abbess Hereburg and Sister Verca could still happen to me. But I will be protected by angels – that is God's word to me."

"Edith, I could talk to the bishop and he might send you to another cloister; one that is far from the border, where you would be safe and where you could praise and give thanks to God without fear."

"Thank you, you are a good man. I shall never forget your kindness. I will think carefully about what you have said."

"I shall visit here again. You can tell me then how it is with you here."

"And Eadred, when do you leave and return to your home minster?"

"I leave for Snailwell with the bishop, tomorrow. He is ill and wishes to go to his own bed and I must travel with him to care for his needs. I wanted to stay a while longer to be with Brother Tatwine. The abbess tells me he may not survive. He cries out and sweats and there is little more she can do, so I pray. If he does not live, he will assuredly go to God's house, but I shall miss him.

"Strangely, I shall miss Elmstow. I have little desire to leave a place where God gave his people a miracle – perhaps more than one. I am a quiet man – that is my nature. When I think of what I have done these past days, I can scarcely believe that it was me. Although I have longed many times to be in Snailwell Minster, I now have no hunger to return. Brother Tatwine told me that he also wanted a quiet life of contemplation, but it was a selfish desire born from his own failings. He reminded me that Christ himself did not hide from the world of men but strove always to walk with them, however base they were, to heal them and to bring them to the Father.

"I suppose I have found in Brother Tatwine a friend who is closer to the heart of God than anyone I have met, but he is also a fearsome warrior and I shall miss him greatly if God calls him home. We all need fellowship – to help others and for others to help us. I have found no-one else in my life to share the journey of faith."

Eadred stared at the floor, reflecting on the words he had just spoken and what they meant for the years ahead of him.

"Perhaps when you return here, we can talk more of sacred scriptures. There is so much that I want to learn. It is important that Brothers and Sisters-in-Christ can share their journeys."

"I would enjoy that very much. And be wary, Edith, for evil men are out there. Be on your guard. For all the world, I wish I could stay here and protect you."

"That would be my perfect life."

How a few words could change a man's heart.

It was a peculiar smile from Eadred – embarrassment, joy, confusion. He reached for Edith's burnt hand and with care lifted it. He sensed no hesitancy; his heart began to pound, and he kissed her hand gently.

Before the priest could withdraw, Edith had taken his hand and touched it with her moist lips.

"Would you sit beside me?"

Edith took Eadred's hands and she kissed his cheek.

"Dear Eadred, I thought this might be as pleasant for you as it is for me. Perhaps not?"

"No, my dear Edith. I wept for you after seeing the moneyer mistreating you in the basest way and when you told me how men had always ill-used you. I am not like them. You owe me nothing."

"My foolish priest, I do not favour you because I owe you anything! And I had no choice with the men who abused me – they told me what to do and it was my duty to do it. But this is my choice; the first time it has ever been."

Edith placed her hands on her lap. She smiled at Eadred, wide-eyed.

"Then I am blessed." Eadred sighed.

Their hands returned to each other and their lips came together tenderly then parted.

"Is this wrong?" Edith spoke with sadness in her voice. "We are unwed, and the bishop would not agree to our marriage." She pulled her hands from Eadred's but he gripped her fingers before they could escape.

"No, we are not married but we share a faith, and we share affection. Should we now share more?" The question was answered.

They shared the tasks of removing their clothing. Their bodies trembled in the cold air and with each touch. Joyfully, hands and lips caressed and explored each other's nakedness. The fear of the past few weeks was finally abandoned. Their bodies quivered and convulsed, rocking together, each serving and indulging the other. Sometimes laughing, sometimes gasping, their passions building ever higher unto rapture.

Smiling and kissing, they vowed always to pray for each other and to find ways of meeting again, so they could give and share – in body, mind and spirit.

THIRTY-FOUR

Snailwell

Eadred joined the bishop in singing psalms throughout the journey back to Snailwell. It was a joyful way to praise and thank the Lord God, and Eadred continued to smile even when he found the activity had become tiring. Bishop Aethelbert seemed to have regained the energy of his youth, while Eadred's voice croaked another verse.

When the priest stood again on the small bridge over the river that curled through the village, his heart exploded with gratitude that he was again within his own community but seeing it with new eyes.

Snailwell Minster rose behind the settlement. Nowhere near as grand to look upon as Elmstow, it exuded a pacifying domesticity. Immediately he saw its walls, Eadred recognised a reflection of his own nature – a temperament that he knew he would need to battle, once in a while, but that thought did not distress him.

The intoxication of his days at Elmstow continued to fill his thoughts. Much had happened and he had learnt much. Eadred's eyes followed the shapes of fish darting under the shining skin of the river. His mind, as it often did, retraced the crimes and how the murderous activities had left their own confusion of ripples. By thinking about how he had come to see the truth, the priest found that his mind, like his eye, could be trained to avoid more quickly the glaring pane of the river and to see more clearly what was happening below. It brought a smile to him.

He left the bridge but, still contemplative, Eadred sat on the riverbank, his mind back at Elmstow. There was one part of the story – the only part – that still confused the priest, although it held no importance in finding those who were guilty. Abbess Hereburg had died from poisoning. Leoba and her brother had administered it in order to stop her from naming them. Yet why not a knife? It would have been faster, with far less risk of her talking. Even if, in her sin-laden misery, Hereburg had arrived at a point where she had abandoned concern for her life and soul, there were quicker methods. It made no sense.

Eadred walked on to the minster and was greeted warmly by the Brothers and priests who came to welcome him. He ate and drank with them and enjoyed telling stories of the battle and the murders and how justice found the killers. There were squeals of horror and solemn declarations of the priest's wisdom and courage.

"What things you have done, Eadred. They must have left their mark on you. You seem the same man we knew but I cannot believe that the Lord God gave you such experiences if not to provide instruction, although I have no inkling what it might be." Brother Godwine stared in unworldly bewilderment.

"Godwine, your mind is indeed sharp. I have thought much about this, myself – and am still thinking. I believe the Lord God has given me a greater understanding of why he wanted me to be ordained and not to become a cloistered man, as I had wished. He chooses all our paths, although it is our decision whether we accept his authority. My path is not only to know God better but to fight against those many parts of my nature that seek my own comfort and to go into those places where darkness prevails to fish for souls for God.

"I will never find this easy. The evil that had taken root at Elmstow risked the souls of many good men and women. I pray that now they are freed of the devil's yoke they will return to God's ways."

"Assuredly, they will!" Bishop Aethelbert came to join them, smiling and rubbing his hands, and sat at their bench. "I owe this priest a great debt," he announced, while shaking Eadred by the shoulder. "A few weeks ago, all I could see was failure. To come to the end of a life and wonder what purpose it served is sad beyond description. Yet God has been merciful and worked through Father Eadred to discover the culprits of those vile crimes and to bring them to justice. Elmstow can now flourish, as the king and queen intended. The weight that has been lifted from me…" The bishop shook his head and wiped the tears away.

"Now, we shall in the next few days have a special service and all give thanks that the kingdom is safe, as well as Father Eadred. We have reclaimed Elmstow for God and saved a pious woman who lost her way from the rope."

It was a joy for Eadred to see the years that had been taken from Bishop Aethelbert. He had thought that the old man might die at Elmstow but now he seemed to move around more quickly. He no longer dozed in many of the services and had become a frequent visitor to Elmstow's gardens and ponds. Now back at Snailwell, he had already expressed his desire to walk again through his home minster's lands and holdings.

*

However, for Eadred, the sights he had witnessed carried an unexpected poison. Nights began to fracture from images of death and decay and screams of pain, imagined but as real as in the flesh.

The young priest had always been Bishop Aethelbert's favourite. Fearing destruction of the young man's mind by demonic forces, the bishop prayed hourly for Eadred's protection. In his wisdom, he also thought a blanket of order, routine and gentle physical work would best heal the memories of violence that were unsettling a receptive, imaginative mind, leaving it open to the devil's attacks.

The strategy may have had some success, but the wounds were deeper than the bishop had first believed, so a far stronger but more risky medicine was needed. Five or so weeks after his return, the priest was summoned by the bishop. He found him seated in the herb garden, relishing the spring sun.

"Come sit with me, my boy." Eadred took the stool beside the bishop.

"I have been thinking and praying about Elmstow.

There is so much there that is now right, but the Lord God has spoken to me and convinced me that I need to do more to secure Elmstow's future as a lamp of faith. Abbess Tetta has done so much to restore the community of holy Sisters and I need to support her. I hear that several women who should never have been admitted have now left or have been removed by their kin. The abbess is bringing the discipline of a prayerful, cloistered life to those who remain.

"Now to the patrons. The three lofty men who made endowments to the minster of land, ponds, woods and meadows have now withdrawn their wealth."

"But they cannot, surely!"

"It is good that this has happened, Eadred. Their gold was tainted. There were no charters signed; the land is still theirs. I think the king told them to spend their wealth on something else. We are freed from the poison they injected, and also from the masses and psalms we were obliged to sing to save their souls. We need to scrape that page and start again. Elmstow is now quite poor."

"Reverend Father, I know such matters are beyond my understanding, but it is known that the king endowed the minster with vast lands."

The bishop shook his head and sighed.

"I wish it were so. They were promised – one hundred hides – but only fourteen were bestowed by charter. The rest never happened – and will not now. There is a lesson for us, Eadred. When the king believed his soul was at risk, he promised the Church everything. I should have had the charter drawn up then.

"I have spoken to someone who knows the king's mind

and condition. His treasury is bare, and he thinks his debt at Elmstow is paid; his only daughter made sacrifice and the minster now purged. So, I must do what I can to secure income for Elmstow.

"When the opportunity arises, I will talk to the new ealdorman and see if I can persuade him to bestow some of his wealth on the minster. He is a good man, still finding his way, and will not impose any heavy conditions on his endowment."

"Will he not despise the very sight of Elmstow? The woman he hoped to marry, and his father, were murdered there."

"It is possible, but he may want to fulfil his new responsibilities by helping set Elmstow on firm rock. We shall see. This brings me to my next idea. A wool merchant passed by Snailwell some days back and gave me a message from the chief moneyer, Regenhere. You remember him?"

Eadred nodded, feeling his chest pound at the memory that name evoked. He began to sweat.

"I was told that he feels the veil of death closing around him and wishes to set matters right for his soul's journey. A man in his position has many worries weighing on him. He has no children now and, of course, he is a wealthy man. He wants to talk to me about an endowment. This is the best chance, Eadred, to set up Elmstow on strong foundations."

"I do not know if he is a good man, Reverend Father. We need better men to support the faith."

"Eadred, I know, but he has been chief moneyer to the king for many years. He has not abused his position. You may not like him – very few of us who have chosen a religious life find men of business attractive."

"It is more than that. There is a dark and unrestrained part of him."

"I am aware. I have heard what he did to Edith and how you freed her. Everyone has heard. He has a weakness for younger women. It is known. His desires can be passionate. Lust is a sin but so is drunkenness. One is not worse than the other."

Eadred flushed.

"I can think of nothing else. Elmstow cannot survive on only fourteen hides."

The bishop's eyes searched out those of the priest and did not give ground until Eadred nodded.

"This pleases me, Eadred. I do not want us to have differences on such important issues. I can feel that the Holy Spirit moves in you. Now, Regenhere will be in Elmstow in several days' time, so I am told. I want you to meet him and to hear what he is offering. I doubt that he will seek to impose heavy conditions. We would be happy to say masses and prayers for him now and after his death – be sure to tell him that. Make sure also that you write down what he offers. If you feel that you can gain more then you should try – men who are staring at eternity think less of the gold and the lands they have acquired, unless their generosity can bring heavenly reward."

"But Reverend Father, I do not want to meet the man again – and I am inadequate in the ways of the world. Send a senior Brother or an ordained man of more experience. I—"

"Enough, Eadred. I am your bishop; do not forget it! You will represent me. Besides, the wool merchant also told me that Brother Tatwine is well again. He lost that eye but otherwise is recovered and staying at Elmstow. I know you became friends, and he would welcome seeing you again.

"Elmstow is not the evil place you endured last time. You will surely be welcomed, and your name raised for your efforts in restoring the minster to its true purpose. You will face no danger and I will be happy for you to tell me on your return how you find the place. Tell Abbess Tetta that you come on my behalf to see how she has improved discipline. She will be sure to show you. You leave tomorrow."

THIRTY-FIVE

Return to Elmstow

Close to midday on the second day, the old mount that bore the priest struggled towards the top of the rise. Eadred spoke encouraging words but with no effect, so he dismounted and led the animal ever closer. As the summit neared, Eadred drew quiet.

In his mind, he had retraced his first journey from Snailwell to Elmstow with a sense of foreboding. Now, a few steps from where he had stood when Ceolfrith, the former ealdorman, had hurled his last crushing abuse before descending to the minster, Eadred readied himself for the bile to rise once more to burn his throat. It never came. Neither was he subdued when he thought of Eanswith's last brutal moments, which occurred somewhere close to where he was standing. A strange healing was happening. There was a new story that connected these events – one of hope and triumph – that even the thought of meeting the moneyer once more could not dim.

Eadred pulled his defiant nag towards the crest and the vastness of the clear blue sky opened as a gate to eternity. He looked across with a smile to the two arms of the ridge, where Tatwine battled with demons in his cave. Then the path levelled and began to fall. Before him spread the burgeoning bounty of Elmstow Minster, set in a sea of green meadows, fields and woods. The river, that had been channelled to feed the mill, curled from beneath him and off into the far distance. Eadred followed the course readily with his eye, for its damp spirit hovered above its body.

Others could see it – and now Eadred felt it. He was a different man since his battles at Elmstow. He had left Snailwell content with his ordered existence, but he was approaching Elmstow eager to be a warrior for his God. The priest felt the blood pump through his body and warm him. He rode through the gate and felt as if he had never left and that Snailwell might well have been another country. Eadred had tasks to undertake for the bishop but he also had a mission for himself. What had been buried by his nightmares at Snailwell was now awakening in Elmstow's morning.

*

"My dear, dear friend, I thought for many days that I would never see you again." Tatwine hugged his companion mercilessly then rubbed the tears from his face. "What happiness this is. It is not good to look at, is it? I weep now from a single eye." The monk fingered the bone-coloured scar that swirled where his left eye had been. "But I can still see. My head throbs with pain a few times each day but I am getting used to it. The new abbess, God bless her, prayed and cared for me, as she did for all the wounded."

"Dear Tatwine, you are a hero to match the greatest warriors of our kingdom. Your deeds are beyond bravery. I prayed many times each day for your recovery; was anxious for news and finally it came. What joy! See, the tears of joy I weep!"

The two friends held each other up and sobbed.

"Now, come and sit, I am exhausted by that welcome. We have much to talk about. See, in your honour, I have three jugs of wine. Sister Burghild was able to free them from the stores for me but in truth no-one would object. She also brought me these." The monk lifted a cloth from his bench. Beneath it were two large joints of boiled and seasoned lamb and two heavy loaves.

"What a feast! I have not seen such fine food since I was last here. This will be an evening to remember."

"Come, tell me about your mission. I am sure that Bishop Aethelbert has sent you here to see if all is well?"

Tatwine poured Eadred a cup and took one himself. They both laughed and drank and rekindled their friendship. They talked about Eadred's task and Tatwine spoke about all the encouraging changes that Abbess Tetta had introduced. The second jug was drained and with good effect. Eadred felt confident he could now raise the subject he had been desperate to talk about with Tatwine – for if he did not, he sensed his mind would bring maudlin thoughts to life.

"My good friend, I have been troubled since I was last here that my mind has not been able to put to rest one part of the web of murder and lies that happened. I would enjoy it if I could share my concern with you, for you have a strong mind that would be able to see what I cannot. It could settle my anxiety if baseless, or you may come to share it. Would you think I might ruin our wonderful evening if I spoke thus?"

"Eadred, I would welcome it and if I can help, all to the better. I missed the times we used our minds to fight against the evil deeds that were done here. It is part of your sacred work and if evil lurks still beneath a stone then let us find it and root it out. Let us start this last jug and then speak as you will."

Encouraged by his friend's words and the effect of the wine on his tongue, the priest offered his empty cup to Tatwine, then continued, "Very well; one of the deaths still perturbs me. I believe what Abbess Hereburg said to the court. She did not try to hide that she had planned dreadful murders. I take it as truth that in her younger days she and Ealdorman Ceolfrith had indulged in illicit deeds and she wanted to live that excitement one more time when she heard that he was to visit the minster. There were others who committed Ceolfrith's murder and Hereburg obviously knew them – Leoba and her brother. It is they who would have deceived the abbess into giving the ealdorman dwale to weaken him, so he could be overwhelmed easily.

"I was certain that they also poisoned her but if they wanted her silenced, why not accomplish it quickly? Why was she given poison that worked slowly? If I were Leoba, I would have used a knife or a rope on the same night as Ceolfrith's murder."

As though the answer to Eadred's question lay in the bottom of his cup, the hermit emptied its contents then stared into the void.

"Someone else gave her the poison?"

"Yes, that is what I now believe. Leoba did not want Hereburg to die on the night of the feast; she had more work for her to do."

If the monk had been happier since realising his injury would not kill him, he could not remember it. To apply his mind in this way was a revelation. The bishop's words stuck in his mind: 'The Lord God uses a bar of hot iron to judge good from evil men, but we must discern God's message.' Eadred's use of his mind and the gifts God had given him seemed to Tatwine to add something. Though he would never say it openly, it seemed as a fine pattern-welded blade compared to a crude piece of hack-iron. It was a joy to witness Eadred using such a blade and to learn from him and for Tatwine to apply his own poor wits similarly.

"But Hereburg's own unwitting hand in the death of the ealdorman so dismayed the abbess that her mind began to fall apart, and the poison would have made the rot even worse."

"Yes, my dear monk. Hereburg's madness would have concerned Leoba, but by then she could do nothing to silence the abbess because she had been captured and was guarded until her trial. So, there remains one page of this dark song that is missing – if not Leoba and her brother, who poisoned Hereburg and why was it necessary?"

"Have you any idea?"

"None, my friend, but as before, we should cast a wide net. It could be any of the inmates here or others who were visitors at the time – Regenhere and his son, even Lord Aelfric."

"And those who are now dead."

"Tatwine, you are right! In a suitable quantity, dwale would poison slowly over a number of days or weeks, which is how Hereburg died. Someone could have planned for her to die even before Ceolfrith and his son arrived here."

One of the heartening qualities of an excess of wine shared with a friend is that the mind and the mouth journey far beyond their usual homes and often without a considered destination. However, the journey can be useful. With searching minds and much for them to ponder, the priest and the monk delved into the characters of many of those who were present in the days and weeks leading up to Hereburg's death. Three people came to mind as possessing a nature that could plan her murder by the purposeful administration of poison.

Mildred had shown herself to be a malicious and calculating woman, capable of murder and of the resolve to hide her steps and to carry on with life as if nothing had happened. Sister Moira was also an unpleasant and vindictive person, who quite happily had delivered Edith into the barbarous hands of the moneyer and others. Of the two, Eadred and Tatwine considered Moira to have more reason to kill the abbess. Her activity of supplying Edith to visiting men would, no doubt, have earnt her some reward, as the nobles and merchants were rich. Hereburg could have tried to curtail her business and Moira would have responded.

The third possibility was the moneyer, Regenhere. He was known to have an indecent liking for younger women. If Hereburg was attempting to deny his access to Edith or others, then his craving could have flared even more uncontrollably.

Tatwine continued, "But what if Hereburg's killer is

another of the Mercian band who killed the ealdorman and whom we have yet to discover? Someone who Edith did not know about? Whoever thought that Hereburg had to die may believe that others must face the same fate because they have knowledge that could identify the killer."

The instant Tatwine said these words, Eadred broke into a shiver. Why had this not occurred to him? He had yet to see Edith anywhere in the minster. She was in danger and he imagined the worst.

"Eadred, my friend, I think you have drunk too much. You look sick."

The priest raised his hand and shook his head.

"No, it is not the wine. Have you seen Edith recently?"

"I have seen her a few times since rising from my sick bed, but I do not think so over the past few days. Why do you ask?"

"I fear she could be in danger. She laid bare the Mercian plot and whoever killed Hereburg may want her dead in revenge or they may fear that she will divulge more when it comes to her mind. It will soon be time for the night service; I must go and see if she is there." Eadred slapped one cheek then the other.

"You are not in the right state in your body or your heart to go to the service, nor am I. The abbess gave permission for us to miss the service; I forgot to tell you. She would not welcome our attendance in this condition. Wait until the service is over and we will watch those leaving."

Eadred nodded. He struggled back to his cell and threw cold water over his head. If his mind had not been so full of concern, he would have likely fallen asleep but when the monk tapped on his door, he was ready.

The holy Sisters glowed under the flickering torchlight

that took them from the church to the dormitory. Abbess Tetta led the way, supported by a stout pole, followed by a single line of cloistered women, and the last to walk from the shadows was Edith. Tranquil, absorbed, prayerful; her face looked to Eadred as heavenly as the Holy Mother of Christ that he had seen in the wondrous books in the minster library.

"She is safe."

"Not yet, my friend. This is the perfect time for someone to attack her. I do not want her to see me thus but watch her carefully and we will follow them to the dormitory."

The journey for the cloistered Sisters was short – across the courtyard then into the dormitory building, where a corridor led past the cells for certain nuns, until it arrived at the communal room, where many of the nuns slept. The first Sisters had already entered the building by a door, now obscured in shadow.

"Look! Quick!" A figure moved from the wall to the left of the door then stopped, shrouded in the darkness. Both Eadred and Tatwine drew their knives and ran.

"In the name of the Lord God, leave her alone!" The abbess came out of the door and struck out with her long staff. "Get away and leave her in peace."

The fleshy barrel that was Regenhere bellowed in pain, as the abbess beat him hard several times. He withdrew with Tetta advancing on him.

"Come on girls, to bed."

Eadred and Tatwine rested their backs against a wall. The monk chuckled.

"Edith is well protected."

Eadred did not feel anywhere near as confident.

"For now, perhaps, but the man is a pig and violent."

THIRTY-SIX

Anguish

"Abbess, thank you for sparing time for me." Eadred blinked several times and made a watery, limp smile. His eyes took a few seconds to accustom themselves to the dark interior.

"It is a joy to see you again, Father Eadred. I have much to tell you about the new condition of this minster. We have some way to go yet but I will be honest about the actions I am taking to remove lax behaviour. Be sure to speak truthfully if you believe there are other areas where improvement is needed." Abbess Tetta pulled the teats of the benign cow several more times, then gestured for one of the holy Sisters to take over the milking.

"Brother Tatwine would have told you that I gave my consent to his request for you both to miss our night services, so you could enjoy your reunion but I expect you at every service from now on during your visit."

Eadred thanked the abbess for her kindness and confirmed that he was looking forward to praising and praying with the community on every occasion.

"Now, walk with me while I talk about what we are doing here. I am certain that the foul murders that occurred in this house were a sign of how far Elmstow had fallen from God's grace. That they affected the highest in the land sadly shows that we failed in our duty to intercede for our noble king and his family. Some may claim that the fault lies with the king, who carries the burden of calling on the Lord God to protect and care for his people. We were all at fault, but my duty is to raise up Elmstow Minster to be a pious, godly house of devotion. We now pray for our king, his family and the whole kingdom at all of our communal gatherings."

The abbess maintained a brisk pace through the minster gardens and gave the impression to Eadred that she had a full day of tasks ahead and was keen to move onto the next duty after her time with him. She spoke quickly. Her language was lean and efficient.

"Elmstow had three problems and I aim to deal with all of them. Firstly, its inmates did not abandon earthly self-love, as those who choose a life of devotion must do, but many of them continued to embrace the fleeting vanities of the flesh. Thus, I gave every Sister the opportunity to leave if they felt they could not live a disciplined, prayerful life and now quite a number have gone. I was not surprised; I knew them well and we are better for their departure.

"As you would have seen, all Sisters now wear the correct habit. I have banned the wearing of ill-considered and lewd clothing on any occasion. Our meals are now frugal, except on the Church's feast days, but even then I will have no

309

gluttony or excess of wine or ale. No longer at our evening meals will there be any reciting of poems with their pagan heroes and heathen gods. We eat quietly, contemplating the Holy Word read by one of our number.

"I have reintroduced scrupulous observance of the daily rhythm of prayer and chanting of psalms, seven times each day. I am encouraging private devotion in addition to these times, coupled with fasting, which I am sure the bishop will approve of." Abbess Tetta glanced across to Eadred as they strode into the dormitory. Eadred nodded to reassure the abbess that he would tell the bishop of all the improvements she was introducing.

"Every cloistered woman is required to undertake useful labour with her hands. The older Sisters, not as much, but I will have no idleness. I find that when I use my hands, my mind and heart can meditate on God's Word. The other blessing of work in the fields, in the mill, caring for our beasts and weaving is that we have useful things we can barter or sell in order to obtain what we need.

"I believe, Father Eadred, we will be able to produce enough of value that we will not be reliant on other benefactors. This was our second mistake; we accepted endowments from men who had no greater desire than to use Elmstow for the pleasures of the flesh. They are, thankfully, gone but I am on guard that they do not return.

"Our last problem – and I shall be blunt – is that we did not have strong, alert and purposeful leadership to stand against wickedness.

"Bishop Aethelbert admitted to me that he felt the weight of his failure to inspect properly the minster and to challenge the powerful lords. I fear he might be getting too old to perform his duties but that is only for your ears. King Athelstan, God bless him, did not rein in his companions and paid an awful price. I feel the saddest for Abbess Hereburg. I remember when she was made abbess, the joy that shone from her eyes. She was abandoned by those who should have stood by her, worn down and made vulnerable to the devil's talk of revenge; then wickedness found a home in her.

"With God's help I shall not make the same mistakes. Now, what more do you wish to know?"

A more senior churchman would have measured his response to demonstrate copious experience and wisdom; to convey that the abbess' achievements were acceptable but not overwhelming. He would have had ready several pointed questions, hopefully to unnerve her. However, Eadred had the honesty and lacked the craft required to feign a lie. Almost breathless with admiration, he spoke.

"Nothing! I have never heard such a strong account of improvements that will bring God back to his house. I wish you well and will advise the bishop of the actions you are taking and of your energy."

The abbess gave a slight bow of her head and smiled.

"You are to meet Regenhere, the moneyer, I hear?"

Eadred blushed.

"It is my responsibility to know what happens in my minster. No doubt you were going to tell me?"

"Indeed, I was, Holy Mother. I am not looking forward to it."

The abbess raised her hand to quell Eadred's unease.

"I understand. When we received news of the moneyer's visit, Edith told me what he had done to her and that you had saved her from his lechery, although I already knew as much. I fear he has not improved. I suppose that the bishop believes that the moneyer's gold will be freely given and will replace the endowments we have lost?

"You have your duty but let me give you my view. Regenhere is ill and will die soon. He has no child and is a broken man, in body, heart and mind. He will, I am sure, give the minster rich lands and gold without earthly constraints on the endowment. Yet, he will expect us to fill the church with prayers, sing psalms and say masses to our Lord God for his blighted soul. My conscience will struggle. I will mouth the words but that is all. What is stronger – the world of man or of God? I am not Regenhere's judge, but I would not take his money to make my short life easier.

"My constant prayer is that we can have a minster built by our faith and our own hands. If the foundations are strong, the minster's light will shine out. If the foundations appear strong in the eyes of the world but were built by men tainted by evil – then darkness will fall again on this minster. Have we learnt nothing?

"Now, I have much to do. If that is all, I will leave you."

The priest thanked the abbess once more and then went to his cell to meditate and pray quietly before his meeting with the moneyer. Again, Eadred felt annoyed with the old bishop. He had not taken the opportunity to talk to the abbess and to be of one mind on the moneyer's proposal. Yet, here was a young priest now caught between the wishes of his bishop and the abbess – and he felt reconciled far more with Abbess Tetta's view.

*

The moneyer rolled out his languid arm towards the stool then leant back to rest against the wall, so his swollen stomach did not spill over the bench. It was a sullen greeting but reflective of both men's moods.

"You know of my message to Bishop Aethelbert?"

"I do. I was sent here by the bishop to agree the terms of your endowment."

"H'm, it would have been better to talk to him. He has the experience needed for these agreements. Anyway, you will do. I will bestow my estate at Barham of thirty hides. I will also endow sufficient gold and silver to buy the land along the river downstream from the minster's only mill and to build a second mill there. All this I will give to Elmstow with only one condition. I need earnest prayers said for my soul every week while I am alive and after my death and four masses a year; one of which shall be on the anniversary of my death.

"I think that is quite reasonable. Elmstow will be able to provide for all its needs now and in the years to come without depending on any earthly lord. It will not be an extravagant life but Elmstow will be master of its own fate if it is frugal and well-managed. You should be grateful. It is my understanding, after talking with the bishop after the trials here, that such an arrangement is considered a blessing. I need your confirmation that my spiritual requests will be met; then the monks at Snailwell can write up the charter and we can have it signed and witnessed, as soon as possible. I am going next to the king's court and will arrange witnesses and a suitable occasion."

"This is what the bishop expected, so it is agreed. When I return to Snailwell, I will have the charter written up. If that is all, I will leave, for I have much to do."

"I am sure you are a very busy man for one so young, but you might spare a few minutes to do one service for me, after my generosity to the bishop and to this place."

Eadred had already gone to the door but he turned and waited.

"Tell me?"

"You can inform Edith to come to my chamber tonight after her evening meal."

The priest stood speechless, staring at the moneyer. Eventually, he managed to utter some words.

"I will not!"

"Then I shall ask someone else to tell her. I pay her well; I always have done. And do not imagine that she is innocent of such behaviour, you foolish, callow boy. You have no idea. Do you know why she did not join her sister in murdering the ealdorman and the abbess? It was not for the reasons she gave but because her life in Elmstow is too good and too rewarding to give up.

"She is a cunning whore – all things to all men. I dare say she has let you eat at her table? That is her way. And now, she has you trapped with her spells and her silky thighs.

"Because of your interruption that night, I am ridiculed. People gossip behind my back, call me vulgar names. I am laughed at because of you – and I am the kingdom's chief moneyer! I swear to you, priest, that while I have breath, I will hound you and it will not stop once I have gone. I have the money to buy problems for you and I will surely spend it wisely.

"Run away, now, boy," the moneyer sneered.

Eadred's stomach knotted. His face must have shown his struggle. The moneyer twisted the knife with a cruel smile.

He waved the priest away and poured another swill of wine.

Eadred's hands shook. He felt for his blade, but it was not there.

*

"Can there ever be peace in my life?" Eadred lay on his bed, exhausted by misery. "Lord, just some happiness; some freedom from the oppression of men."

Eadred was powerless against the moneyer's wealth. The priest saw the days ahead of him darken, watching against an attack. This was not life. The bishop would not listen. The desire for the wealth of the wicked lay at the heart of the Church's failure. Regenhere had said it himself – the Church would never be free from the worst vices and sins of men while it depended on their gold. That corruption had birthed a torrent of death and yet the bishop was about to sanction the same evil once again. The curse that fell upon Hereburg was about to fall upon her successor – worse, Tetta knew it was coming but was powerless.

What of Edith? Eadred had lost trust in his own feelings. He was so easily duped by her deception. In fury, the priest threw his wine cup against the wall. He knew what he had to do.

THIRTY-SEVEN

The Last Stone

"Father Eadred." Another tap on the door. "Eadred, the bell has been rung for the night service. Would you come? It is Edith. Please."

The priest lay on his back, staring into the darkness. He had listened to her appeals in silence. Finally, she went. Her time with the moneyer had passed. He could act now or closer to daybreak. Eadred chose the latter.

He knew that the devil had gained control of his mind and heart, but he did not care. There was no other way out of the misery he saw for himself. His impotence in the face of power and ridicule had to end – and it would – in the killing of the moneyer.

Eadred had thought through how he would achieve the deed. A gentle knock on Regenhere's door. The old lecher would open it, probably expecting Edith, then the priest would pounce. A punch to the stomach then he would throttle the winded pig. It would look like a natural death. Regenhere was fat and ill and expected to die soon.

Despite the hatred within him, Eadred's hand shook when he went to knock. He held his wrist with his other hand. He could not make it work.

What possessed him? He stood back, ashamed of what he was contemplating.

"Forgive me, Father, for such a thought. Help me banish it."

A voice – feeble and gasping – whimpered. Eadred stood silently, his ear close to the wood. The speech was shallow with a sense of desperation. The priest pushed and the door creaked open.

The moneyer lay supine upon his bed, his face red and glassy with sweat. Eyes flitted uncontrollably. Regenhere clutched at his stomach and right side. He groaned miserably and his few words were muddled and senseless. The stench was overwhelming – a smell the priest knew – dwale. It pervaded the bile, the piss and shit soiling the blanket. Eadred smelt the cup that rested on the bench; the dark wine stain stank of the poison. The moneyer was beyond recovery.

*

"I was walking to the church to pray alone and passed the moneyer's door. There were pitiful sounds coming from inside. When I saw him, he was close to death; I prayed for him until he breathed his last. His wine had been poisoned with dwale. He must have drunk heavily. I am afraid we have another murder."

Abbess Tetta nodded in response to Eadred's account.

"Perhaps. Father, I spoke to the moneyer after I talked to you yesterday. We did not spend long together. I tried to change his mind about an endowment. I told him that we had no need for his money or lands. He spoke sadly about the weight on his soul. Although I had no liking for the man, I had some mercy in my heart towards him. Even more so when I saw the pain that afflicted him. He cried out with the spasms in his chest and head and said he could bear them no longer and wished to die, and for his soul to be freed from its distressing house of flesh.

"I wonder whether he poured dwale into his wine to lessen the pain and, in his agony, he took too much? I am far from convinced that this is murder. Do we need to inflict the ordeal of hot iron on us all for no purpose? The minster needs to heal."

The priest turned to the wall for a few seconds.

"No, Reverend Mother. You have much wisdom. There is no need to create any more misery in Elmstow."

Eadred left the abbess and went straight to the church in disbelief at what he had just done. He pushed the door closed and fell against it. A single candle flickered.

"Eadred, at last. I have missed you so much." Edith rose from her knees and hurried towards him, her arms open.

"Come no closer. Stop!"

"Eadred, it is Edith. I am alone. What has happened?"

"Leave me alone." The priest covered his eyes with a trembling hand. "What is happening?" Edith started to reply. "Do not talk. Listen to me and answer truthfully, as God is your witness."

"I swear I will speak honestly. I always have with you, sweet Eadred."

"Do not use such words. Answer me this. Did you poison Regenhere when you were with him last night? For he is dead."

"I was not with him! Why do you speak like this?"

"Swear on the precious blood of Jesus Christ that you were not with the moneyer last night and you did not poison him."

Edith fell to her knees.

"I swear by the precious blood of Jesus, which was shed for us all, that I did not go to the moneyer last night or any time since I saw you last. I have been with no man since you and I have not sought to harm anyone. If I lie, may demons take me now and may this hand, which proved my innocence, rot before your eyes.

"Eadred, who has filled your heart with such spiteful thoughts? You know me and know that I am not capable of such evil."

The priest slumped to the ground. Edith wrapped the shield of her arms around him and he collapsed into her.

"Who has said such things?"

"The moneyer, when I saw him yesterday."

"My dearest Eadred, you know how he hated you. He used words to harm you. Now, you are free of him. Come, we must heal each other with tender words and embraces." They kissed and held each other closely and talked of occasions they could find to be together before Eadred had to leave for Snailwell. Edith spoke of the changes at Elmstow and how her life was now filled with light and promise.

"The abbess is a wonderful mother to me. I attend all the services and am improving my reading and writing. I learned some words when I was growing up in Mercia, but now I have a teacher in the abbess.

"She is even showing me how to make balms and medicines, which is a great skill she has. The abbess made me laugh with a story about Bishop Aethelbert. When they were younger and she was just starting to learn, she gave the bishop a potion of dwale to cure an illness – and it almost killed him! Now, she knows every measure; those that lead to healing and those that harm. She makes no mistakes."

Eadred's body stiffened.

"What is wrong, my dear priest?"

"Nothing. Just a strange thought. Come, we must both go to our labours."

*

In the solitude of his cell that night, deep in thought and worry, no answer came to his dilemma. Eadred dared not pray for guidance for all paths ahead of him were painful. The moneyer that the abbess said she saw – full of pain and misery, seeking death – was not the callous and vindictive man that the priest had seen. It was a lie. Regenhere did not give medicinal dwale to himself – it had been administered as poison.

The abbess had sought to protect the minster and Edith from the odious moneyer. She would have been skilful and careful in hiding the deed. She had done what Eadred could not. He was alone in this awful knowledge.

Then he turned the last stone. Hereburg's death had never made sense to him.

She had been poisoned, not to ensure her silence, but to remove her blighted occupancy. The ache for strong and pious leadership had led to a terrible crime.

But the killer was worse than Hereburg. It was murder by a ruthless, practical and sure hand. It was the hand that had given back his life to Eadred; it had done likewise for Edith and it had saved Elmstow from tainted gold. Here was a sinner and a saint in the same body.

*

Eadred woke to the sound of the bell and wearily prepared for the night service. Sisters-in-Christ smiled and acknowledged him along the short journey to the minster church. He responded as best he could. The voices rose in praise of the Lord God and joy filled the air.

But Eadred hid a tear. He had no strength to pursue the final murderer. He doubted if it were even possible. For now he would keep his silence. Had the devil been forced from Elmstow or was he still there?